*Jacki,
Some things are worth
the punishment!*

# PRISONED

## MARNI MANN

Copyright © 2016 by Marni Mann
All rights reserved.

Cover Designer: Mad Hat Covers, www.madhatcovers.com
Editor: Steven Luna
Proofreader and Interior Designer: Jovana Shirley,
Unforeseen Editing, www.unforeseenediting.com

No part of this book may be reproduced or transmitted in any form or by any means, electronic or mechanical, including photocopying, recording, or by any information storage and retrieval system without the written permission of the author, except for the use of brief quotations in a book review.

This book is a work of fiction. Names, characters, places, and incidents either are products of the author's imagination or are used fictitiously. Any resemblance to actual persons, living or dead, events, or locales is entirely coincidental.

ISBN-13: 978-1535397896

*For Brian.
You're my strength. My light.
My everything.
I love you more than love.*

# PROLOGUE

## GARIN
## SIXTEEN YEARS AGO

"Sorry I'm running late, guys." I tossed my jacket on the bed before I sat on the floor between Kyle and Billy. "Show me what you all got tonight."

"It wasn't a good one for me," Kyle said. She was still wearing her jacket, rubbing her arms like she couldn't get warm.

I reached behind me, lifting my coat off the bed so that I could hand it to her. "Here, put this over you; it'll keep you warm."

She was always cold. I figured it had something to do with her being so skinny. And that was because her ma didn't have the money for food. She sold her food stamps for cash.

Same as my ma.

Same as Billy's.

Us kids who lived in The Heart—that was the name of our housing project—had to earn our own money and buy our own food.

Four long streets with over two hundred apartments, and no one would even give up a box of mac and cheese. It may have been named after the muscle that kept us alive, but there wasn't any life around here.

The Heart sucked the life right out of everyone.

"Thanks, Garin." Kyle crossed her legs in front of her, tucking the jacket over her lap.

I smiled at her. "Tonight was real good for me," I said, grabbing the cash and change from my pocket and dropping it all on the carpet. "Three hundred and forty-eight dollars."

"Damn," Billy said. "Look at all that drug money." He pushed the coins together to make a pile. "Lots of panhandlers tonight, huh?"

Panhandlers used change to buy their dope. Most of the time, they'd hand me a full cup—the same one they'd collected it with. I'd keep the cups in the alley, stacked against the wall, and dump the change into my pockets when I left to re-up. Mario, my boss, owned a corner store. It was where he stashed all the dope. I'd go there and pay Mario back my advance, and then I'd refill my pockets with balloons and baggies.

Dope was way lighter than that heavy change. It didn't make my jeans sag either.

"You should've seen all the junkies lined up tonight," I said. "I thought for sure the cops were going to get called."

"Any of the hookers try to give you head?"

I didn't look at Kyle when I answered Billy's question, "Not tonight." I hated when he talked about that kind of shit in front of her. "I wouldn't let those hookers touch me. Half of them don't even have any teeth."

"I hear that means they give better head, all gums and suction. Can you imagine?"

"Fuck no. I don't want to imagine."

I felt Kyle staring at me, but I kept looking at Billy. "How'd you do tonight?" I asked him.

"I couldn't find nothing to pawn besides a CD player and some old drills. Cheap bastard at the pawnshop only gave me twelve bucks for it all 'cause the drills were so rusted. Fucking winter. People keep their shit locked up 'cause it's so goddamn cold."

"Twelve isn't all that bad," Kyle said.

# PRISONED

Billy threw a wad of cash onto the floor, his grin telling me he wasn't quite done. "Nah, but sixty-two is better. I got fifty bucks for the tires."

"Tires?"

"You're gonna lock your car up, so I can't steal nothing. Then, I'm going to take your tires, so you can't go nowhere."

"Oh, man." Kyle laughed.

I punched Billy's shoulder. "That's messed up. You know that, right? I'd beat your ass if you stole my tires."

Billy would steal anything. It didn't matter if it had sentimental value, if it was the cheapest thing you owned, or if it was the tires on your car. Family and friends were all he cared about. He had no fear.

None of us did in The Heart.

Except for Kyle.

"You mean, you'd beat my ass if I stole your *ma's* tires since you ain't even old enough to drive."

"Neither are you," I shot back. "Besides, Ma's car got repo'd a long time ago, so she doesn't have any tires you can steal."

"You know I wouldn't take nothing from either of you." Billy looked at both of us. "But those fuckers I steal from, they can try to beat me all they want. They'll never catch me. I'm too fast."

"Garin!" Ma yelled from downstairs.

"What?" I shouted back.

"I'm going out. Make sure you get your ass to school in the morning. I'd better not get another call telling me you skipped again. You hear me?"

"Yeah, I hear you."

I finally looked over at Kyle. She was smiling at me.

The last time I'd skipped school, we ditched together. We smoked a joint in my room and took a cab to Mario's house, so we could go swimming in his indoor pool. That was after I'd taken her bathing suit shopping. The only suit she owned was a bikini with a giant hole in the bottom that showed her ass crack. She wasn't comfortable wearing it, but God, I'd wanted her to, even if that meant holding my breath and going underwater and opening my eyes until they burned from the chlorine. I'd do that if it meant I could see more of her body. I didn't tell Kyle that. Instead, I offered to buy her a new one. She couldn't afford one, which meant she wouldn't have gone swimming at all. And that meant she wouldn't have gone to the beach that summer. I couldn't let that happen. The beach was the best part about this hellhole town.

"How much did you make tonight?" I asked her.

Her hair had fallen into her face. As much as I wanted to tuck it behind her ear, I didn't. Not now and especially not in front of Billy.

She held out her closed fist and slowly unfolded her fingers. There were a few crumpled up dollars in the middle of her palm. "It's winter. There's no beachgoers that I can sell bottles of water to and no tourists walking the boardwalk. And, when I try to panhandle outside the casinos, everyone has lost so much money in there, they won't even give me their change. I'm not as good as you guys."

"Then make 'em look at you, Kyle," Billy said. "Stick out your tits, hike up your skirt, and make 'em want to open up their wallets."

"Shut it, Billy!" The look I gave him told him I wasn't messing around. Another word, and I'd rip his fucking face off. I didn't care if he was my best friend. He would never give that kind of order to Kyle. "You want some dude to grab her off the street and rape her? Because that's what'll happen if she does that."

"Damn, Garin, you're right. I wasn't even thinking. Course I don't want nothing like that to happen to Kyle."

Kyle dropped the cash onto her lap and buried her hands inside her jacket. "It's okay. I know you didn't mean it, Billy."

"You've been trying real hard to earn money, and I know that," Billy said to her.

She nodded. "I just don't know what else to do until summer." Her voice was so soft, and I knew she was trying not to cry. "Garin, you're so good at dealing, and you make a ton doing it. And, Billy, you're the best hustler in our whole school. You could steal a diamond ring off a woman's finger, and she wouldn't even know it. I can't do that. I can't do anything."

"Bullshit," Billy barked. "You're smarter than me and Garin, and you got more talent than the both of us combined. Those things you make on the computer ain't like nothing I've ever seen."

"You mean my designs?"

"Yeah, those."

"But they need so much detail, and I need so much more practice. The only time I get to work on them is during Mr. Gunther's second period class...unless Mom plans on getting me a computer, but we all know that isn't going to happen."

"Well, whatever. They're good," he said. "Real fucking good."

I waited until Billy was done redeeming himself. "He's right," I said. "You're too good to be out there, hustling, and definitely too good to be dealing. You just figure out how to sell those designs and leave the street stuff up to us."

She finally tucked her hair behind her ear. I was glad it was out of her face, but I wished my fingers had done it.

"You guys pay for everything, and that's not fair," she said. "I've got to help out somehow, and I've got to come up with a way to pay you back."

We didn't give her much—food, mostly, some clothes, taxi rides around the city since none of our mas had a car. I was happy to do it. I'd buy her food every day if she'd let me. But there was no way she was paying us back.

"You do help," I said.

"How?"

"Yeah, how?" Billy asked.

I gave him another nasty look to shut him up. "Just trust me, Kyle. You do."

Kyle was the reason I hadn't dropped out of school to go live in one of Mario's apartments and deal all the time. That would have been better than living in The Heart with Ma and my sister. But Kyle lived just a few apartments over, and she was in most of my classes, so I stayed.

I just wanted to be close to her.

"You can pay us back when you're making the big bucks from selling those designs while me and Garin are still here, hustling," Billy said.

"I won't be here," I said. "I've got four years left, and then I'm getting the hell out of Atlantic City."

"Where you going?" Billy asked.

"Vegas. Mario's been getting me ready to work at their hotel out there. Once I turn eighteen and get my diploma, I'm out."

Kyle didn't know it yet, but she was coming with me. So was Billy. There was no way I was leaving them here. Going to Vegas meant more money for all of us, and I could probably get them jobs at the casino.

"Well, I'm going to college," Kyle said.

Our heads jerked toward her. The kids around here didn't go to college. Most didn't make it to their junior year of high school.

"That's..."

"A big goal to have," I said, finishing Billy's sentence.

"I have to try to get a full academic scholarship. Going to college is all I've ever wanted. Somehow, I'm going to make it happen."

I had to talk to Mario and see if he or any of his boys had connections at the colleges around Vegas. Maybe he could get her in. I'd pay for her schooling, and I could make it look like she'd gotten a scholarship. That was the only way she'd take my money and probably the only way I could make sure she came to Vegas.

"If that's what you want," I told her, "it'll happen."

"It won't be happening for a while," she said. "And since summer is still a ways away, maybe I could help you deal down at the boardwalk." She looked over at Billy. "Or I could help you hustle—"

"Not gonna happen, Kyle," I said. "I told you, leave the street stuff to us." I grabbed my money off the floor and shoved it into my pocket. I usually took twenty bucks from whatever I earned each night and bought food with it, and then I saved the rest. But tonight, I was going to spend a little more. "Come on, guys."

"Where we going?" Billy asked. "I've been running all night, and my feet hurt. You'd better not be taking us too far."

Kyle handed me my jacket, and I slipped it on as I walked to the door.

"It's not far," I said.

"Should I grab a sweater or something?"

The worry in Kyle's voice made me stop in the doorway and turn to face her. The shirt she was wearing underneath, I'd bought for her, and it wasn't thick enough to keep her warm.

I grabbed a sweatshirt from my closet. "This is warmer than anything you have at home."

She took off her jacket, put the sweatshirt on over her head, and zipped her jacket over it. She tucked her nose under the front of the sweatshirt. "It smells like you."

"It's my favorite. I wear it a lot."

She pulled her face out and smiled. "I know."

# PRISONED

"Are we gonna talk about your stank ass all night, or are we gonna get going?" Billy barked.

I rolled my eyes. "Yeah, come on."

"Where are you taking us, Garin?" Kyle asked, walking a bit behind me.

We went down the stairs and out my front door, passing Kyle's and Billy's apartments on our way out of The Heart. "I'm taking you guys to the diner 'cause we all could use something to eat. Then, we're going someplace where we can have some fun."

I'd have to call Mario when we got to the diner. He let me use his indoor pool and hang out in his basement arcade whenever I wanted, but I needed permission to bring my friends. And then I'd have to have a talk with Billy. I'd never brought him to Mario's before. I was afraid he'd steal something. I needed him to promise that he wouldn't. Billy wouldn't break a promise—not to me anyway.

"I'm down for some fun," Billy said.

I waited for Kyle to say something. When she didn't, I slowed down, so she could catch up to me.

"What about you?" I asked her.

Her smile was even bigger than it had been in my bedroom even though she was shivering now. "Of course I'm up for it."

"Good." I stopped walking, the three of us forming a tight circle.

Kyle's teeth were chattering loud enough for Billy and me to hear. I had to get her out of this cold.

"You sure you can't run, Billy?"

"Ahh, fuck. I can always run if I have to."

I grabbed Kyle's hand, and we took off.

"Then, start running!" I yelled at him from over my shoulder.

Once Kyle was sipping some hot chocolate at the diner, she finally stopped shaking. The three of us wolfed down bacon cheeseburgers with extra orders of fries and onion rings and headed over to Mario's.

I knew Kyle had a good time at his place; she didn't stop smiling or laughing the whole night. Mario even let us make eggs for breakfast and gave us a ride to school. Kyle fell asleep on my shoulder before Mario was even out of his neighborhood. I didn't want to wake her when we pulled up in front of the school. She needed the sleep. But, when I did, I liked the way her eyes looked when she opened them real slow and rubbed the corners with her small fingers.

Shit, I liked it a lot.

But there weren't many more nights like that one—the three of us together, sober, earning on the streets and celebrating with our shares. The nights that followed weren't fun at all. They were tragic. Devastating.

They were really fucking dark...

# ONE

## KYLE

There was so much paperwork. I couldn't see my glass desk. Piles and piles of folders and printouts and designs and mark-ups. My hands stayed frozen in my lap. There was too much. I didn't know which project to work on first, which deadline required my immediate attention. My to-do list would have told me, but it was buried somewhere in there, too. So were my keyboard and cell phone. Someone must have been calling because the stack on the right was vibrating. I dug around until my fingertips hit the hard plastic and held it up to my ear.

"Anthony, hey. Can I call you back tonight? I'm about to step into an important meeting."

Telling my brother that I couldn't talk because I was completely overwhelmed would have gotten me a nasty response. I didn't need nasty. Not now.

"I'm not calling to talk about money or the business," he said. "I have news, and it's something I think you'll want to hear right now. But if you have to call me back…"

I wheeled around in my chair, so I could face the window, taking in the sight of downtown Tampa. My brother was hours away in Atlantic City, but it felt like he was standing next to me, looking at me with a disgusted stare.

"What is it?" I asked.

"Billy Ashe was found dead last night."

I rested my hand over my chest to try and stop the ache in my heart. "Oh my God."

Billy Ashe.

*Dead.*

"How? He wasn't shot…was he?"

"Overdose." He paused, and I felt myself relax just the tiniest bit. "Heroin, from what I hear."

Twelve years ago, when I had been a senior in high school, we had lost Billy's brother. Paulie's death was a night I would never forget. It was the reason *home* wasn't my home anymore.

Now, both brothers were gone.

The thought made my chest ache more and more as each second passed.

Heroin had the power to freeze pain, and Billy had lots that needed to stay iced. We'd all hurt back then—Billy, Garin, and me. But I had kept my pain frozen by burying myself in homework, and Garin had kept his in check by sinking himself into women.

A part of me had always expected Billy to get sober. To be saved somehow.

*Why didn't Garin save him?* I wondered.

"The funeral is in three days," Anthony said. "It's been a while since you've been home. Maybe you should plan on coming."

*Home.*

There was that word again. But Atlantic City hadn't been my home since the day I left for college. I hadn't returned.

Not even once.

Could I return for Billy? It had been years since we'd spoken, the last time when I was a senior in college. It was the anniversary of Paulie's death, and I wanted to let Billy know I was graduating soon, something he'd never thought I would do. He let me go a few minutes into our call. There was a cop driving behind him, and he said he was in a stolen car.

# PRISONED

After Paulie's death, things changed between the guys and me. I had backed away from our relationship, and they had fought me on it for a long time. They hadn't won. But that didn't mean I stopped caring—then or now. I cared more than I would ever admit. And had I run into Billy in the years following, I would have embraced him, and I would have told him I wanted more for him. I would have offered to help even if it would have gotten me in trouble. It was the least I could do.

Now, it was too late.

"I'll be there," I said.

"You can stay at my place."

Anthony may not have lived in The Heart, but he didn't live too far from it and was still deeply involved in every illegal activity that went on there. I didn't want to see it, I certainly didn't want to be around it, and I didn't want to spend that much time with my brother.

"I'm going to stay in a hotel and fly out the next morning. One night there is plenty. I'll—"

"You'll talk to me later."

"Right."

I ended the call and immediately pulled up a travel website, knowing that if I didn't book it now, I'd miss the chance and end up not going. It showed a nonstop from Tampa that got me into Atlantic City before ten in the morning and departed the next morning at eight. I added on a hotel room at what had been my favorite casino on the boardwalk. I'd never actually been inside. I'd only admired the facade and the flashing lights and the ornate glass door when I panhandled out front. I wouldn't be panhandling this time. I wouldn't be selling stolen bottles of water on the beach either. I would be staying in one of the rooms I had dreamed about as a kid, eating a huge meal in one of their restaurants, and having an expensive drink at one of their bars. And then, less than twenty-four hours later, I'd be back in Florida.

Far away from the memories…far away from The Heart.

Far away from everything I'd been forced to give up.

# TWO

## KYLE

When I finally reached the front of the line, I walked up to the counter and rested my arms over it. "Kyle Lang," I said, "checking in for one night." I handed her my credit card.

"Thank you, Ms. Lang. I see you've booked a king-size bed. Will you need one key or two?"

"Just one. Thanks."

I looked around the lobby, at the faces of all the employees, but I didn't recognize anyone. I wondered if any of the kids from my school worked here. The only person in this town I kept in touch with was my brother. I did know that no one from The Heart was employed at any of the casinos. Their records were too long to work in a place that dealt with so much cash.

"Your room was prepaid, so I'm scanning your card to keep it on file for minibar purchases, room service, or incidentals." She handed the card back to me along with a room key. "You'll be on the twenty-sixth floor. The elevator is just to the right, around the bank of boardwalk-themed slots. If you left your luggage with the bellboy, it will be delivered to your room."

I pointed at the small suitcase by my feet. "I've got it right here."

"Do you have any questions, Ms. Lang?"

"No, I'm fine."

That wasn't the truth. The feeling inside me was far from fine. But having her tell me where the ice machine was wouldn't make me feel better.

My feet moved on autopilot as I pulled my suitcase around the slots, into the elevator, and down the hall of my floor. Once I was inside my room, I dropped the suitcase by the door and rushed over to the windows. At some point, I would hopefully appreciate the suite I had spent a fortune on, but right now, I needed to see the view.

The window was thick glass, rimmed with black metal bars, like the ones that had been in our apartment in The Heart. There was a cloudy buildup in the corners from the sea salt, similar to my windows in Florida. The beach sat right below, the water extending as far as I could see. The sand wasn't like the beaches I went to now. I remembered it being grainy and coarse, mixed with small pebbles and shells, especially sharp after high tide.

Even the sand was harsh in Atlantic City.

The three of us—me, Billy, and Garin—would spend our summer days at that beach below. After months of cold and shivering, the sun had felt so good on my skin. Those were the only months my body didn't shake. There was barely enough meat on me to keep me healthy and definitely not enough to keep me warm.

My phone rang from inside my purse. I kept my eyes on the ocean as I reached for it, trying to shake the memories away. "Hello?"

"Have you checked in?" Anthony asked.

"Yes."

I'd told him not to worry about picking me up from the airport. I didn't want to have to talk during the ride to the hotel. I just wanted a second alone with my thoughts. Anthony wouldn't have given me that. It would have been order after order, and I didn't want to hear it.

"I'm on my way," he said. "We'll get something to eat and then go to the funeral. I figured we could hit up the diner. I know you liked that place, so—"

"No diner."

# PRISONED

That was where I'd always gone with the guys. I didn't need to open those memories, too.

"Then, we'll eat at your hotel."

"Fine."

"I'll see you in the lobby in twenty."

"Anthony, wait." I hadn't thought of it when I talked to him a few days ago. But now that I was here and the service was in a few hours, I had to know. "You're coming with me? To the funeral?"

There was silence on the other end of the phone. Maybe I shouldn't have asked. Maybe I should have just let it play out, like the rest of today would.

"Yes." His tone was so sharp. "Meet me downstairs in twenty."

The phone then went dead.

I wished the window had a frame or a sill, so I had something to hold on to. Just a small ledge, wide enough for my fingers, so I could grip it tightly. So I could squeeze. Something that could bear my weight. Because, suddenly, everything felt so heavy. So thick. So foggy. Even more than when I'd stepped off the plane. Heavier than when I'd walked into the suite. Heavier than before I'd answered the phone.

But there was nothing to grip. Nothing to hold me. Only a warm pane of glass and a full view of my ugly past. So, I tilted forward and rested my head against it, hoping it would keep me from falling.

I checked my suitcase to see what I had packed. I didn't remember throwing in clothes or shoes or cosmetics. It had been another autopilot moment, my brain in a much different place than my body. But as I dug around, I found everything I needed. I pulled out a pair of black pants and felt myself putting them on. My arms slipped through the holes of a black tank top and then through the sleeves of a matching blazer. I placed a long necklace over my head, bracelets on my wrists, heels on my feet.

In the bathroom, with my makeup bag open and my cosmetics spread over the counter, my hand shook as I drew a strip of liner over my lids. I didn't know why I was making such an effort. This was a funeral, not a reunion. Anyone who recognized me had seen me at my worst. I'd been twenty pounds thinner back then, my skin gray, my hair ratted. But still, I added more makeup to my face, curls to my long strands of dark hair. Perfume to my skin.

When I ran out of things to put on, I finally paused and took the time to really blink, to take in the face that stared back at me in the mirror.

I could dress her up. I could cover her face in makeup. I could brush her hair and make her skin smell clean. I could fix her teeth and add twenty pounds to her frame. I could fly her first-class and book her in a hotel suite.

I'd done all of that already.

But, under this cosmetic blanket, I was just a girl from the projects.

A girl who had been holding in the biggest secret. A secret I had never spoken to anyone.

The secret lived in this state, so why would I ever come back here?

If I were smart, I would grab my purse and rush off to the airport, catching the first flight out of here and pretending the last hour hadn't happened.

I was smart. I just wasn't as strong.

Anthony and I stood against the back wall of the chapel. There weren't enough chairs for everyone in attendance. They were at least thirty short, maybe more. And no one here was dressed up...but me. I was in a roomful of torn jeans and wrinkled shirts. There was a thick breeze of stale cigarette smoke and heads full of greasy hair. My brother had at least put on a clean shirt.

Had I not been on autopilot before I left Tampa, I would have packed less black, shorter heels, and a jacket that wasn't so starched. I should have known better. I should have paid attention. This wasn't the kind of crowd who wore black suits and shiny shoes. This was the crowd who looked into the open casket and thought, *Fuck, will I be next?*

The only other suit in here was worn by the man who stood next to the casket. His was blue—blueberry blue—with a stain in the middle of his tie. I just stared at it while he spoke about Billy and tried to decide if it was salad dressing or pizza grease.

It was either that or stare at the casket, and there was no way I could look at the latter any longer than I already had. Billy was in that box. A shiny dark brown box that glistened from the corner of my eye with a puffy white fabric that lined it.

This wasn't the Billy I remembered. He was too clean. Too ironed. Too tucked in.

Too at peace.

Billy was the only person in this room who *was* at peace. The rest of us were from The Heart, and The Heart didn't allow it. And, for those of us who were close to Paulie and were around after he died, we definitely weren't at peace. The aftermath of his murder, the mourning. There was enough pain to last the rest of our lives.

But those weren't the only things I remembered, the only things that made me hurt.

There were the things that had happened just moments before Paulie's death and the second after, like the sound of the car's engine, Paulie's footsteps, the gun, the gasp, the feeling of the car door, the tires squealing on the pavement.

The words that echoed in my ears.

*His* words.

The ones that had haunted me since the moment they'd been screamed at me.

I sucked in a deep breath and turned my head away from the stained tie and the shiny casket. I'd had enough of both. Obviously, Anthony hadn't. He was looking straight at them. He was so calm, as if he were listening to a friend speak about plans for the weekend. How could he not be shaken by this? How could he not look at that casket and think there was something we could have done to stop Billy from overdosing? I assumed Anthony was here because he thought it was the right thing to do.

But it wasn't right. Not even close.

"We should go," I whispered.

When he faced me, there was so much anger in his eyes. "Stop it, Kyle."

"This is wrong."

"Go outside if you can't handle it, and I'll drive you back when the service is over."

I should go outside. I couldn't handle it.

My thoughts, my panic, my fear—it all came to a halt when I felt another set of eyes on me. Eyes that caused a whole new set of emotions. My heart was hammering so hard inside my chest, it felt like my lips were vibrating. My face filled with heat. My lungs felt too heavy to take a breath.

I slowly looked away from Anthony and searched for those unforgettable dangerous eyes. They weren't always emerald; they lightened and darkened, depending on what he was wearing. I'd seen every shade on him. But it had been years—twelve—since I'd heard his voice and seen him in person.

He was the reason I survived The Heart. He was my happiness. He was my best friend, my family. He kept the three of us together.

And then he was nothing.

He sat in the last seat of the second row from the front, looking at me from over his shoulder. My dark brown eyes connected to his sea-green ones—lighter than emerald, thanks to his blue shirt. My lips tugged into the smallest of smiles...another autopilot moment. I had lost complete control of my body.

He had the power to do that to me.

*Garin Woods.*

His name echoed in my head. Over and over.

I'd expected him to be there, but I hadn't considered what it would feel like when I saw him, that I'd be reacting this strongly, or that he would have changed so much. Before this moment, I could have drawn his face from memory or from the few faint pictures I'd seen online. But what I would have sketched was a boy—one who was underweight, who filled his belly with sugar just to make it feel full, who barely shut his eyes because he was always running, fighting, hustling his way through the dark.

My image wouldn't have captured the gorgeous man who was staring at me now. He looked healthy and fit. He had color in his skin and shadowy black scruff on his cheeks and chin. Deep lines etched across his forehead and between his brows. There was even a difference in his eyes. They had a light to them, a glow that told me his life wasn't full of darkness anymore.

# PRISONED

Seconds ticked away, and still no smile, still no expression, besides the intensity of his stare. Then, he turned back around.

I was finally able to take a breath again, the heat in my body starting to cool, the tingling in my limbs subsiding.

"Do you want to wait in line to see him?" Anthony asked.

See him?

I blinked, realizing everyone had stood from their chairs and were moving toward the front. When I checked Garin's seat, it was empty. He wasn't near the casket, and he wasn't on either side of the room. But, each time my stare crossed that shiny wood and that puffy white fabric, it felt like someone was clawing into my chest.

The happiness Garin had caused was completely gone.

"Kyle?"

"Yeah," I said, looking back at Anthony. Guilt was darker than any memory I had. "No, I mean. I don't want to get in line. I think I need some water."

"There are drinks in the next room. I saw them when we came in. I'll take you."

I walked next to Anthony, keeping my eyes down, not wanting to make contact with anyone. When we reached the refreshment table, I poured myself some water. I never brought the cup up to my lips. I just kept my fingers wrapped around the plastic and let the coolness soak into my skin while I concentrated on my breathing. It was becoming more labored than I liked.

"You should eat something," Anthony said. "You barely touched your lunch."

I looked at the trays of cookies and finger sandwiches. "I'm not hungry."

I wasn't thirsty either. I just needed to get away from that room, from the casket.

From all of it.

"I think I should go," I said.

"You need to go say something to Billy's mom first, and then I'll take you back to the hotel."

My breath…I couldn't catch my breath. "You want me to talk to… Billy's mom?"

Anthony nodded.

"Not a bad idea, Kyle," Garin said from behind me. "I'm sure she'd like to see you since you never said good-bye to her either."

I turned around, my eyes finding his. The spark of happiness that had shot through my limbs earlier quickly turned to guilt.

I squeezed the cup between my fingers and palm, so I wouldn't drop it. "Hi, Garin."

He broke contact to look at my brother. "Anthony," Garin said. The two of them shook hands. "It's been a while."

"It has been," Anthony agreed. "I didn't expect to see you here."

He didn't?

It was so strange to be standing in this circle. Anthony, almost identical to the person he was twelve years ago. Garin and me, nothing like the shells we once were. There were so many secrets between the three of us now.

"The old gang back together…how sweet," Anthony said.

The sarcasm was so thick in his voice. It made me shiver.

Why the hell would he say that? Now? When Billy sat in a coffin in the other room?

It felt like Anthony's hand had just torn at the hole that was already gaping in the middle of my chest. And, when I took a breath, it felt like he ripped it open even further.

"A funeral isn't the kind of reunion I had in mind," I said.

"Oh no?" Garin said. "I'm surprised to hear you even talk about a reunion."

Now that I was standing so close to him, I could finally see the pain in his eyes. The anger. The coldness. There were so many layers to it, and they'd all been caused by me.

"Saw your sister the other day," Anthony said. When he coughed, I could smell the weed on his breath. "Her kid's real cute."

I wasn't surprised Anthony hadn't told me he had run into Garin's sister, Gina. He never talked about Garin or Billy to me.

But I was surprised to hear that Gina had a child. She was the same age as Paulie and Anthony. The three of them had been as close as the three of us. And Gina was into everything they were—hustling, drugs, and all the violence that went along with that lifestyle. The last I'd heard a few years ago was that she was in pretty rough shape and had been admitted to a rehab center in California.

"She had a baby?" I asked.

# PRISONED

"She adopted one."

Garin's teeth weren't gritted, but they may as well have been. The pull of his lips, the look in his eyes, the tone of his voice all told me he didn't want to discuss Gina or her daughter. He wanted to say something to me, and I had a feeling it wasn't going to be pretty.

I didn't deserve pretty.

I knew this was going to get me in trouble, but I didn't care. "Do you want to talk?" I asked Garin.

"Not here."

"Well, I'm—"

"Not here, Kyle. We'll go to a bar or something."

I was afraid of what he would ask, what he would want to know, but I owed him this. Even though I couldn't tell him the truth, I owed him at least something.

I tried to calm the emotion in my chest as I looked over at my brother. "Are you going to come with us?"

His phone beeped, and he pulled it out of his pocket. "Fuck," he said, reading the screen. "Something happened with work, and I have to go take care of it." He glanced between Garin and me. "I'll pick you up from the bar later."

"I'll give her a ride," Garin said.

"Then, I'll pick you up at the hotel in the morning and take you to the airport."

"I have to be at the airport by six. I'll just take a taxi."

I'd spent more than enough time with my brother today. But I'd be seeing him again on the first when he made his monthly drive to Florida. He'd stay at my house for about twenty minutes, checking things out, leaving what he needed to, and then heading to my mom's. She now lived on the other side of Tampa, and that was where he would sleep until he drove back to Jersey.

"Kyle, you sure about this?" Anthony asked.

It was a warning.

"Yes," I said, giving him a hug that was all for show. "I'll see you soon."

Anthony gave me a final glare, and he went over to Billy's mom. I wondered what he could possibly say to her to make this right. How he could look her in the face and lie. It was all so easy for him. He had no hole in his chest, no guilt in his heart.

We had nothing in common.

"I can't believe you came back home," Garin said.

*Home.* There was that dreadful word again.

I slowly shifted my attention to him. Those eyes. That face. So much dark scruff I wasn't used to seeing on him. So much anger that was warranted.

"Honestly, I can't either."

That was the most honest I'd been all day.

"You're heading back tomorrow?"

"Yes."

"Flying out to..."

"Florida. I still live there."

"Right."

I knew he was living in Vegas, that he was the general manager of The V, a high-end hotel and casino on the strip. I Googled him more often than I should have.

Silence passed between us, but I still felt his emotion, his questions. I most definitely felt his coldness. "Garin—"

"Don't. Let's go."

"Aren't there people here you want to talk to?" I asked, grabbing his arm to stop him from moving. His eyes told me I needed to get my hand off him, so I immediately lifted it. "I just meant, I can wait for you outside if you want."

"I've spoken to everyone I need to."

And I'd spoken to no one but him and Anthony, which was more than enough.

"My car is out front," he said, turning around and walking toward the door.

My anxiety built as I followed him, keeping my eyes on the floor, knowing I would be away from that shiny box in just a few seconds. From that puffy white fabric that lined it. From the still face of Billy, who never should have been inside. But I would also be alone with Garin, the man I had thought about every day since I left Atlantic City. The man who deserved so much more than I was about to give him.

The man I could never tell the truth to because I would be in a box next to Billy's.

# THREE

## GARIN
## TWELVE YEARS AGO

I opened my bedroom door and shrugged out of my jacket. As I rounded the corner to the bed, I saw Kyle sitting on the floor. She was tucked between the end of the mattress and my window, a blanket wrapped around her, sleeping on her arms as they rested on her bent knees.

"Hey," I said, kneeling in front of her. I waited until her eyes opened. "You okay?"

No one was at my place tonight. Ma was probably partying at some other apartment in The Heart, and I'd seen my sister down at the boardwalk with one of the guys she liked to hustle with. Kyle must have used the spare key I kept hidden.

"I'm okay."

"Come here." I held out my hand.

When she grabbed it, I lifted her out of the corner and sat her on the bed. She brought the blanket along, tightening it around her.

"I couldn't fall asleep at home."

"Too cold?"

She nodded, sleepy-eyed and cute.

I paid our heat bill, but Kyle didn't make enough to help out with her ma's bills. If Anthony gave his ma any cash, I was sure she'd spend it on dope rather than making sure their apartment stayed warm. That was the kind of bitch she was. My ma was no better.

But that didn't matter because I wanted Kyle here anyway. I liked that my place was where she went to get warm and go to sleep.

"Lie down," I said. "I'll take the floor."

She kicked off her shoes and rested her head on the pillow. I sat on the carpet and leaned my back into the side of the bed.

"Is your ma home?" I asked.

"No, she went out before I got home from school."

"What about Anthony?"

"I haven't seen him for a few days."

Kyle's fridge was always empty. If her ma was home, she'd get Kyle something to eat. But, with her being out, that meant Kyle had skipped dinner. And there was no way the turkey sandwich and apple she'd eaten for lunch would hold her until tomorrow.

"I'll be right back."

She grabbed my hand when I tried to stand up. "No, don't leave. I know you're going to go get me some food, but I'm not hungry. I just want to talk." Her eyes pleaded with mine. "So, stay with me and just talk to me, okay?"

"You need to eat, Kyle."

"I will in a little bit. I promise."

She let go of my hand, and I sat down again—this time, on the bed right next to where she was lying.

"I'm worried about Billy," she said, resting her chin on her palm. "He's using more and more."

I knew she had noticed. It was impossible not to. But, shit, I didn't want Kyle to worry about him, too. Billy was my responsibility, and somehow, I'd get him straight.

"He'll be okay."

"Are you sure?" She scratched her cheek and down her arm and rubbed around her elbow.

# PRISONED

I knew she didn't itch. Kyle was just fidgeting. She did that sometimes when we were alone together and sitting real close.

"Because I'm not sure he's going to be okay," she continued. "He doesn't just use on the weekends when we're having fun. He uses before school and right after last period. He's always high now. And I've seen what happens when people use that much. We're surrounded by it."

She was talking about the people in The Heart. Her ma. Mine. They'd probably use a hell of a lot more if they could afford it. But she was right about what Billy's using would eventually lead to, and the sadness in her eyes fucking killed me.

It killed me even more because it was my fault.

"I'll talk to him, Kyle."

I had to fix it. I'd already tried. But I'd try again and again until I got our friend back to the way he used to be.

"Okay."

I could tell there was something else on her mind. She was acting too timid, too restless, for there not to be.

"Tell me what you're thinking about." When she didn't answer, I put my hand over hers to stop it from moving. "Kyle?"

She looked so pretty as she glanced at me. She didn't have any makeup on. Her hair was a little tangled and messy, and her eyes were puffy from rubbing them when she'd woken up.

"I don't want to go home."

She said that to me every time she came to my place. I never once made her leave. But this time felt different; it felt like there was something she wasn't saying.

I pulled the blanket higher until it wedged under her chin.

When I tried to stand again, she stopped me. "Don't go."

"I'm not leaving. I'm just going to sit on the floor."

She shook her head, her fingers squeezing mine. "No. Don't."

My dick hardened from the sound of those sweet words. It rubbed against my boxers, painfully pushing against the inside of my zipper.

"Where do you want me?"

Her skin was so soft, so perfect in the light that shone in from the streetlamp. I wanted to rub my face against her cheek, to kiss it.

"Here." She patted the small space that was between us.

I kicked off my shoes and swung my legs onto the bed.

"No." She was fidgeting again—this time, combing out the side of her hair. "I want you under the covers."

She'd never asked me to do that before, never looked at me the way she was staring at me now. If I lay down as close as she wanted me, she'd feel how hard I was. I didn't want that to scare the hell out of her. I had to know what she wanted before I got under the covers.

"Come here," I said, reaching for her hand, pulling her until she sat up.

She didn't fight me. She didn't question what I was doing. And, when my fingers cupped her cheek, she didn't pull away. My thumb traced the corner of her lips. After a few passes, she leaned into me, nuzzling my hand.

"I want to kiss you." I wouldn't have warned anyone else, and I never had in the past. But Kyle was my best friend. That made this different. And it made me more cautious.

Her teeth stabbed her bottom lip. "Do it. Please."

Her lips were so hot. So full. So delicate, like the rest of her. I'd been checking them out for years, and now, she was telling me I could have them.

I didn't want to wait a second more.

"Kyle," I groaned right before I kissed her. I was gentle, not knowing how she'd react even though this was what she'd told me she wanted.

She moved much quicker than I expected, wrapping her arms around my neck, pressing her body into mine. When I felt her tits rub against my chest, I thought my dick was going to bust through my jeans.

"Garin." It was a whisper. Tiny and breathy. Almost as tiny as her.

I pulled back just enough, so my tongue wasn't inside her mouth. "Yeah?"

"Why are you being so gentle with me?"

I glanced down at her lips. They were wet—from me. They were red and puffy—from me. It looked so good on her.

"I don't want to scare you."

The problem with being her best friend was that I knew everything about her. I knew this was her first kiss. That was my doing. The guys at school didn't fuck with her. They barely even talked to her because of me. So, I wanted to make sure she was comfortable, that her first time wasn't rushed and heavy. She was making that almost impossible.

"You could never scare me, Garin." Her voice was still so tiny. "Because I already love you. I always have."

Girls had said that shit to me before. It was different with Kyle. It meant something. It hit me in the chest and stayed there. That was a feeling that had never been in there before.

"I—"

She put her finger over my mouth. "Don't say it." She smiled. "I already know how you feel about me. So, when you do say it, I want to be surprised."

I kissed the inside of her finger. "Then, I'll tell you that I want to kiss you more, and I don't want to wait any longer to do it." I pulled her out from underneath the blanket, turned her until she faced me, and sat her on my lap.

She spread her legs around my waist, her arms wrapped around my shoulders, and she moved her face much closer. "Kiss me, Garin. I mean, *really* kiss me."

I gripped the back of her head and pushed it forward until her lips were on mine. Then, I gave her my tongue, and hers swirled around the tip of mine, softly sucking it. My hands slowly dropped down her body, feeling the spots I'd wanted to touch for so long. Her flat stomach, her narrow waist. Those perfect thin thighs. Each breath, each tiny moan, told me how good she was feeling.

And she felt so fucking good to me.

When I reached her chest, I brushed my thumb over her nipple. Back and forth. Just the very edge of it and only using the pad of my finger.

"Garin," she groaned against my mouth. "Ahh."

I switched to her other nipple, and her back arched. She was breathing her moans into me, and I swallowed every one. Her scent, her taste, her sounds—all of it made my dick even harder. And I was sure she felt it as she jerked her hips forward and sat right on top of it.

"Ahh," she groaned again. Her fingers were running through my hair, tugging it so hard that I thought she was going to pull it out of my head.

I fucking loved it. I wanted her to pull harder. Because everything I heard, everything I felt, told me how good she was feeling, and that was the only thing that mattered to me. Except I knew I could make her feel even better. It would just mean that my hands would have to dip down to her pussy. Once they touched that part of her, I didn't know if I could stop what would happen next. There had already been a lot of firsts tonight. I didn't want to take her virginity, too.

I held her waist still and pulled our faces apart. She squeezed my shoulders as she tried to catch her breath, gnawing on those wet, puffy lips.

I couldn't get enough of her innocence. That was something that didn't exist around here. But I'd protected Kyle and made sure she didn't lose hers.

I'd be the one who eventually took it.

"Why did you stop?" she finally asked.

There was hurt in her eyes, and that was the last thing I wanted.

"I'm out of self-control. I've been trying real hard, but I want you so bad, it hurts. If I don't stop now, I'm going to take things much further, and you don't want that yet."

"Maybe I do."

She was so fucking sweet. And so naive.

Rubbing her nipples and grinding against my dick had made her horny, and I hadn't given her any relief. But if we had sex, there was a chance she'd regret it in the morning. Until I was sure it was what she really wanted, the only thing she was getting from me was more kissing.

That would have to come tomorrow though. I needed to jack off before I trusted myself around her again.

"I'll give you everything you want, Kyle. Things just need to move slowly."

The hurt returned to her eyes. I needed to fix it.

"You're my best friend. Nothing is going to ruin that. I want this." I pushed my hips up, so my hard-on pressed into her pussy. "You can feel how much I want this. But I want more than just sex, and that's why we have to go slow."

"I do, too." The hurt started to dissolve when a grin spread over her lips. "More than anything."

I lifted her off my lap and set her feet on the floor, standing in front of her with my arms on her shoulders. "If you stay here tonight, I won't be able to keep my hands off you."

# PRISONED

"I kinda figured." She was hiding her smirk by chewing her lip again.

I sucked it into my mouth and ran my tongue across it to heal it. "Stop chewing," I said when I finally pulled away. "That's my lip, and I'm the only one that's allowed to bite it."

She laughed, and it was the sound I'd been waiting to hear. A sound that caused my hands to wrap around her face and pull it toward mine. I knew I shouldn't be kissing her again. It was too dangerous to keep tasting her. But I had to. I hadn't gotten enough. I would never get enough of her, not when I'd waited this long to have her.

This was just a tease.

Hours with my mouth on her wouldn't even give me the satisfaction I was craving. I needed days, months, with her. I needed to know that every part of her was mine. And I needed to feel that over and over. And ravishing her mouth was making that need intensify.

"You have to go."

I licked the wetness off my lips and got another taste of her.

The want rushing through me made me want to fucking growl.

"I'm never going to sleep tonight," she said so softly.

"Neither will I." My thumb traced that curve around her mouth again. "But it's not safe for you to be here a second longer."

She tried to touch my chest, but I clenched both of her hands between mine.

"I'll walk you out."

I stopped by my closet before I took her downstairs, grabbing a plastic sleeve of powdered doughnuts. I always kept a few boxes of them in there. They were my favorite—Kyle's, too—and we'd eat them every morning on our way to school.

I put the sleeve in her hand when we reached the bottom step. "Stay here," I said.

"Garin?"

I opened the fridge. "Yeah?"

"I know you're getting me more to eat, but I'm really not hungry." She rubbed a finger over her lips. "I just want to taste you tonight. I'll eat in the morning before school, I promise."

I wasn't used to her speaking this softly, but I liked it. Hell, I wanted so much more of it.

I shut the fridge and moved over to her. With her standing on the first step, we were almost the same height.

I leaned forward and nibbled her bottom lip. "Is this what you want?"

"Yes," she sighed as I pulled my teeth away. "Keep eating me."

"I want to." I gripped her hips. "Every bit of you." I lifted her off the step and set her by the front door. "Eat those doughnuts before you go to bed. All of them."

The only way she'd get some sleep was if she put food in her body. The hunger pangs would keep her up all night if she didn't. She knew how to convince herself she wasn't hungry, that it didn't hurt. We all knew how.

I wouldn't let it happen anymore.

"But—"

"Eat them for me, Kyle. No excuses."

"Okay."

I opened the front door and held on to it while she stood in the entryway. "If I kiss you again, there's a chance I won't let you leave."

Her teeth slipped out of her mouth and rubbed across her bottom lip.

"That's mine," I reminded her. "Chew on something else...like those doughnuts."

She laughed. "Got it."

"I'll see you in the morning."

I closed the door behind her and rushed up the stairs to the bathroom. I stripped off my clothes and jumped into the shower. The freezing water hit my chest as I wrapped my hand around my hard dick and tugged. I didn't have to search my head for an image to jerk off to or picture one of the porn scenes I'd watched. Kyle's face was what I saw when I closed my eyes. It was her moans I heard in my ears. It was her body I could feel under my fingers.

She was so fucking sexy.

I gripped my dick tighter and twisted my hand as I got closer to the tip, that familiar warmth already starting in my stomach. I pushed my other hand against the back wall and aimed my cock toward the water stream.

*Boom!*

# PRISONED

My eyes burst open, and I froze as the sound vibrated across my body.

A sound I'd heard too many times before.

Motherfucker.

I left the water on and hurdled the short step of the tub. I grabbed the towel that hung on the back of the door and threw it around my waist as I ran down the stairs. When I got outside, someone was lying facedown in the middle of the road. The clothes and short hair and the size of the body told me it was a guy.

I hurried over to his side and knelt on the icy ground. "Hey, buddy. I'm going to turn you over, so I can help you."

He didn't respond.

I squeezed the back of his jacket and slowly rolled him toward me. There was so much adrenaline running through me. I could barely feel the cold air on my naked skin or the ice and rocks scraping against my knees. The only thing I felt was the stab in my fucking chest when I saw his blood-splattered face.

"*No!*" I screamed. "Paulie, open your eyes!"

I held my hand against his chest to feel if it was rising and falling and my ear to his face to hear if he was breathing. There was nothing—no movement, no sound.

"Paulie, open your eyes and talk to me!"

I unbuttoned the top of his jacket and saw the bullet hole. It was on the right side of his chest. And there was blood. On his shirt. On the ground. On my hands. A puddle of it pooling around my feet.

"Paulie, come on, open your eyes, buddy." I checked his pockets for a phone. I didn't find one. "Help!" I shouted, looking up and down the street.

There was no one on the sidewalk, no one standing on their front steps, no one at their front door, no one looking at me through their windows. Where the hell was everybody?

"Help me!" I put my hands over the bullet hole and tried to stop any more blood from coming out. "Paulie, I'm going to get you some help, and they're going to take you to the hospital and make this better."

I was holding his wound hard enough where he should have been groaning from the pressure. But he wasn't making a sound. He wasn't moving. There was just silence and so much fucking blood.

I didn't know when I saw the plastic sleeve—if it happened while I was holding Paulie's chest and waiting for the ambulance to come or if it was when Billy showed up and broke down when he saw his brother or if it was after I got back from the hospital. But, at some point, I saw it lying on the ground halfway between my apartment and Kyle's. The sleeve was open, and the doughnuts inside were crushed. There was a single doughnut smashed onto the sidewalk. Sugary white powder was all over the pavement, like little piles of coke.

And Kyle?

She was nowhere to be found.

# FOUR

## KYLE

"Bring us another one, *please*," I said to the waitress, pointing toward our half-empty glasses. Or maybe they were three-quarters full or only a quarter. Or there were more than two glasses on the table. I wasn't really sure. I'd stopped caring after the fourth round. That was when I'd stopped seeing straight, too.

But I didn't really need to see straight. I only needed to see to the right of me—where Garin sat. My childhood bestie. The boy I'd been in love with for as long as I could remember. And the boy I'd given up because I was forced to leave New Jersey.

I hated that.

I hated it more than anything.

When I looked in his direction, I couldn't believe he was here, sitting so close, his face filling my vision. Those eyes...their intensity.

I wasn't cold, but my whole body was covered in goose bumps.

He was cold though. Freezing, icy. He hadn't warmed even the tiniest bit since we'd gotten to the bar and the drinks started flowing.

"Maybe I should have ordered a water," I said. "And gotten you some coffee to melt all your icicles."

"You know what would make me less cold?" His eyes narrowed. "If you slowed down on the drinking and started answering some of my questions."

I laughed, covering my mouth with the back of my hand, so I wouldn't say anything stupid. The last time he'd said *slow* was during a sexy memory...the only sexy memory I had of us. "Slow doesn't apply to drinking." My hand must have fallen away because something incredibly stupid had slipped out.

His tongue swept over his bottom lip, reminding me of a time when he had been so possessive of my mouth. "It only applies to when I tried not to fuck you on the same night I kissed you for the first time." His tongue swept in the opposite direction. "The first and only night I ever got to kiss you."

So, he was thinking about it, too.

A shiver passed through my entire body, leaving a tingling sensation in my chest. I could still feel his hands and that kiss. The tingling wouldn't budge when I tried to rub it away. It grew instead, spreading to my breasts and down between my legs. I crossed them, squeezing my thighs together, hoping that would help alleviate it.

It only made it worse.

So did the way he stared at me. His gorgeous eyes looked straight through me, the alcohol practically unzipping my soul so that he could get a better view.

A view that needed to stay hidden, so I looked away.

"Yeah...that night," I breathed.

"And then you ended everything."

There was the sound of anger again.

I lifted the glass to my lips. "Something like that." I swallowed however much was left. I couldn't feel it go down my throat. I couldn't taste it. I was completely numb, except for the tingling, and the tingling was only getting worse. My body shouldn't have been reacting that way. This was all wrong. So wrong.

"I'm back in Atlantic City, drinking my face off, and Billy has died from an OD. This is so fucked."

"Kyle..."

I liked the way he said my name a little too much.

# PRISONED

I set the glass down, my hand still clinging it for support, and I slowly met the eyes that made me so unsteady. "I know my face is still on. It just feels like it's off."

"Tell me why you left."

"I left to go to school. You know that."

"That's not what I'm asking. *You* know that."

He wanted to know why things had changed after the night Paulie died. Why I had left our relationship. Why I had never allowed him to kiss me again.

But I couldn't tell him any of that.

My face reddened. "That kissing though…"

I could tell by the way he glared at me that he knew how he affected me. My flushed cheeks just confirmed whatever he thought. I was even sure he could sense the tingling in my body, the goose bumps, and the wetness between my legs.

"And then Paulie died."

His gaze shifted to my mouth.

"And now Billy…" The tingle briefly turned to an ache. "Why did it happen?" My voice trailed off as I answered my own question.

I'd watched Billy's using go from a few times a week to several times a day. That was back then. I was sure it had only gotten worse. Garin had told me not to worry, that he would take care of it. But he couldn't fix Billy, especially after Paulie died.

No one could fix us after Paulie died.

Now, it was too late.

"He lost his fucking brother, and that ruined him."

"It ruined all of us," I whispered.

It especially ruined me.

"It didn't have to," he said.

I wished that were true.

Garin fed me, he bought me clothes, and he made sure I always had a little cash in my pocket. He made sure I stayed safe. He was my family. My everything.

And then…he was my nothing.

"You saved me, you know." I could hear my words start to slur. "I don't know what would have happened if you hadn't taken care of me."

He gritted his teeth. "Then, why didn't you stay?"

Why didn't I stay?

My legs were bouncing underneath the table, and my hands couldn't sit still. I only fidgeted this badly when I thought about him or when I was around him. "My mom was a mess, and my brother used way too much. Drugs made them feel good." That was the truth, but it wasn't the reason I left. "And what made me feel good was you." I wished my hand were back over my mouth instead of playing with my napkin. I didn't know why I was saying any of this.

"Bullshit."

He didn't believe me. That absolutely killed me.

I guessed I wouldn't believe me either. But he had made me feel good; that part was pure honesty.

"It's true, Garin. Even when I slept, I always wanted to be close to you. And then I left your apartment and…"

"And what?"

"And I just couldn't stay anymore."

A lie.

The drinking didn't ease the hurt of the lie, nor did it ease the guilt. That was always there, no matter what I tried to tell myself or what I put in my body.

"I just couldn't, Garin. It hurt too much." Another lie. I shook my head to get rid of the memory and rubbed the center of my chest. That was where the pain lived, where the gnawing started. I wanted the tingling back. The tingling was so much easier. "I struggled so much with it, and I was only—" I cut myself off. I'd already said way too much.

"You were only what?"

I raised my glass, but there was nothing in it. So, I twirled the base of it over the table.

"You were only what, Kyle?" He didn't shout, but his voice was so stern.

I finally looked at him again. "They're both dead now. The two brothers. Almost a whole family. It's such a tragedy."

"Stop avoiding this."

He was right. I was avoiding.

And, if he continued staring at me, he'd see the truth. And the truth needed to stay where it was—hidden behind years of scars.

# PRISONED

I pulled out my cell to check the time. The numbers were squiggly, thanks to the liquor, but it looked like it was close to midnight. Or ten past one. Either way, we'd been here for hours, and I couldn't remember the last time I'd gone to the restroom.

"Ladies' room," I said, getting up from the stool. "I'll be *back*."

I hurried into the restroom and locked myself in a stall. The buzz hit me even harder now that I was standing, and I had to use the walls to hold myself up. It felt like they were getting narrower, the longer I hovered over the bowl, my ankles becoming wobblier in these heels.

*Only a few more hours*, I reminded myself, *and then I'll be on a plane heading home.* Away from Atlantic City. Away from the secrets. Away from the lies that stared me in the face. Away from Garin Woods, who made me feel as unsteady as these damn shoes. God, he was sexy.

*Hiccup.*

And he'd been the best kisser.

*Hiccup.*

And his hands had known just how to touch me, just the right amount of pressure to use on my nipples. Hands that, I was sure, had only gotten more talented in the twelve years that had passed.

Hands that needed to find their way out of my head.

I wasn't here to be touched or to think about being touched. I wasn't here to feel any pleasure at all. I wasn't here to remember how much I missed Garin, and I couldn't miss him when I left. I'd have one more drink, go back to the hotel alone, and sleep for a few hours before I got on the plane.

*Hiccup.*

I wiggled my panties back up my legs, ignoring the wetness that had soaked into the fabric. Wetness that Mr. Hands had caused. Wetness that needed to dry and not be added to.

The automatic flush roared behind me as I stumbled out of the stall and washed up at the sink. The lighting showed my eyeliner had smudged a little, giving my eyes a sultrier look. My hair had loosened out of their curls and was wilder than normal. I didn't bother to tame it.

*Hiccup.*

When the restroom door shut behind me, someone moved right in front of me and gripped my waist. It took me a second to connect the arms to the hands and the chest to the arms and the face to the neck.

But, when I finally made it all those inches above me, I realized they belonged to Garin.

I shivered. "You're so cold," I breathed. The tingling was now back in my chest. "Why are you so cold?"

His icy glare didn't stop the wetness. It was still on my panties. But I wasn't drunk enough to mention that part.

"Because you still haven't given me what I want."

He was holding me so tightly. I didn't mind. I should have. I should be pushing my way out of his hold and returning to our table. But I didn't. It had been so long since a man had really held me. I missed the feeling of a pair of strong hands. Hands like Garin's.

I missed him.

"Were you waiting for me?" I asked, ignoring what he'd said.

He took more of my weight, making my body feel even lighter. The thumping, the tingling, the wetness—I wished I could give him some of that because it was becoming unbearable.

"Garin?"

His hands moved up my sides, over my shoulders, and cupped my throat. It was already hard to breathe. This made it worse. But the hold he had on me was so sexy. It was like a punishment for what I had done to him.

"You like this," he whispered angrily over my face.

I closed my eyes and let his statement simmer through me. He didn't phrase it like a question because he obviously already knew the answer.

"What if I squeeze harder? Will you like that just as much?"

It was a threat. One that I liked more than I should have.

He didn't wait for me to respond before he tightened his grip. Air was stuck in my lungs. Fear was pulsing through me—not because I was worried he would hurt me, even though I should have been, but because I was worried I was on the verge of telling him the truth.

"Yes," I finally replied. "And I want more of it."

My mind showed me what more felt like. It took me back to that night in his bedroom when he'd kissed me for the first time. I'd had zero experience before that moment. Garin had plenty, and I found that intimidating. So, before I'd gone to Garin's that night, I'd taken a few sips of vodka from the bottle I'd found in my freezer. I'd wanted him, and it was time to finally tell him.

# PRISONED

Vodka was now running through my body, but that was where the similarities ended.

Now, there were secrets between us.

And lies.

And years of anger over me leaving Atlantic City.

And coldness.

I was lost in a wind of dark memories and guilt, and it was all thumping inside my chest. His eyes were tearing through me, and I was losing the ability to keep it all hidden.

"Kyle…" His grip tightened once again, bringing me back to him. Bringing me back to the feelings his hands caused. Bringing me back to the tingling and wetness.

"Yes?"

His thumb grazed the base of my neck where my pulse hammered away. His eyes told me the thought crossed his mind. A harder squeeze was all it would take.

"Tell me what I want to know."

If I could lean forward and kiss him, I would. But the way he was holding me wouldn't allow for that. I was caged, unable to move, barely able to breathe, and all I wanted was his lips on mine. So, if I couldn't take it, I could ask for it. "Kiss me."

"That's what you want?" His jaw flexed when he ground his teeth together. "My hands are around your fucking neck, and you want me to kiss you?"

"More than anything. Give me all your anger."

His chest was rising and falling. His lips were parted in a way that they looked enraged.

"I can take it. I can take all of it, Garin."

Seconds passed.

They felt like the longest seconds of my life.

Then, squeezing my throat even tighter, his mouth crashed against mine, and he slammed my back into the wall. Where I had once been overtaken by numbness, I now felt everything. From the gentle sparks in my toes to the throbbing in my nipples. The roughness of his lips owned me, and my entire body was responding to each lashing. I did nothing to fight it.

What I did was beg for more.

My hands went to his chest to feel the man he had become. In high school, he was so scrawny. Now, my fingers skimmed across planes of pure muscle, ripples that bulged under his skin. He was so much harder, so much more dominant than I'd expected.

He deepened our kiss as I slid my hands up his neck, his tongue swirling around mine. I combed through the thickness of his whiskers, stubble I'd never felt on him before. A coarseness that I fantasized scratching up the inside of my thighs. I reached his cheeks, and suddenly, I was in the air, my legs wrapped around his waist, my back still on the wall.

The space between us was gone. We were shirt against shirt, breasts against chest. Lips so intertwined, it felt like they'd never been apart.

And it was perfect.

It was too perfect.

All these years, I'd wanted to know what it would have felt like had I not left his apartment that night and had begged him to take my virginity. I was getting a taste of that now. It made me want more.

And it made the guilt grow.

And the guilt made it hard to breathe.

"Garin…"

I pulled my mouth away, but his didn't go very far. It moved to my neck, biting across my throat and down my collarbone and over the tops of my breasts.

"Mmm," I moaned.

"You want this to stop?" He lifted his face, his eyes holding mine.

Was I capable of telling him to stop? Not at this point. Not after being reminded of how good he could make me feel.

"No," I said.

He sucked my bottom lip into his mouth, pulling it away from the teeth that were grinding into it. "I want to torture this fucking lip." His eyes only confirmed his words. "Let's get the hell out of here."

"And go where?"

He kissed the outer edge of my cheek, his deep voice tickling around my ear, turning me on even more. "To a place where I can give your body everything it needs."

He set me on my feet as he waited for my answer.

An answer that was already on my tongue.

A tongue that watered to taste more of him.

## PRISONED

I was going home tomorrow where I could dwell on the guilt for the rest of my life. But, tonight, I wanted to feel some pleasure even if I didn't deserve it. And I wanted Garin to give it to me.

I took his hand and led him to the door.

# FIVE

## KYLE

My throat was so dry. I couldn't swallow. Every time I tried, I choked on the thickness of my tongue. It was swollen, stuck to the roof of my mouth. The taste was worse than morning breath. More like days' and days' worth of morning breath plus bile.

I rubbed my cheek into the pillow, not understanding why it was so firm. Why there was no give. Why it felt like muscle, not feathers or fluff.

"Don't open your eyes too fast," a man said. "Whatever they gave us was some heavy shit."

I pushed away from whatever my head was lying on and opened my eyes as I sat up. *"Ow!"* I screamed, covering them with my forearm.

He was right; I shouldn't have opened them too fast. The light stung and made my head pound. The little I could see was all blurry and rushing in circles, like I was inside a washing machine on full spin. Sweat covered my skin. My mouth watered.

I was going to throw up.

"Take some deep breaths. It will get better," he said.

I leaned back into what must have been the headboard and sucked in mouthfuls of air before blowing it out through my nose and inhaling more. I knew the voice that kept speaking to me. Even though it had changed over the years, it was a voice I would never forget. It was deeper now. Sexier. I just didn't understand how he was able to talk to me in person. I had a flight to take me back to Tampa early this morning, and there was no reason I shouldn't be on it.

Maybe I was on it, and he'd decided to come with me. Maybe the spinning in my head was really turbulence. But then, why didn't I remember checking in at the airport?

"Tell me we're on the plane."

"We're not."

"Tell me I didn't miss my flight."

"You missed it."

"Shit."

Still covering my eyes, I tucked my head between my knees and tried to take more deep breaths. "Was I that drunk?" My stomach churned. "Don't answer that. I don't want to talk about what I drank. It hurts too much."

"We were both pretty drunk."

I remembered both of us drinking. I remembered ordering more drinks. I didn't remember much else besides...him kissing me. It was a little cloudy, but I could visualize the hallway we were in. My back was against one of the walls. His hands were around my throat, and there was tongue and biting and moaning.

Lots of moaning.

Had we done more? I reached down and rubbed my thighs. I was wearing pants. They felt like the same ones I'd worn to the funeral. I wiggled my butt and felt the pull from my panties. My shirt and bra were on.

That didn't mean I hadn't been naked at some point.

I sucked in the walls of my pussy, trying to feel for that familiar tenderness that was usually there the day after I had sex.

"We didn't fuck."

How did he know what I was thinking?

"If I'd fucked you, Kyle, you wouldn't have to try to remember it. It would be the only thing you'd be thinking about."

## PRISONED

I rubbed my temples, trying to dull some of the pounding. "A little conceited, aren't you?"

"I've wanted to fuck you since I was fifteen years old. If I got the chance to finally be inside you, I would have fifteen years of making up to do. And it would be something you would never, ever forget. So, no, I'm not conceited. I just know what I'm capable of and how I'd want to make you feel."

I didn't care how much it hurt or how badly everything inside my head was spinning, I had to see the expression on his face. So, I spread my fingers slowly, letting in a little light at a time.

The sweat on my skin was starting to dry, and the dampness in the air was hitting me now.

"Why do you have the air-conditioning on?" I asked. "It's freezing in here."

"The air isn't on."

I had one eye open, focusing on him, while I gradually opened the other. Everything was hurting even worse now that I could see, but that didn't take away from his gorgeous face. A face with long scruff and messy hair that was leaning against a wall.

A wall...not a headboard.

And beneath him was a cement floor that was the color of dirt.

"Where are we?" I asked, slowly peeking around the room.

There was a toilet just to my left with a pedestal sink, both made of rusty metal. A bottle of soap and a tube of toothpaste lay on the sink. The door across from us had a square cutout in the center, filled with thick rusty bars. On the next wall was a rectangular window directly under the ceiling.

No color, no tile, no paint. Just metal, rust, and dirty cement.

"Is this your bathroom?" I asked although he still hadn't answered my first question.

My bathroom in The Heart was nicer than the one in Garin's hotel, which seemed really odd.

He shook his head. "No."

Why was I so cold?

"Then, where are we, Garin?"

"From what I've been able to piece together, I think we've been taken."

"Taken? Taken where?" Everything inside me was suddenly shaking, including my voice. The sweat was back; the churning had returned. The whole room was spinning.

"The guy who opened our cell wouldn't tell me, and he shut the door too quickly for me to grab him."

"OUR CELL?"

I pushed myself off the ground and wrapped my arms around my stomach. My chest was heaving, my pulse racing. The air was closing in on me. It felt like there were hands squeezing my throat. And then there was this awful taste in my mouth, like I'd been sucking on a piece of hard plastic. But there was nothing between my lips, nothing around my neck.

Just me, Garin, this cell, so many unknowns, and not nearly enough air.

*Stop fighting it, Kyle.*

"I can't breathe."

I tried yanking my collar away from my throat, but my tank top wasn't anywhere near it. The movement only made it feel tighter. Three clumsy steps, and I was at the sink, splashing cold water on my face, gulping it down. It didn't help. I still couldn't breathe.

Tiny flashes of light sparkled at the corners of my eyes as I paced in a small circle. They weren't pretty; they were a warning that I was going to pass out. I needed to breathe. Nothing was going in; nothing was coming out.

*Breathe.*

Garin's hands were on my shoulders.

*Breathe.*

"What's the worst design you ever made?"

"What?" I panted, looking up through the pieces of hair that had fallen over my eyes. I was holding my chest because my throat was too tight to touch.

"Worst design," he said. "Tell me about it."

*Relax, Kyle.*

I shook my head. The plastic taste wasn't as strong, the tightening starting to loosen just a little. "It was supposed to be a calla lily."

"And?"

The shaking stopped, and the room was no longer spinning.

## PRISONED

"It looked more like a tulip." I inhaled through my nose and exhaled slowly out through my mouth. "Client hated it. Made me redo it, and the second one was just as bad."

"Why?" He gripped my shoulders even harder.

"I can't do flowers. Never have been able to."

"Too detailed?"

"I'm just not a fan."

"I've never heard a woman say that before."

I shrugged, feeling his fingers bear down on me. "They die too fast. I'd rather have something that lasts a little longer."

"So, no chocolate?"

I laughed, enjoying the warmth I was feeling from him because I didn't know how long it would last. "Oh no, chocolate lasts. It goes straight to my ass where it has the potential to stay forever."

"You're breathing again."

"I know."

To make sure it stayed that way, I focused on Garin. He was in the same clothes he'd worn to the funeral, but now, his shirt was untucked, and there were stains on his pants. His scruff had definitely thickened, and the look in his eyes had deepened. As deep as when he had been kissing me.

"How long have we been here?" I asked.

"At least a night. Maybe more. I woke up only a few hours before you. It took you longer to sleep off the meds."

He'd mentioned something about that earlier, and I'd ignored it. At that point, I thought I was in his hotel room. I wished I could go back to that thought. That image was perfect.

"What do you think they gave us?"

He sat us down on the floor, turning so that he faced me. His hand left my shoulder. I missed it the second it was gone.

"I don't know, but something strong enough where they were able to transport us without us waking up."

Air had fully returned to my lungs. It was my stomach I couldn't get to relax now.

"Who's *they*?"

"I've only seen one guy. I don't know who he is."

Garin was over two hundred pounds of muscle. It wasn't just one guy who had drugged and transported the both of us. There had to be at least a few guys. If they took us, they wanted something from us. And if they wanted something from us, something told me they'd do anything to get it.

*Anything.*

How much time had I lost in this cell? How many days had I lain on that dirty cement while our captor watched us, planning on what he was going to do?

I glanced down at my hands. They looked so yellow in this dim light. Yellow and sickly and unwashed and shaking.

I was shaking again.

This wasn't real. It couldn't be.

I rushed over to the door, wrapped my hands around the bars, and pulled on them as hard as I could. There was no budge. Not even the slightest movement.

"It's locked. I already tried it. The fucker has no give at all."

"No!" I shouted. I lifted myself until the bottoms of my feet were driving into the door, and I tugged with all of my weight. "We can't be locked in here. There's no reason for it. We didn't do anything wrong. We…"

There was no *we*.

Garin hadn't done anything wrong.

There was only me.

"I've tried, Kyle. Trust me, it won't open. Don't use all your strength; you're going to need it."

My feet dropped to the ground, and I turned around to press my back against the door. My hands stung from the metal, my palms now tinged a deep orange from the rust. I felt myself falling until my ass sharply hit the cement.

"Ow," I cried out. It wasn't just my ass that was stinging from the fall. My bladder was full and burning, too. "It all hurts."

"It's the meds. Once they fully wear off, you'll be better."

"Will I?"

He was sitting across from me, staring into my eyes, his face so stoic.

"Because I don't know how either of us can feel better in here," I said.

"Come here."

I shook my head.

# PRISONED

"Come here, Kyle."

He'd seen the man who had come to our cell. He'd had a few hours to stare at every corner of this room, every inch of the floor, every speck of grime, every bit of rust. Maybe he didn't have answers, but he had some time to process.

I needed time, and I needed to process somehow.

"Kyle, come—"

"What? Are you going to give me some of your warmth? Or are you going to turn cold again? I can't take that and this, Garin. And I can't move." It must have been the drugs that made my limbs feel so heavy, my head so cloudy. I could see, I could hear, I could feel, but none of it was crisp, and none of it felt like it was under my control.

Finally, warmth shone over his beautiful features, and he rose from the floor and walked over to me. "Come here." He wasn't asking me to do anything now. He was telling me what he was going to do, which was lift me from the floor and set me on his lap.

I molded to his body until I was snuggling into his chest with his arms wrapped around me.

I no longer felt the dampness in the air or the unforgiving hard floor.

I no longer felt his coldness.

I just felt him.

All of me felt him.

"I feel like a kid again, stuck inside The Heart, your comfort promising me that there's a way out."

"I can't promise that."

I sighed. "I know."

I finally smelled him. His skin, clothes—whatever it was, it was a taste. A taste of something delicious inside a flavorless room. A taste that reminded me of years of memories. They embraced me as much as he did.

I needed that...even if I didn't deserve it.

"I don't know why we're in here, but I'm happy they didn't put us in separate cells."

"Me, too," he whispered.

Even if he was being wrongfully accused, I didn't want to be in here alone. That made me selfish. That made me a horrible person. But

I closed my eyes and soaked up whatever he was giving me. If things were about to get bad, then at least I had this minute of good.

"Garin?"

"Mmm," he grumbled across the top of my head.

"You're squeezing me so hard. My bladder is about to burst."

"Then, get up and go to the bathroom."

I slowly looked at his face. "I've never peed in front of a man before. Not even you when we were kids."

His expression didn't change, but his grip lightened. "I'm sorry."

"Sorry for what?"

"That you've never felt comfortable enough with a man to be able to pee in front of him."

In all the time I'd been dating, I'd never peed with the door open. There was no pimple-popping. No shaving. Nothing personal, besides putting my clothes back on and walking out the door.

He was right; I wasn't comfortable enough.

It was a sad reminder of the truth.

"Stop overthinking it, Kyle. Just go over to the toilet, drop your pants, sit on the seat, and pee. I won't look."

"But you'll hear."

"Yes, I'll hear."

"That's just as bad."

Considering where we were and what had happened, it should have been the least of my worries. The problem was, I was worried about everything.

He pressed his hand over my cheek, his fingers reaching well past my ear, his thumb dipping to the corner of my lip. Even when he was soft, he was still so rough. "I don't know how long we're going to be in here, but you're going to hear me pee, you're going to see me wash my body, you're going to watch me get fucking pissed if someone doesn't bring us some answers and some food pretty soon." When he paused, it felt like he was reading my face. "If it's fear, get over it. Right now, it's just you and me and this goddamn cell. The only thing I care about is keeping you safe and comfortable."

I wiggled out of his lap and moved over to the toilet. There was no lid, just a big hole and a flushing handle. On the floor was a single roll of toilet paper. I didn't know if we'd be getting any more, and building

## PRISONED

a nest would use too much of it, so I dropped my pants and sat on my hands.

Before I peed, I glanced at Garin. His legs were stretched out and crossed, the back of his head resting against the wall, and his eyes were closed. He was giving me the privacy he'd promised.

I shut my own eyes and relaxed my body, feeling the relief almost immediately. When I was done, I washed my hands at the sink and used my pants to dry them. Then, I stayed in the corner, staring at the bars. There were eight of them, at least an inch apart, and through them, all I saw was darkness. "Why are we here?"

I felt his eyes on me, but I didn't get an answer.

# SIX

## GARIN
## TWO YEARS AGO

I pushed my chair back, reclined into the soft cushion behind me, and crossed my shoes over the edge of the desk. This was the first time I'd sat down in the last twelve hours, and there wasn't enough scotch in my wet bar to dull the ache that was throbbing behind my eyes.

It had been a long fucking day.

My marketing director had quit this morning, gone to work for the casino at the end of the strip, challenging his non-compete just one month before the largest poker tournament my hotel had ever hosted. A cocktail waitress had been sexually harassed by a player while taking his drink order. The finger he'd used to rub her cunt with was no longer attached to his hand. When my men didn't get enough satisfaction from that, they sawed off his whole goddamn wrist. And, to make matters even worse, three of the slot machines had paid out jackpots in the last six hours, totaling over ten million.

As soon as Mario saw that number, he'd be all over my ass. Every night, he received a detailed report of my daily numbers. Those numbers were then sent to all the other bosses in Atlantic City. The board was for show; the bosses were who really ran this casino. They called the shots from back home, and I made sure they were carried out. With them being so far away, there was a lot I could hide. The fucking numbers weren't one of them.

And, when the bosses got angry, they didn't take hands.

They took lives.

Someone's ass was going to get it because three jackpots in six hours wasn't typical. That was what we usually averaged a week. So, someone was either tampering with my machines, or they were faulting. I had everyone working on getting me that answer.

But, until that answer was in my hand, I needed to distract myself. Maybe I'd call one of the dancers from downstairs and have her come up to my condo that was on the top floor of the hotel. I'd chain her to my bed and pour scotch all over her tits. Her dripping tight asshole and a buzz would help dull this ache in my head.

When I picked up my phone to call the club, it started ringing in my hand. Billy's name was on the screen.

"Not a good time—"

"It's never a good time." He blew into the phone, which I knew was a mouthful of cigarette smoke. "Isn't it around eleven there? You should be balls-deep inside some slut, not picking up my call."

"Then, why didn't you just send me a text?"

"'Cause I knew you'd answer. You always do. Listen, I've been talking to some of the guys down at the boardwalk, and I've learned some shit."

This wasn't making my day any better. The guys down at the boardwalk were a bunch of street thugs who slept on the beach and ate from dumpsters. If Billy was hanging out down there, something told me he was sleeping down there, too.

"Did your Ma get evicted?" I asked.

"That's not why I'm calling, Garin."

"Answer me."

"She's been crashing with some dude, so she stopped paying the rent. Landlord tossed all our stuff. It ain't too bad, being down at the beach."

# PRISONED

I couldn't give Billy cash. He'd use it to buy as much black tar heroin as he could and have himself a shooting party until it was all gone. But there was something else I could do. It wouldn't get him out of The Heart; that was what I wanted even if he didn't.

"Call the landlord tomorrow morning, first thing. He'll either give you the keys to your old place, assuming he changed the locks, or keys to a new place."

"I don't need no charity."

He was homeless, and in a few days, when that guy kicked out his ma, she would be, too. I couldn't let that happen. Paulie wasn't alive to help them, and there was no one else who cared enough. Billy had his pride, and I respected that, but it wasn't going to stop me.

"It's not charity. It's a place to live. Take it, Billy." I walked across the room and leaned into the window.

Lights from the strip flashed below me. Sometimes, I needed a reminder—that piece of scenery Vegas was known for—so I wouldn't question where I was. When I was on the phone with Billy, it was easy to forget that I'd gotten out of Jersey, and I wasn't back living in that fucking hole.

"Fine. Whatever. But about those guys at the boardwalk, they were talking about Paulie, saying he was down there a lot. They said he wasn't hustling or slinging rock or anything like that. He was doing something; they just don't know what."

"We knew he hung out there, Billy. We all did back then."

"But he wasn't hanging out. He was by himself, like he was looking for someone…or trying to recruit someone."

Billy had never recovered from Paulie's death. If my sister had died like Paulie, I wouldn't have gotten over it either. It had hit Kyle and me just as hard. Harder than any of the other deaths in The Heart—and there were a lot of them. Losing Paulie was the catalyst that made Billy's addiction spiral out of control. And, each year, it seemed to have gotten worse.

"Looking for those answers isn't going to bring him back."

He blew another cloud of smoke into the phone, and a long stretch of silence followed. I could tell he was high. I heard it in his voice.

I always heard it.

And, every time I did, the guilt would gnaw at me a bit more. I was responsible for his using. I was the reason he had become a junkie. His voice was my punishment, and I had to live with it.

"I know," he finally said. "But I still want you to look into it. Ask some of your guys if they ever saw Paulie down there. Maybe they'll remember something."

After Paulie's death, we all asked around to see what we could find out. I started with the people who lived in The Heart and then the guys who sold and hustled on the streets. No one knew a thing, and the police didn't do shit. Mario and I came to the conclusion that the murderer had worked alone because no one in this town could keep their mouth shut, and it had been timed perfectly to make sure there were no witnesses. Asking around again wouldn't get Billy what he wanted, but I'd do it for him.

"I'll make some calls."

"Thanks, man. Now, when are you coming home for a visit? It's been too long since I've seen your ass."

"Not for a while. Things are a little heavy here."

"Is Mario going out there anytime soon? Maybe I could hitch a ride with him?"

Whenever one of the bosses came out, I'd meet them in Phoenix or Santa Fe or Denver. If the gambling commission found out they were in Nevada, our entire operation would be shut down, and we'd all be in jail. Mario would bring Billy to one of those spots if I asked him, but I couldn't have him here. Not with him shooting that shit into his arms all day, hustling every goddamn dollar that crossed his path.

During my years of dealing, I'd learned never to trust a junkie. Billy was as bad as any of them. I couldn't trust him in this city, and I sure as hell couldn't trust him in my casino.

"He doesn't have any plans to," I said. I hated lying to him. It ate at me almost as badly as the guilt. "Hey, my sister told me they just started having NA meetings down at the old church by—"

"I know where it is."

"Have you been?"

"Nah. When I'm ready to get clean, I know where to go. Don't worry; I got this shit handled."

I'd been hearing that for years. It was nothing more than an excuse. An excuse that would eventually be the cause of his death.

"Don't tell me not to worry."

"Why?" He laughed. "I ain't worried about you. I figure, the worst that can happen is you get inside some nasty pussy. You'll slide right out of it and run your ass home." He laughed again, which turned into a deep cough. "Just like I'd get out of it. Nothin'—not dope, not pussy—is gonna get me down."

"That's what you call handling your shit?" I couldn't hide the anger in my voice. "Because it has gotten you down, Billy. And it's holding you down, too."

The guys on the streets reported back to me—not the scum down at the boardwalk, but the guys who sold to them. The same guys Billy got his junk from. So, I knew how much he was buying, how much he was slinging, and how much he was using.

And I knew he was using more than he was slinging.

"I don't want you to end up in the same place as Paulie. You keep this shit up, and that's what's going to happen."

"You want to fight with someone? Is that it?" he barked back. "Then, fine, fight me. Say whatever you need to say, and let it all out. As soon as I hang up, I'm going to do what I want, you're gonna keep on worrying, and nothing is going to change."

"Fuck that."

I didn't want to get angry and sound like I was attacking him. But why the hell didn't he want to get help? Why didn't he worry about overdosing? Why did he act as though he were invincible when he'd witnessed so many guys like him drop dead?

It was because he didn't fucking care.

"Let me know if the guys say anything about Paulie. I'll call you in a few days," he said and hung up.

The phone felt so hot in my hand. I couldn't hold it anymore. I reached back and threw it as hard as I could. It flew through the air, hit the wall, and fell to the marble floor. The screen smashed, the case shattered, throwing tiny pieces everywhere.

When I walked over to my desk, it was covered in papers and reports and contracts. None of them mattered. Not at this moment.

Neither did the stress from worrying about the jackpots or the marketing director I had to replace. Not even the poker tournament that was going to draw our biggest crowd yet.

All that mattered was Billy.

If something didn't happen soon, I was going to lose my best friend.

# SEVEN

## KYLE

When I heard the lock unlatch, I jolted upright, my head swinging in the direction of the door to watch it slowly open. It was the first time there had been noise inside our cell that hadn't been created by Garin or me. The first time anyone had been in here since I'd been awake.

A man walked in, taller than Garin, his shoulders almost as broad as the doorway. His wifebeater showed a set of arms that were twice the size of my thighs. Every inch of them was covered in the most colorful tattoos. A full-grown thick beard hung from his chin, a feature I had once considered extremely sexy until I saw it on the face of my captor. And in his hands were two trays filled with small mountains of brown slop.

"¡A comer!" he barked, his voice so deep it vibrated through the cell.

The two years of Spanish that I'd taken in high school weren't going to help me out at all. I knew ten words, fifteen tops.

"What did he just say?" I asked Garin, not at all expecting him to answer.

"He's telling us to eat," Garin said.

Later, I would ask him how he knew that, but now, the bearded guy had my full attention. He dropped the trays on the floor, and he kicked them toward us. The brown sauce spilled over the sides from the rush of movement.

My stomach growled, and I wanted so badly to crawl forward and lap up the puddle off the dirty cement. I didn't know how long it had been since I'd eaten, but the hunger pangs were clawing through my belly so fiercely that I had to stop myself from crying out.

Garin stood and walked toward the bearded guy. "Tell me why the fuck we're in here and when we're getting out."

"*¡Siéntate!*"

"No, I'm not going to sit down!" Garin shouted back. "I want to know why we're in here. And I want to know when the hell you're going to let us out."

Beard unlatched one of the two guns that was holstered at his waist and pointed it at Garin. "*¡Que te sientes carajo!*"

I wrapped my arms around my navel and squeezed some of the pressure away. I couldn't breathe. I had the biggest fear of guns. I couldn't stand the sight of them. Not after what had happened, not after one had been pointed at me.

"Garin, get back!" I screamed. "Do what he says before he pulls the trigger."

"*Siéntate*," Beard said again.

"Jesus fucking Christ," Garin barked as he took a seat on the floor next to me.

A few seconds passed before Beard started walking back toward the door. I needed to try something to get him to talk. Maybe coming across a little sweeter would get me further than Garin.

"Are you in charge?" I asked him.

He held on to the door and stared at me. His eyes were black and terrifying, his mouth set open like his teeth were about to tear through my flesh.

"I'd like to talk to whoever is in charge…if that's not you." My voice was so weak. I barely recognized it. "I want to talk to them about why we're in here and—"

"*¡Cállate!*"

"He's telling you to shut up," Garin said.

# PRISONED

"But—"

"*Haz que se calle*," he snapped.

"He's had it, Kyle. He doesn't want to hear any more of our questions."

But I wasn't trying to sound bossy. I wasn't even being a smart-ass. I just wanted answers. I didn't think asking a few questions was too much, considering I was locked in a cell with no memory of how I'd gotten here.

"Can you please—"

"*Le voy a dar lo que se merece y después se muere*," Beard growled as he backed out of the cell.

The sound of the lock echoed, sending a shiver through my whole body. A sharp pain started gnawing at my stomach. It wasn't hunger. That was suddenly gone.

I waited a few seconds and turned toward Garin. "What did he say?"

He ground his teeth together, the blacks of his eyes as venomous as Beard's had been.

"Garin?"

"You'll get what he gives you."

If that was all he'd said, Garin wouldn't be grinding his teeth. He wouldn't be wringing his hands together and staring at the door like he was going to beat his way through it.

"What else did he say, Garin?"

"It doesn't matter."

I stood up, holding my stomach as I looked down at him. "Yes, it does matter. You can't protect me in here, so at least you can be honest. Don't shelter me. I can handle the truth."

He slowly glanced up. The anger and rage replaced with something else. I almost gasped when I realized what it was.

Fear.

"He said you'll get what he gives you…and then you're going to die."

It felt like everything had dropped from my body. Not just my hunger. That was long gone. But my questions, my voice, my emotions, my hope—those were gone, too.

Everything was gone.

I heard Garin behind me. He was moving the trays, probably to the far wall, placing them next to each other like he was setting a goddamn table.

"Come over here, and eat."

I didn't turn around to face him. I didn't move. My feet were paralyzed, my knees shaking so badly that they weren't going to hold me up for much longer. When I opened my mouth, my throat convulsed, and tears poured from my eyes. It was the first time I'd cried since I'd woken up in here. The first time I didn't actually believe I would get out.

His arms circled my waist, and he pulled my back against his chest. "They're not going to kill you. They need you. That's why you're in here."

"But..." It was the only word I could muster through the sobs.

"If you don't eat, you won't have the energy to fight. We need our energy, Kyle. We need to take everything they're willing to give us and figure out how to get out of here."

"I'm not getting out of here." My voice was becoming louder, and I didn't know why. None of this was his fault, but he was the only one in here who I could blame. "You're the one who told me what he said. You're the one who told me I was going to die. You can't honestly believe I'm going to get out of here, Garin."

I didn't wait for him to speak. I pushed my way out of his grip and moved to the other side of the cell, squeezing into the small space between the toilet and sink. I tucked my knees up to my chest, wrapped my arms around them, and rocked.

*Relax, Kyle.*

I had no breath. I had no feeling. I had numbness. I had an entire pit of emptiness.

And I had tears that wouldn't stop flowing.

"I'm going to give you a minute to sit there and feel sorry for yourself. Then, I'm going to pick you up, set you over here, and force food down your throat." He sat at the mock table, stretching his legs out in front of him, crossing his shiny shoes. "The minute starts now."

# PRISONED

"Do you think it's poisoned?" I asked him, holding the tray onto my lap, staring at the mountain of slop that was in the middle of it. It had cooled and flattened a bit since my pity party—or whatever Garin had called my mini breakdown.

"No." He dipped his finger into the sauce and stuck it into his mouth. "It's not that bad...as long as salt and metal are flavors you don't mind."

The tray was broken into three small compartments, similar to the ones they used in the lunchroom at school. Beard didn't give us any silverware, so I waded through it with my fingers. The mountain was actually a pile of shredded beef with thick rectangular noodles smothered in a brown sauce. The next compartment held a roll. The outsides were hard and a little moldy. Once I broke it open, the middle was actually quite soft. Four canned peaches were in the final compartment, sitting in a juice that was much redder than normal.

"Stop playing with it, and eat."

I pinched a few noodles between my fingers and dropped them onto my tongue. He was right; they were salty and almost metallic-tasting, like they'd been marinating in tin. As that layer of flavor dissolved, the aroma of plastic spread through my mouth.

I held my breath, trying to block it, and swallowed. "I think I'm hungrier than I realized."

Garin looked up, licking the last bit of peach off his finger, the only surviving morsel. "I could eat five more trays' worth."

"I wonder how long it's been since we've eaten."

"I don't want to know." He kicked the tray toward the door and went to the sink to wash his hands.

I shoveled in the noodles and mixed them with mouthfuls of roll. The brown sauce dripped down my fingers. I felt it on the sides of my mouth, and beef was in my teeth. I didn't care. My stomach was so desperate to feel full.

"Slow down, Kyle. Let your body get used to the food."

I ignored him and sucked in a peach, mashing it between my teeth before swallowing. When I felt it slide down my throat, I tossed in another until the only thing left on my tray was the juice. It wasn't red, like maraschino cherries. It was blood red. Way too red to drink.

I pushed the tray away and reclined against the wall, rubbing my stomach as the food moved around inside. Garin sat next to me, and I knew I needed to get up and use the sink. My fingers were sticky, and my face needed to be washed. But I was too full to move.

"How do you feel?"

His sleeves were rolled up to his elbows, and his hands were resting on his thighs. They were still wet; we didn't have a towel to dry off. I couldn't stop staring at them.

"I ate too fast. My mouth tastes like plastic, and this wall is miserably hard." That wasn't all of it. I hated to admit the rest, but not mentioning it seemed like a lie. "I'm really scared."

"Come here."

He tapped his chest, and I fell against it, feeling his breath blow onto my neck. He was much more forgiving than the wall. Much warmer. Much more caring. But his affection didn't hide the truth.

*"Le voy a dar lo que se merece y después se muere."*

I shivered from Beard's words as they played over and over in my head.

*"You'll get what he gives you...and then you're going to die."*

He hadn't said anything about Garin dying. Just me.

Actually, Garin's presence made no sense at all. Maybe he was here to comfort me before they killed me. Maybe our captors believed I'd told Garin the secret.

But one thing I knew for sure; he was prisoned because of me.

His life was put at harm...because of me.

My mouth began to water, and I could feel the food rising in my throat. "Oh God," I whispered, saliva dripping from my lip.

I pushed off his chest and rushed toward the toilet. Like my lips were the rim of a hose, chunks of food and liquid poured out of them. With each purge, I squeezed my stomach tighter, the cramps hurting as badly as the burning in the back of my throat. When I heaved nothing but air, I stuck my face under the faucet and let the freezing water cool my scorching skin. I kept it there until my body shivered.

"What can I do to help you feel better?"

I held up a finger, and using my other hand, I sucked in palmfuls of water. Once my mouth felt rinsed out, I swished around some toothpaste and swallowed a few gulps of air, trying to calm my stomach. It settled just enough to know I wouldn't be sick again.

## PRISONED

"Your body couldn't handle that much food at once," he said. When I sat next to him, he pushed his arm against me, so I could lean into it. "You have to eat slow and give it time to adjust."

Eating fast wasn't the only reason I had thrown up. But if I allowed my mind to go back there, I'd be sleeping in front of the toilet tonight.

"We have to get out of here," I said, "before something happens to one of us."

"I'm going to come up with a plan. I just need to feel out that guy a little more and find his weakness. I'll also memorize the times he drops off our food. Don't worry; I'll get us out of here."

But I did worry. "I trust you." I needed to get my mind off of it before it made me even crazier. "What would you be doing right now if you weren't in here?"

He looked up at the window. There wasn't any sunlight coming through. The only light was the overhead bulb that buzzed and sometimes flickered. "I'd probably still be working."

"Me, too."

"In the shop or behind the scenes?"

I'd told him about my job when we had first gotten to the bar. It wasn't like he had researched me the same way I had Googled him... unless he had been acting and really did know.

"Behind the scenes," I said. "My employees work in the shop and handle the walk-ins and the retail side of the business. I manage the large orders and anything custom. I don't use stock images. I draw everything."

"You enjoy it." He said it like he already knew the answer, which was ironic because it was one I really needed to think about.

Art was all I'd ever wanted to do, and college had taught me how to make my craft more mainstream than having just a struggling paint-and-canvas career. Business was the part I didn't enjoy as much, especially having my brother as my business partner. He took away all the fun, and he sucked out all the passion.

"Yes," I finally answered. "I love the creative part."

"Have you had any business deals go wrong?"

"A few." I searched his eyes. "Why?"

"I was thinking that could be the reason we're in here."

As much as I wanted to believe that, I couldn't. It didn't make any sense. Arguments over pricing and wrong colors wouldn't land me in a prison cell.

"Then, why are we in here together?" I asked.

His eyes narrowed. "Maybe it's something we did as kids."

Garin was dominant; he always had been. He was someone who wouldn't give up control in any situation unless he was locked in a cell with a captor who had two guns on his hips. His edges were hard, and his stare didn't waver even slightly. Someone like that had enemies. Big enough ones who would have put us in here.

I still didn't believe it.

I looked straight ahead, unable to hide the guilt from my face. "I'm sure there are endless reasons for why we could be in here."

He would hate me once he found out it was because of me.

*I* would hate me.

I already did.

"I'm going to get you out of here," he said. "I told you not to worry, so don't."

"How do you know that?"

"I've been in enough situations to know."

"But what if—"

He was so fast that I barely felt myself move. I only felt the landing, which had me straddling his lap, his arms fully wrapped around me.

"Wow," I gasped.

I couldn't move my gaze from his. I was frozen. There was so much intensity between us.

"You were starting to panic again. I needed to stop you."

What a strange thing it was to be looking at his face again, a face I'd known since I was a child. But, now, it had hard lines and small imperfections, the evidence of age on both of us.

The eyes that stared back weren't childlike. They were the eyes of a man.

A hungry man.

"You did," I finally said.

He glanced down, and I felt my skin flush, my nipples slowly hardening and poking through the thin fabric. He noticed and gradually looked up at my face. His erection was pressing into my ass, my mouth opening from the size of it.

# PRISONED

"If you need a minute, take it," he said. "Now."

"I…"

His gaze was so strong; it felt like it was stroking me the same way his fingers were. Fingers that shouldn't have been touching me because I didn't deserve it. Fingers that should have been locked far away from me because I had been such a coward.

Before I could process my next thought, he was moving me once more. This time, he placed me on the floor, a little farther away from where I had been before.

"When I kiss you again, there isn't going to be any uncertainty in your voice. I'm going to feel the answer in you and know it's what you want."

I couldn't tell him that what he felt in me was the guilt.

He had his own emotions and his own demons and his own reasoning for why we might be in here. It didn't stop him from wanting me.

And I wanted him. More than anything.

I always had.

But I also wanted to tell him what I had been holding in. I just couldn't do that. I couldn't tell anyone. Where I was from, spilling a secret like that could get you killed.

It was no different inside this cell.

I tucked myself into the corner and rested my forehead against the cold cement. My knees pressed into my chest, and my arms crossed over them. My smile grew as I thought about the way he had looked into my eyes, the feeling that had come through his fingertips, how his dick had hardened beneath me.

I needed a minute, just a minute to get this ridiculous smile off my face and to cool my body down to the right temperature. And I definitely needed more than a minute to get my chest to stop beating so hard.

I hid the grin under my arm and closed my eyes.

It took less than a minute to remember the reason we were in here and the fear that I would never be getting out.

*Sleep now, Kyle.*

# EIGHT

## KYLE

Light had been seeping in through the top of the window for hours, but I barely had the strength to lift my arms. Whatever they had drugged me with had to still be in my system. I had never been this exhausted from doing nothing.

At some point during the morning, Beard had delivered more food. This tray had a heaping pile of meat in a red sauce that was extra plastic-tasting, overcooked carrots, and a roll. Still no silverware. No napkin. Nothing to drink besides water from the sink. I'd been drinking the rusty liquid though. Garin said I had to. I needed to stay hydrated, or I'd get extremely sick. Sicker than I'd been the night before when I threw up my entire dinner.

When Beard dropped off the trays, he'd also given us a blanket. No pillows or cot or even a blow-up mattress. All we had for comfort was the cold concrete floor and a single gray wool blanket that stared at me from the corner of the room.

I was surprised Beard had been so giving after the confrontation he'd had with Garin. In his profession, maybe he was considered a forgiving man, or maybe he just wanted to give us one last luxury before he pulled the trigger.

Whatever the case was, we needed to get out of here.

And I told Garin that at least once an hour.

"I would kill for a popsicle and a fluffy pillow right now," I said.

"That's an odd craving."

"My throat is on fire."

It didn't just hurt when I swallowed; it hurt constantly. I was sure it was from throwing up. I had retched so hard that I was surprised my chest wasn't sore, and my eyes weren't bloodshot. The reflection in the sink showed me they weren't. But it had shown that I looked like a mess, which I'd done nothing to fix.

I was too tired.

"I can't give you either, so how about you use my shoulder?"

I grinned. "I would love that."

He grabbed the blanket and returned to my side of the room as I went over to the sink. I'd been sitting in these clothes since I arrived, and I hadn't done more than swish a bunch of toothpaste around my mouth. I squirted some on the pad of my finger and took my time brushing it over the front and back of each tooth. Then, I used my nails to scrape in between them. When I was done, I soaped up my hands and rubbed them over my face, across my chest, and down each arm. It wasn't nearly as good as taking a shower, but I was surprised at how much better I felt once I rinsed all the suds off.

Now facing Garin, I saw that he had opened up the blanket and spread it out over the floor, folding the top several times to make it thicker where our heads would lay. I hadn't felt his eyes while I was washing up, but it was all I felt now.

"My turn."

His hand grazed my waist as he passed me. It was brief. Gentle. Unneeded because there was enough room for him to walk by. I stopped breathing when I felt it. There wasn't any panic this time, just a warm tingle that dipped between my thighs.

I hurried to the blanket and sat in the middle, unsure of which side he would want. I crossed my legs and tried to focus on my hands. He'd given me minutes of privacy whenever I'd asked for it by looking the other way. It was the least I could do for him. But when I heard the water turn on and his hands rub together, as though he were lathering the soap between them, I wanted to peek.

I put every bit of effort into keeping my face pointed down...but still, I glanced up.

His shirt was draped over the corner of the sink and his sudsy long, strong fingers were washing his neck. My eyes traveled to his forearms. They were covered in a dusting of dark hair, the grooves in his biceps and triceps so well defined. His shoulders were wide, squaring off the top of his back, and the muscles narrowed at his waist. From this angle, with his pants sitting low on his hips, I could only see the side of his abs. They were lightly covered in hair, and there was more across his chest.

"You've seen it all before."

Now that he was looking at me dead-on, I saw the true sculpture of his muscles. They were tighter. Stronger. So much more powerful than I had thought.

How could something look so beautiful inside this cell?

I shook my head. "I haven't seen that."

"It's just me, Kyle."

"No." I looked him over again. "It's not just you. It's a very different, very built, very manly version of you."

He left his shirt on the sink and walked over to me, grabbing my hands and lifting me to my feet. He grasped my neck to hold my face steady, squeezing like he had outside the restroom at the bar.

"You're a much different version of you, too, Kyle. You fought to get that business. You're fiercely independent. You're healthy. You take care of yourself. You can afford to, and you want to."

Clearly, he didn't know anything about me. I hadn't fought, nor was I independent. But I couldn't tell him any of that.

Discussing our weight was a much simpler and safer topic. "I was so skinny back then. We both were."

"You were gorgeous back then. You're even more gorgeous now. And this body"—his eyes dipped to my mouth—"is fucking perfect." His hands moved down my sides, stopping at my waist, squeezing my hips. "You've filled out in all my favorite spots." His body seemed to move closer, my chest pressing into him. "The ones I like to touch"—

he leaned his face down, his lips kissing the outside of my neck—"and lick."

A shiver ran through me when I exhaled. I didn't know how I wasn't naked already, stripped of everything, including my ability to make a decision. But, in my mind, there was no decision to be made. There was no guilt. No fear. Whatever Garin wanted to do to me, wherever he wanted to touch me, I wouldn't deny him. I couldn't. We'd gone through too much. We had survived The Heart. I had been pulled away from him, and we'd been brought back together and put in this cell. That all had to mean something.

"Let's get some sleep," he said.

He didn't wait for me to answer before he slipped his body away from mine and sat me on the blanket. Then, he moved in behind me, his head resting on the makeshift pillow. "Come here."

I kept my back to him and cuddled into his chest. He was so warm, his grip so strong in the way he held me. The scent of the soap was different on him than it was on my hands. It turned so masculine on his skin, tasty and almost erotic.

He slid me further back, our bodies now pressed together. He didn't ask if I wanted to be moved. He just read me and gave me what I needed.

But he hadn't given me everything.

Everything would have been his mouth on mine.

Maybe it wasn't time for that just yet. Maybe this wasn't the right place for it. Maybe I was losing focus and should have been concentrating on how we were going to get out of here instead of how good Garin's arms felt. But he had said he was going to work on an escape plan, and he promised he was going to get us out of here.

And, in the meantime, his embrace and his presence were the only two things that made this feel good. Without one, there was no other.

"I think they're going to give us some answers soon."

His voice startled me.

"How do you know?"

"I know the game."

The whiskers from his chin brushed across the back of my neck. It reminded me of the nights I had stayed in his bedroom, how the sound of his breathing was enough to put me to sleep.

"I just wanted to warn you. You'll be fine. Don't worry."

## PRISONED

*You'll be fine.*

I closed my eyes as the light above us hummed and flickered. I blocked it out and focused on sleep.

Focused on his breathing.

Focused on the way he rubbed my hand.

*Sleep well, Kyle.*

# NINE

## KYLE

"*¡Despierten!*" Beard barked.

I flew into a seated position while Garin still lay behind me, his hand protectively resting on my hip.

"*¡A comer!*" He slid both trays into the room and ran his fingers through his beard. "Vendré por ustedes más tarde."

Then, the door slammed shut, and he was gone.

"What did he say?"

Garin sat up and leaned his back against the wall. "He wants us to eat and says he'll be back for us later."

"Back for *us*?"

His hand moved to my thigh. "If we're going to get answers, he has to come back. And, every time he opens that door, he makes himself more vulnerable for an attack. I'm learning his habits. I've got this, so stop worrying."

The dampness in our cell wasn't the reason I was shaking. Beard made me nervous. Not just his size, the guns he wore, the attitude he had, or my inability to communicate with him, but the fact that there wasn't even the tiniest bit of tenderness in his eyes. I could never win against someone who had no heart. My tears would go unnoticed; my pleas would go unheard.

I would confess, and then I would be dead.

That meant I couldn't tell the truth. The second I did, my life would be over.

Garin didn't seem affected by Beard's threat. Maybe that was because, as a kid, he had run drugs for the mob and now managed their casino and was used to the way gangsters thought, how they threatened, what they carried through on, and what was meant to just scare. Maybe he was trying to stay strong for me.

The panic in my throat was making it hard to breathe again. I wrapped my arms around my stomach and swayed, trying to ease the air in and out of me. I felt the heat spread over my cheeks and the gripping around my throat. It was tight.

Everything was so tight.

"Have you been to Vegas?" he asked.

I continued to rock, trying to find the breath to grunt out a response. "Huh?"

"Get your mind off what you're fearing and concentrate on what I'm asking you."

"Yes," I panted. "I've been to Vegas."

"Did you enjoy it?"

"It was fun." The pounding in my chest started to subside. "Lots of lights and noise. The food was delicious."

"You've become a foodie now? I could barely get you to eat anything, other than powdered doughnuts and bacon cheeseburgers when we were kids."

I laughed at the memory. "I like food. Probably a little too much." I stopped rocking and took some deep breaths. My hands were no longer shaking. "Do you like your life there?"

"I work. A lot."

"Do you date?" The question came out before I could stop it.

"I wouldn't call it dating."

I wasn't going to ask him to elaborate. I understood perfectly what he meant by that.

## PRISONED

"What about you, Kyle?" He moved over to the sink and squirted some toothpaste over his finger, brushing his teeth, while he stared at me.

"I doubt my life in Tampa is even close to as interesting as your life in Vegas."

"I meant, do you date?" he spoke through the side of his mouth and spit when he was done.

"I go on dates. They don't turn into anything, but I go on them."

"Too picky?"

I wanted to laugh at his question, but in all actuality, it wasn't really funny. Maybe I was too picky. It didn't seem like the case when I drove myself home at the end of each date. It was more like none of them made me feel anything. We lacked chemistry. If there was a slight physical connection, which we pursued, I'd quickly learn that our personalities clashed.

Maybe in some strange way, I'd been comparing them all to Garin.

"Not compatible is a better way to put it," I said.

"So, you live in Tampa. You go out on dates. You work. You work out, obviously. You like food. What else do you do, Kyle?"

I held a secret that should have been spoken from my lips many years ago. Instead, I kept it inside, allowing it to fester and morph into so many different emotions that it caused panic attacks.

"I have a small group of friends I hang out with," I said, trying to hide any trace of those thoughts from my voice. "I read. I decorate my house and think I may like it, and then I decide I don't and redo it all over again."

"You're not happy."

My mouth opened and immediately closed.

I couldn't lie. He'd see right through it.

"There are some things missing from my life." Some things that were controlled too tightly. "But I'm not unhappy. I just can't say I'm completely satisfied."

"What would you change?"

I couldn't be completely honest with him, which was making this conversation harder than I thought.

"I wanted college, and I got it. I wanted to be able to turn my art into a business, and I got that, too. I wouldn't change any of that."

"But you'd add in love. That's what you're missing."

His eyes were a darker green today, maybe picking up some of the brown from the floor or the gray from the blanket. I felt them inside my soul.

I slowly nodded. "Yes." I took a breath, surprised by how easy the air passed through my lungs. "What about you? Are you happy?"

"I'm happy enough."

"What does that mean?"

"It means I've accepted the way my life is, the amount of work that's involved, the people I have to report to. It will be that way until I grow tired of it all, or I get killed."

I tucked my knees against my chest and held them there. "You say it so easily, like you're talking about someone else's death and not your own."

"Because it is that easy. I knew what I was signing up for when I went into business with Mario. I suspect you knew the same."

He was talking about my career and opening my shop, but there was so much he didn't know.

It wasn't the path I'd chosen.

It was the path that was chosen for me.

And, now, after all the time I'd put in, all the sacrifices I'd made, I didn't expect forgiveness. I didn't expect redemption. I sure as hell didn't expect a fairy tale. But, when I looked around the cell, this wasn't what I expected at all.

"It's not that easy for me," I said.

"That might change when you get out of here."

I had been staring at the trays that Beard had set on the ground. Several orange slices, four grapes, and a heaping pile of what looked like yogurt sat on each.

I wasn't hungry.

I finally looked up at him. "You mean, *if* we get out."

*You'll get out of here, Kyle.*

---

Beard delivered another blanket a little while later—only one though and still no toothbrushes or towels or anything to drink. I'd held my breath the whole time he was in our cell, waiting to be plucked out or grabbed or hurt in some way. It didn't happen. He just tossed the blanket inside, grunted, and left. I tried shouting out a question, hoping that while he was still inside our cell he would at least give me something. But he didn't. He ignored me and slammed the door shut.

All of this was so strange.

But we now had two blankets, and we'd eaten three meals today. Whoever prepared our food somehow managed to make yogurt taste like cottage cheese and beef taste like fish. And all of it left a terrible aftertaste of plastic. It didn't matter how much toothpaste I smeared across my teeth, I couldn't get rid of that flavor.

I stood at the sink, finishing my evening routine of washing down my body, but this time, I stripped off my tank and hung it over the back of the toilet. I left my bra on as I soaped under my arms, across the tops of my breasts, and over my stomach.

"I know you're watching me," I said, keeping my eyes on my hands.

"I am."

I finally glanced in his direction. "There are three other walls, a floor, and a ceiling."

"I don't want to look at them, Kyle. I want to look at you."

It wasn't just what he had said; it was the way he had said it. The sound of his need. The roughness in his voice. It was deep enough to make me shiver. Sexy enough to make his words flutter underneath my bra and between my legs.

I looked away, knowing my reaction was showing on my face, and reached for the button and zipper on my pants. Things hadn't progressed with us physically, but I still wanted to be clean. So, I laid my pants over my tank top, dropped my panties into the sink, and squirted more soap on my hands.

As I used my palms to scrub, I felt the heat from his stare start to scorch my skin. I expected nothing less. I was only wearing a bra. The side view he was getting was more of my body than he'd ever seen.

I wasn't aiming to tease him—although I'd be lying if I said I wasn't enjoying it. He didn't even have to say anything or make any kind of sound at all. I could feel his response in the air.

It was turning me on.

Once each area of my body had been lathered at least twice, the suds completely washed off, I waited for the droplets to stop falling before I grabbed my tank to get dressed again.

"Don't put it on."

I looked across my shoulder at him. "I'm practically naked, Garin."

"That's the way I want you."

I had never seen such hunger in a man's eyes before.

"Come here," he said.

"But—"

"Come here." His voice had deepened even more. "Bring your clothes with you."

It was as if he could sense my worry that Beard may walk in again at any minute and see me standing here, naked. Leaving my panties by the sink to dry, I lifted the tank top and pants and moved over to him.

As I sat down, he stood.

"Cover yourself with that blanket." He pointed at the one on the ground that he'd folded in half. "I just need a minute."

While he turned on the water, I climbed beneath the fold and propped myself up on my elbow, so I could watch him. He'd already taken off his shirt and pants, and he was wearing only his boxer briefs. There was something incredibly sexy about watching a man rub suds all over his skin, the way they slowly trickled down his sides, mixing with his tanned flesh and dark hair. His hands moved so fluidly, so confidently.

I wanted those hands on me.

His boxer briefs fell to the ground, and my heart started pounding so hard that I could feel it in my throat. The side angle gave me enough of a view to see the length of his cock, the thickness of it as it laid against his sack. I squeezed my thighs together, needing the heat and friction to satiate the throbbing inside my pussy.

But there was no relief. Just more tingling as my body starved to have him inside me.

A sigh gradually poured from my lips.

Garin looked at me. "Getting impatient?"

I felt my face flush. "No. I—"

"Want me."

Was I that obvious? Did that mean he finally felt the desire in me and would give me that kiss I wanted?

# PRISONED

He carried his clothes over and dropped them on the floor on top of mine. I slid forward under the blanket, so he would have enough room to move in behind me. And he did, sending me a rush of air filled with his scent, and his skin pressed against mine, making me even hotter than I already was.

*Kyle.*

I tried not to moan as he breathed into the back of my neck. His breath trickled lower and lower, my bare flesh covered in goose bumps.

"You're wiggling."

I finally felt his lips. They were pressed between my shoulder blades.

"Every time you wiggle, you grind your ass against my dick."

"I can't…help it."

"You're making it difficult to take things slowly."

His words vibrated across my skin, causing my hips to buck forward and back.

"Jesus, Kyle."

Slow was my past. Slow wasn't what I wanted anymore. He had to know that. He had to feel it. He had to be able to put all of this in the back of his mind—the painfully hard floor, the dirt and rust, the fact that we were prisoned—and just focus on what was happening between us in this moment.

"Touch me," I begged.

His hand spread over my navel, gently running up my side and down my thigh.

*Kyle.*

"Garin…"

"That was the sexiest sound I've ever heard."

"I'm trying to be quiet, but"—I gasped as he moved around my arm and squeezed my nipple—"it feels too good."

His teeth grazed the outside of my ear as he pinched harder, the tip of his cock rubbing between my ass cheeks. Something had changed in him. The hunger, the starvation, the need that pulsed through me, I now felt in him, too. But it was stronger, more powerful, than I'd ever felt from a man before.

"We're surrounded by cement walls and steel bars, so no one can hear you," he hissed. "Show me how long you've wanted this."

He was still pinching my nipples, still pushing the head of his hard cock into my cheeks, still nibbling the outside of my ear, and I was overwhelmed with how good it all felt. Moans—that was all my mouth could produce. They came out with every breath. It only took a few breaths before his hand moved down to my pussy.

*Kyle.*

"Garin, this is—"

"What you need. What we both need."

He slid between my lips and gently rubbed my clit. I didn't expect it to feel this good. He was only using his finger, nothing else. But those expert hands knew just how to touch me, how to bring the most intense sensations to the surface.

And they were there...already so close.

His middle finger wandered down through my wetness and into my hole.

"*Yes*," I moaned.

*Kyle.*

Long, deep shuddering breaths came through my mouth while he added a second finger inside me.

I reached for his hair and used it to pull his face even closer to my neck. "Give me more of you, Garin."

When I felt his teeth, I tugged harder. They were biting the bottom of my earlobe. Just when it felt like he was going to tear through my flesh, he licked it, soothing it with his tongue.

*Stop fighting it.*

"Give me what I want first."

"What"—I panted—"do you want?"

"I want your pussy squeezing my fucking fingers as you come on them, and I want your body shaking so hard from it that your ass pinches the tip of my dick."

I was there before he had even requested it.

But the build had already passed. I was at the peak now, holding on to the pleasure, trying to control it from leaving my body. I wanted to stay at the top. I wanted to wrap myself in this feeling of bliss and warmth and euphoria because I didn't know if I'd ever feel it again.

What if things inside this prison were about to become unbearable? What if Garin was about to be taken from me?

I didn't want to lose him.

I didn't want to lose this.

I didn't want to lose us again.

"Come for me, Kyle."

I released his hair and flattened my hand over the back of his head, using his power, his presence, the sound of his demands to push myself over the edge.

And, when I did, I screamed.

*Kyle.*

His fingers pumped out my orgasm, twisting and sliding inside my wetness. My back arched, my ass pushing further into him, opening just enough to take in his tip and squeeze it, like he'd asked. Then, the shuddering hit, waves and sparks passing all the way through me, the pleasure slowly lessening, until there was complete stillness.

Stillness and sedation.

"I've waited half my life to hear that"—he kissed the top of my shoulder—"and to feel it."

I groaned. "Then, I guess you got everything you wanted."

"Not everything."

"I hoped there was more." I was smiling, but because he was behind me, he couldn't see it.

"There is but not now."

"Garin—"

His teeth nipped my earlobe. "You're going to fall asleep because it's what I want."

"What about what I want?"

"That guy is going to be back soon, and I don't want to have to stop. When my cock is inside you, I want to be able to take my time."

My eyes were getting so heavy that I couldn't keep them open. "Will you be able to sleep?" I felt him slide my tank over my head and shimmy it down my stomach. Then, I felt him tuck something over my legs.

"I have the smell of you on my fingers. I'll sleep just fine."

"Mmm," I murmured.

*Good night, Kyle.*

# TEN

## KYLE

My body was so cold that I couldn't stop shaking. My skin felt wet, and my hair clung to the back of my neck. I didn't understand why my bones ached so badly or why my wrists and ankles felt like they had been rubbed raw, the skin around them burning with a heat that was almost intolerable. My eyelids were heavy, as though someone had taped them shut. When I finally opened them, it felt as if they were still closed. Darkness surrounded me. Not a murky gray or a translucent charcoal. It was pitch-black.

Our cell was this dark, but it wasn't this cold.
I had been taken.
Again.
*Where am I?*
*Why do I hurt?*
*Am I alone?*
I blinked, waiting for my eyes to adjust.

One, two, three, four seconds passed. I still couldn't see anything. Not my legs. Not my chest. Nothing.

My breath...I couldn't find it.

*Relax, Kyle.*

I tried to rub my eyes, but I couldn't lift my hands. They were tied behind me, and my legs were shackled as well.

*Tied...to what?*

I rocked back and forth and realized I was on a chair. There was little give. I figured it was bolted to the ground, but it moved enough that I could feel its sturdiness and weight. It was metal, heavy. It had no cushion.

*Breathe.*

When I tried to pry my wrists out of the rope, it tightened even more, chafing over the raw skin. I felt my skin crack open, and the pain seethed. I cried out loud and gasped when I inhaled. My throat was closing.

*Breathe, Kyle.*

Each breath hit my bare thighs. I tucked my chin to my chest and felt even more bare skin. When I exhaled again, the burst of air hit my naked breasts.

Someone had taken off my clothes.

Someone had soaked me in something that made my skin and hair wet.

Someone had tied me up.

Someone...

"Let me go!" I screamed, rocking in the chair, hoping the momentum would loosen the bolts. "Help me."

Each pump of my body caused the burning in my wrists and ankles to intensify. It felt like they had been sliced with a razor and doused with alcohol. When I stopped moving, I felt the drizzle. Too warm to be water from my hair and too thick. It had to be blood. It was running down my fingers and stopping as it reached the tips of my nails. And then...

*Drip...drip...drip* onto the floor.

"Garin?"

Silence.

"Garin, please answer me if you're in here."

More silence.

# PRISONED

I would have heard him breathing. I would have seen the window by the top of the ceiling if I were in the cell.

So, where the hell was I?

I tried to take a breath and couldn't. The air...it was gone. Not around me, but in my lungs.

If Garin were here, he'd tell me to breathe. He'd try to take my mind off the tightening of my throat, the pressure in my chest.

*Breathe.*

I shook my head, and strands of wet hair clung to my cheeks and to the spit on my lips. I hadn't licked them, so why were they still wet? Why hadn't my skin dried? Why was my hair soaked?

Whoever had taken me from our cell had drugged me. I couldn't remember a thing past going to sleep there. And, now, I was waking up here. I felt so out of it, so out of control. I wasn't sure what were thoughts and what was actually happening. But I knew only that I was in a chair, and my hands and feet were tied.

And there was pain.

"Kyle..."

"Ahh-ahh-ahh!" I screamed. My heart pounded so hard that it made me stutter. "Wh-where are y-you?"

I didn't recognize the voice, but I had to find where it was coming from. I turned my head from side to side, slapping more of my wet hair onto my cheeks. The freezing strands made me shiver even more. I couldn't see him. I couldn't feel him.

"I'm *here*."

His breath was hot. It scorched my ear.

"W-who are y-you?"

"That's not the right question."

He had an accent—not as thick as Beard's and a different tone. This guy's was deeper. As far as I knew, Beard didn't speak English.

"Wh-what did y-you do to me?"

"Still not the right question."

I couldn't stop my chest from heaving, and I couldn't draw in a breath. I expected to pass out at any second, the lack of oxygen causing my brain to shut down.

"But I'll answer it because I like you, Kyle." He moved to the other side, to my other ear. His mouth smelled like rotten fish. "I ripped you away from the bed that Garin had you tucked into and slowly, *very* slowly, took off all your clothes." His lips moved down to the base of my neck. "You were dirty. So very dirty. So, I dropped you in a bath. It was a special bath, you see, filled with special things. And I made sure the water was very cold. Ice cold." His laugh was so sinister. "I liked watching the way your nipples hardened when they got wet. They wrinkled around the circles and pinched together in the middle."

Every time his tongue curled around an R, my stomach churned.

"Nice, tight pink nipples, big enough to fit and tug between my front teeth. Most nipples are too big to fit between there. Not yours. You have small tits and one hell of a fucking ass." He licked the length of my neck and stopped at my earlobe, flicking it with the tip of his tongue. "Mmm, that cunt of yours. Without a razor in your cell, I was surprised to see it was still bald."

He moved down to the top of my shoulder and chomped into my flesh. It was impossible to hold in my scream.

"It was a good surprise though; don't worry. I didn't punish you for having a bald cunt. I admired it, and I took pictures of it...after I rubbed my cum all over it."

My body shook, as though I were being electrocuted. Tears ran into my mouth as they streamed from my eyes. He had violated my body. He had taken something that wasn't his. He had...

"You ra-raped me."

My tongue suddenly felt too large for my mouth, and I gagged. I turned my head and urged whatever was in my throat to come out. Saliva pooled around my teeth and on my tongue. I spit it on the ground. No food came up, no bile.

I was empty. Again.

How long had I been in here? Naked? With him doing whatever he wanted to my body? With whatever objects he deemed appropriate? And whatever secret bath sauce he had marinated me in?

"I didn't rape you." Two long breaths and a lick on the inside of my ear. "You're my prisoner; your cunt isn't lucky enough to feel my dick." He laughed again. This time, it sounded like it served as a confirmation. "I won't fuck you until you give me what I want. Until then, I'm just going to use you as a landing pad for my cum. But, mmm, my cum looked so fucking sexy on your bald cunt."

I should have felt relief. I should have started breathing. But knowing he had seen my body naked, had touched it, had put me in the most vulnerable position hurt almost as badly as the thought of him raping me.

Could I really trust anything he said though?

I squeezed in the walls of my pussy, searching for that small ache that always came after sex and lingered for at least a day.

I felt nothing.

Maybe he was telling the truth.

"What do you wa-want? Wh-why am I h-here?"

"Wrong questions. Again."

The smell in the air told me he was now in front of me.

"I want you to listen," he said.

"Li-listen for wh-what—"

*Whap.*

I screamed as his hand slapped my cheek. I screamed again as the sound echoed in the room. Each repeated noise felt like another slap. The pain seared through my jaw and behind my eye, like it was going to fly right out of the socket.

"Don't make me punish you, Kyle. When I tell you to listen, that means shut your fucking mouth."

I just wanted to rub my face. I just wanted to soothe the ache. All of me was hurting, and I needed relief. Just the tiniest bit of tenderness before he hit me again.

A grunt filled the silence, pulling me from my self-pity. It was much louder than my scream had been. It didn't sound like it came from a place of sadness or anger. It was far beyond pain or hurt.

This was the sound of someone being tortured.

And the sound had come from Garin.

"What are you doing to him?" I yelled. "Don't hurt him. Please don't hurt him."

"QUIET!"

"Wh-what do you want from m-me?"

He reached inside my mouth and clamped my tongue between his fingers, pulling it so hard that I gagged again. "I told you to be quiet. One more sound, and I'll rip this fucking tongue out."

Tears were falling even faster. I didn't know what was causing me to cry harder—the torture Garin was going through or the fear of what this guy was going to do to me. But I wasn't stupid enough to make a sound. I cried silently, holding it all in, the sobs causing tremors in my stomach and chest.

I was so tempted to bite down on his fingers. Resting under my teeth like they were, I'd be able to gnaw right into the muscle and tear off a piece of his flesh. But I worried about what would happen to me if I did that and what would happen to Garin. There could be someone else in this room with us or someone waiting outside the door. I was sure this guy carried a gun like Beard.

I was defenseless in this prison.

"Do you hear that?" He knelt at my side, his fingers still in my mouth. His lips were uncomfortably close to my cheek.

The muscles in the back of my throat tightened as I prepared to grunt my answer, but I stopped myself. What if this was a test? What if he was goading me into disobeying him?

I shook my head.

"Listen, *puta*…"

I squinted my eyelids together and tried to calm the pounding in my body, so I could really focus. The sound was quiet, just barely above a whisper.

"Kyle…Kyle…Kyle…" Garin said my name over and over. It was like someone was standing on his throat, and he was exhaling his final breath.

His last words.

*No*, I wanted to scream.

They needed to stop hurting Garin, to leave him alone, to release him from this hell we were both in. It wasn't Garin who they wanted. He had done nothing wrong.

It was me.

I was the guilty one.

But, like a coward, I kept my mouth shut and said nothing. Instead, I let the anger simmer inside me, slammed my back into the chair, and thrust my hips forward to try to loosen the bolts that held it in place.

Breath, who was still at my side, laughed at me. It was the most evil sound I'd ever heard. It made my skin prickle like swarms of ants were crawling all over me.

Tears dripped down my aching swollen cheeks. Spit foamed around my lips as he held my tongue between his foul fingers.

I only stopped rocking when he yelled, "Enough!"

# PRISONED

I froze, and he rubbed his nose along the bottom of my jaw.

Breath was breathing me in. "Next time I come for you, I want you to ask the right question."

I nodded, the movement causing his fingers to tighten around my tongue until I gagged again.

"Next time, I might not come only on your cunt." He moved in front of me and licked across my bottom lip. "A big load right on your mouth will look so fucking sexy."

I held in my sobs, but they racked my whole body.

"Good night, Kyle."

*Good night, Kyle.*

There was a prick on the side of my arm, and then I felt the liquid drain into my muscle. A warmth immediately spread through me. It was a kind of heat I'd never felt before.

My fear was gone. The pain had dissolved. There was happiness even though it wasn't caused by Garin. Happiness and contentment and coddling. The shackles felt soft. His fingers felt tender, and his breath smelled like pineapple.

And then everything went black.

# ELEVEN

## KYLE

Cold—that was the first sensation I felt. Stiff was the second. Not just in my legs and arms, but in my jaw. It was like I had been chewing gum for weeks straight. Even my tongue hurt and the roof of my mouth. I didn't know where all this aching had come from. It couldn't have been from just sleeping on the floor. I'd been sleeping on it every night. I'd...

It all came back to me as fast and as sharp as the slap Breath had given me across the face.

The chair. The ropes. The clamping of my tongue.

*"Wrong question."*

Garin's screams.

My eyes shot open. The only thought on my mind came flying out of my lips, "Garin!"

"I'm here," he said.

He was standing in front of the sink. I could relax a little now. He must have been the one who tucked me under the blankets and folded one under my head. But had he gotten me dressed? I feared that was Breath. That those vile, repulsive fingers had grazed my skin while he slipped my clothes back on. I was worried his fingers weren't the only things that had touched me...or dropped on me.

"What happened to you?" I asked Garin, waiting for him to finish so that I could wash my body. "Where did they take you? How long have we been back?"

He said nothing. He didn't even look in my direction. He just moved his hands under the water.

"Garin?"

He still didn't answer, so I rushed over to him and grabbed his shoulders, trying to turn him around. The burns and cuts on my wrists stung, but I ignored the pain. I needed to find out what was wrong with him. He wouldn't budge.

"Show me your face."

"Why don't you go lie back down? They gave you some heavy drugs and—"

"Show me!"

"Kyle, I don't want to scare you."

"It's way too late for that." He still didn't move, so I dipped underneath his arm and squeezed myself into the tiny space between his body and the sink. "Oh my God." I did everything I could not to cringe at the sight of him.

He had bruises everywhere. There wasn't a section of skin that wasn't darkened to some shade of purple. I couldn't tell if the imprints on his cheeks were from someone's fist or the sole of a boot. There were open cuts around his eyes and forehead, dried blood surrounding every one. There was a scrape by his lip. Gashes ran the length of his throat. The wound by his ear looked like it was becoming infected.

"What did they do to you?"

"It doesn't matter."

"You're right. You're alive, but..." I remembered the fear that had crippled me when Breath made me listen to Garin's whispers. "I thought..." My voice trailed off, unable to finish.

"You thought they killed me?"

I nodded.

"They wanted to."

I touched the sides of his face gently. "How could they hurt this?"

# PRISONED

I brushed my fingers over the bruises, staying clear of the cuts so that I wouldn't dirty them. There were more than I thought. Some were even hidden in the thickness of his beard, which had grown so much since we'd been in here. He didn't make a sound the whole time. He didn't even wince.

"Let me clean it for you."

"You don't have to."

The guilt was almost unbearable. All of this had happened because of me. I owed him much more than just the cleaning of his skin.

"I want to."

I grabbed several squares of toilet paper, soaked them under the faucet, and gently rubbed the clump across his chin. I was only able to get off a tiny bit of blood before he grabbed my hand and squeezed it.

"Stop. Just leave it."

I could tell how much pain he was in. He just didn't want to admit it. And even though I was trying to be so careful, I was hurting him. So, I got up and flushed the toilet paper, watching it swirl around the rusty bowl before it disappeared down the hole.

The next time we were taken, would he return to the cell at all? Would I?

I hadn't asked Breath the correct question. What if I was only given so many chances to get it right?

"What did they do to you?" he asked, holding my hands, palm up, rubbing his thumbs across each mark.

There wasn't any blood on my wrists. I suspected that was because Garin had cleaned them while I slept.

What if this was our last moment together? The last time he'd ever touch me?

When I didn't answer, he picked me up and rushed me over to our bed, covering me in a blanket. "You're shaking."

He was right. My entire body was convulsing, my teeth chattering. I didn't know how the fear would ever leave me, how I would ever stop trembling with these thoughts in my head.

"Tell me what happened to you, Kyle."

As I tucked the blanket under my chin, he found his way underneath it and ran his hands over my legs to try and warm them. He never stopped touching me, not even when my shaking calmed a little or when I described everything that had happened—at least the bits I could remember before Breath had stuck a needle in my arm.

"He didn't rape you," he said through gritted teeth. "Are you sure?"

I crossed my legs, squeezing my thighs together. Once again, I searched for that familiar soreness that came after sex. "Yes. I'm positive."

The relief was in his face and in his touch. "They're prepping you."

"For what?"

"So, when they ask you, you'll give them what they want. It's a mind game. They're trying to break you, weaken you through fear." As he paused, it felt like he was looking through my eyes, straight into my soul. "They're getting to you. I can feel it."

Every tremor in my body told me Garin was right.

Breath knew I cared about Garin. I had to believe that was why he was in here with me. Now, those feelings were being used against me.

Garin's whispers, *"Kyle...Kyle...Kyle..."* were all I could hear.

His bruises were all I could see.

Breath was torturing me. Again.

"Was it Beard who hurt you?" I asked.

He shook his head. "There were two guys. I didn't recognize either of them."

That meant there were at least four men holding us captive. The more men, the less chance we had of escaping this prison.

"Did they ask you anything?"

It took him a minute to answer. "No."

I couldn't tell if he was being honest or telling me what he thought I could handle. Garin was a protector, so it didn't surprise me that I was getting very few details.

"Then, why did they hurt you? Just because?"

"They can beat me and torture me all they want. I can take it. They're not going to break me, Kyle."

I stared at his cuts, at the bruises, at the gash on his throat. He was trying to hide the pain he was in by acting unfazed by it all. Dealing drugs on the streets, running the casino in Vegas, working with the bosses—it had all prepared him for this...whatever *this* was.

I wasn't used to this at all—not the torture or the threats. Not the uninvited touching.

Not someone coming on me.

# PRISONED

My whole body shook as I thought about Breath's cum.

"What is it that they want?" I had asked him that so many times before. I doubted this would be the last time either.

"I don't know."

I looked up at the window, wondering what I would see on the other side of it. Was there such a thing as normal beyond the bars of this cell? What was my brother doing right now? My employees?

"What's the date?"

I was sure Beard or Breath or some other bastard had our cell phones and had texted a lie to our employees, so they wouldn't be worried and call the police. They'd probably sent the same message to my mom and Anthony. My mom and I weren't close at all. She lived on the other side of Tampa, and we barely saw each other. That was just the way things had worked out after she'd gone to rehab and moved to Florida. But Anthony called me every day. I really wondered how he was handling my absence and who he was trying to strangle to find where I was.

"The funeral was on the twelfth," he said. "So, maybe it's the fifteenth or sixteenth. I don't know how long we've been in here."

On the first, Anthony would be making his drive down to Florida. If I wasn't home, if he didn't talk to me before then, he'd start looking for me, if he hadn't already. And he wouldn't stop until he found me.

"We just have to hang on a little longer," I said.

"You've got a plan?"

"They have until the first. Then, things will get interesting."

# TWELVE

## GARIN
## TWELVE YEARS AGO

I waited for Kyle in the alley. She didn't know I was here, but I knew she'd pass me because this was the route she took to get home from school. I used to walk it with her every day. But since Paulie's death, she walked home without me. She'd run right out of that fucking schoolyard before I even got a chance to get to her locker.

But not today. Today, she was going to walk with me. I'd skipped my last few periods, so I'd be here when she strolled by. So, I could join her, and things could go back to the way they used to be because things were all fucked-up now. I'd bang on her front door; she wouldn't answer. I'd call her place; she wouldn't pick up. I'd wait outside her class; she'd walk the other way.

Something was wrong, and I was going to find out what it was.

I heard her humming as she came down the street. She hummed when she drew, and she hummed in the shower. I'd hear her from outside the bathroom when I'd wait for her in her room. I'd poke my head out of the doorway just so I could hear her. And I'd hope she'd open the door just a crack to let out some of the steam, and by chance, I'd catch a glimpse of her in her towel. It had happened a few times but not enough.

At least now I knew what her body felt like since we'd hooked up in my room the other night. Shit, that needed to happen again real soon. Maybe even tonight, and I wouldn't make her go home. I didn't know if I could have her spend the whole night without getting her naked, but I'd try.

Her humming got louder the closer she got, and when I finally saw her foot step across the entrance of the alley, I grabbed her waist and pulled her inside, pushing her back against the building.

"Ow!" she screamed, flailing her arms, her legs trying to kick me in the shins.

"Kyle, it's me." I grabbed her hands, and she stilled.

"Garin? What the hell? What are you doing? I thought—oh God, I thought you were going to hurt me."

"Sorry." I should have planned this better, and I probably shouldn't have scared her. I was just afraid she'd run the other way if she saw me. "But you wouldn't talk to me, so you gave me no other choice."

"Let me go."

"No, Kyle. Not until you talk to me."

Her chest pumped real hard, as though she were trying to catch her breath, but she was breathing just fine. Her eyes were just a little watery. "What do you want to know?"

"I want to know why you've been avoiding me and why you haven't been answering your door and why you've been acting so different since Paulie was killed."

Her eyes started to really fill up, and her chin was quivering. "I can't do this. Let me go."

She tried wiggling out of my grip, and it only made me hold her tighter.

"What is wrong with you?"

"I need time."

She was crying now, tears running down her cheeks. I just wanted to wipe them away, brush all the hair out of her face, straighten her jacket, and tuck it up under her chin, so she'd stop shaking. But if I let her go, I feared she'd take off running.

# PRISONED

"I need time," she repeated. "You need to give me that."

"Time? Are you upset about Paulie? What is this about?"

When Paulie was killed, Kyle and I had both lost a friend. We'd known Paulie as long as we'd known each other. We'd grown up with him. At times, we hung out with him as much as we hung out with Billy. I knew Paulie meant a lot to Kyle. Shit, he meant a lot to all of us.

But she needed time? For what?

Nah, I didn't believe that. Something else was going on here. She just wasn't telling me what it was.

"It's too much," she said. "All of this is too much."

She stopped looking at me, and her head now pointed toward the ground. I saw the tears dripping down the front of her jacket. She was pushing her back against the wall, holding herself as far away from me as she could.

"Kyle?" I softened my voice, hoping it would make a difference. "Talk to me. Tell me what's wrong."

She finally looked up, but her expression had changed. She looked pissed off and irritated—a look I didn't see from her all that often. And, even though her cheeks were wet, she had stopped crying. "I can't do this anymore."

"Do what?"

"Us. This. All of it. You need to give me a break, Garin." The tone of her voice was the same one she used when she spoke about her ma, and she and her ma didn't get along at all.

"Kyle, what the fuck are you saying? You're done with me?"

"I'm asking you to get your hands off me and respect the space I need."

I kept my hands on her wrists, waiting for her to change her mind, for the look on her face to lighten, for the tears to return.

None of that happened.

She wanted nothing to do with me?

She'd change her mind. The second I let her go, she'd take it all back, and we'd walk home together. She'd ask me to kiss her like I had the other night, and all would be good again.

I lifted my hands and waited.

With her eyes still pointed toward the ground, she pushed herself off the brick wall and said, "Good-bye, Garin," as she passed me.

My mouth opened, and not one fucking thing came out of it. I watched her walk out of the alley, turn at the sidewalk, and head toward her place in The Heart.

I didn't move because she was going to come back. She was going to rush into my arms and kiss me, and this whole thing would be behind us.

She was going to come any second.

So, I waited.

I waited until it turned dark. I waited until the streetlamps flickered on.

I waited until I knew she wasn't coming back.

And then I ran to Billy's apartment. I didn't talk about Kyle to anyone. She wasn't just some girl I fucked in the bathroom behind the gym or some chick who gave me a blow job in between English and Trig. Kyle was my best friend. She was the girl I'd cared about my whole life. The one I wanted to take things slow with when I'd never taken things slow with anyone before.

"Quit the racket, will ya?" Billy's ma shouted when I banged on their front door. "He's upstairs, for fuck's sake."

I took the stairs two at a time and burst through Billy's bedroom door without knocking. He was on his bed, his shirt off, lying in just a pair of ripped boxers. His belt was tied around his bicep, and there was a tarred-up spoon and needle right next to him. His head was leaning back against the wall, a line of drool coming out of the corner of his mouth.

"Billy," I said, standing beside the bed. I shouted his name again when he didn't answer, shaking the arm that wasn't being squeezed by the belt.

"What?" he groaned. As he woke up, he scratched his chest and his stomach and his thighs. I'd heard the last batch of dope that had come in made everyone real itchy. He looked all around his room until he saw me. "What did you wake me up for? I was just catching a good nap."

"You were fucking nodding out, not napping."

"Whatever."

I knew he was shooting a lot, but I hadn't realized things had gotten this bad. He usually came to my place, so I hadn't seen his room in a while and all the shit that was lying around in here. There were wax

# PRISONED

paper packets all over his dresser and covering most of the floor along with orange needle caps all over the rug in his closet.

It was a junkie's fucking paradise.

And my best friend was the junkie.

"I need to talk to you. Shit is all messed up with Kyle, and I need some advice and—Billy?"

His eyes were closed again, his head starting to lean forward.

"Billy, wake the fuck up."

"Mmm," he groaned, scratching his forearms.

He was too gone to talk. Too high to even give a shit.

*Fuck.*

"I'll see you tomorrow, Billy." I shut his door, ran down the steps, and let myself out.

Some of the old-timers were hanging out in front of my place. That probably meant my ma was home, banging one of them for a hit while the others waited their turn.

I couldn't see it.

I sure as hell couldn't hear it.

So, I walked right past my place, past Kyle's apartment where I saw her bedroom light on, past the Stop sign at the end of the street, and I turned down the next block. I was still in The Heart, but I didn't know many of the guys who lived on this street.

If it was even possible, this block looked worse than ours. There were needle caps all over the sidewalk and empty balloons of junk. Broken crack pipes crunched under my sneakers as I stepped on them.

If hell had dirty siding, chipped paint, leaky roofs, boarded up windows, and paraphernalia lining the street, then I was fucking in it.

Every row of two-story buildings that made up this neighborhood was the same. I heard it and saw it as I walked past—screaming on the inside of the apartments, most of them dark from not paying the electric bill, kids outside trying to hustle in the streets because their parents were getting high.

Kyle made it worth staying. I would have left and gone to live in one of Mario's apartments a long time ago. Maybe I would do that until this little break of hers was over.

But I didn't like the way she had looked at me in the alley.

Or the way she hadn't looked at me at all.

Something about this didn't feel right.

"Watch it," some guy said to me as I passed him.

Our shoulders smacked against each other.

I turned around. "You fucking watch it. Who do you think you're talking to?"

It was the wrong hour to piss me off.

"You got something you want to say to me?" he barked.

I told myself to turn back around. I told myself he wasn't worth it. I told myself not to pay attention to anything this dude said.

But Kyle didn't give a shit about me anymore. Heroin was more important to Billy than I was.

So, I stopped caring, too.

I wasn't going to give a fuck about anything—not that guy's face or what my knuckles were going to do to it. I clenched my fingers together to make a tight fist, and I aimed right for his goddamn nose.

# THIRTEEN

## KYLE

When I woke up, there were two trays on the floor. Beard must have delivered them while we'd both been asleep. I was surprised the sound of the door hadn't woken me. It was the scariest noise inside our cell, and it was a sound I had quickly come to fear. I must have been too mentally worn to hear it, or the drugs had kept me knocked out as they worked their way through my system.

Garin was still sleeping, so I carefully wiggled away from his body and carried the trays over to our bed. He had told me not too long ago that I needed to eat to keep up my strength; so did he. We didn't have antibiotics or first aid. We had rusty water and food that tasted like plastic. It would have to do.

I traced my fingernails up and down the dark hair on his forearm. "Garin, you have to wake up and eat."

He stirred slowly, eventually looking at me through his long black lashes. "I was dreaming."

"About?"

"Us. That night. The sound of the gun."

My throat started to tighten.

*That night.*

It had been significant for so many different reasons.

"I dream about it often, too," I admitted.

"Does the outcome ever change in your dreams?"

I shook my head. "Never. Paulie…doesn't ever make it."

The truth was, I didn't just have that dream often. I had it constantly. I figured it was one of my punishments, and I'd accepted that.

"Eat." I handed him a piece of cantaloupe, hoping the presence of food would keep him from talking about that night. "This actually isn't all that bad."

I swallowed the bite after mushing it around my mouth. Maybe I was just getting used to the plastic taste. At least they'd also given us two small paper cartons of milk, which was the first time they'd ever set drinks on our trays.

He ripped off a piece of the toast and put it in his mouth. His hands stayed near his lips, touching the cuts, feeling around some of the bruises.

"Your face looks worse today."

The bruises under his eyes seemed to have darkened, or the lighting in here had gotten worse. The cuts had started to heal a little, the wide dotted scabs showing how deep and long each gash was. His beard hid the marks on his cheeks, but because I had stared at him for so long, I knew what lay beneath the hairs.

I continued to watch him as he took a bite of the cantaloupe. My tray sat mostly untouched, besides the fruit. Eating meant I would have to look down at my food, and I didn't want to move my gaze from his damaged face. I wanted to save this moment. Hold it. Live in it for as long as I could. I would use this moment the next time I was taken from my cell. The next time I was slapped and jizzed on. The next time I needed to feel something beyond my own pain. Because I feared we didn't have many more moments like this together.

"Do you have guilt, Kyle?"

And then the moment was over.

The truth stared into my face, and I hated the way it made me feel. I didn't want him to see it, so I walked over to the sink and washed the juice off my hands. I couldn't look at him when I answered, "Yes. Every day."

"I gave Billy his first bag. I'm the reason he started using."

I looked at him as he stirred the oatmeal with his finger. He wasn't going to eat it. Neither was I. I couldn't imagine putting anything in my stomach at this point.

This was his guilt, the part of our pasts that ate at him, and from what I could see, it was just as deep as the part that gnawed at me. I couldn't let him take the blame.

"That's not true."

"It is." He pushed his tray away and moved over to the wall next to me, leaning back against it, as he glared down at me. "He wanted to try it. He wanted to know what all the hype was about. He wanted just a taste…and I fucking gave it to him."

"He would have tasted it whether you'd given it to him or not."

He didn't seem convinced.

"It was all over The Heart. His mom and Paulie used. He could have gotten it from either of them. Stop blaming yourself, Garin."

"I deserve the blame. It's mine." He slammed his fist against the wall. "Aside from you, I was the only person in his life who truly gave a shit, who wasn't whacked out of their mind on drugs, who was supposed to keep him safe." He punched the wall again, but it wasn't out of anger. This time, his face was filled with sadness. "I didn't keep him safe. I led him straight down the path that the rest of his family took."

"Stop. Garin—"

"For years, I begged him to go to rehab. I offered to pay for it. I offered to get him a job once he was clean and buy him a house and make sure he never wanted for anything ever again. He wouldn't go." He rubbed his hands against his thighs, like the friction would take away his pain. "I couldn't fix him, Kyle. It's all I wanted. It's all I ever wanted."

The room went silent, but the lack of noise didn't hide the emotion that pulsed inside here. It was in Garin's eyes. It was in me.

"Once Paulie died, there wasn't anything we could have done for him," I said. "If he hadn't already been using, he probably would have started then. That pain…it was too much."

I remembered all the times Anthony had found me on the floor of my closet. There weren't any windows in there; there wasn't any light. It was just my tears, my shaking body, four walls, darkness, and guilt. Anthony would pull me off the floor and tell me to stop crying and demand that I get my shit together. It had taken me months before I had found my breath again.

"I wish it hadn't changed everything between us."

We'd talked about this before, but it felt different now. More personal. Much more intimate.

"Me, too," I whispered, wrapping my arms around my stomach to dull the ache.

It wasn't from hunger but from all the regret I felt. I wished more than anything that things hadn't changed between the guys and me. My whole life would have been different. I wouldn't have been in this cell. I wouldn't have been living in Florida. Maybe I wouldn't have even had my shop.

"Then, why did we let it?" he asked.

There was no *we*. It was all *me*.

If I gave him an answer, I would be confessing every bit of truth I'd been hiding. It would be the biggest relief. It would probably eliminate all of my anxiety. I wouldn't have a hard time finding my breath ever again.

But I couldn't do it.

"Some things are so destructive that they're impossible to recover from. I think losing Paulie showed us the scary reality of what could happen to any of us and…" Lies. All lies.

We knew how dangerous The Heart was; we knew the possibilities. We'd seen them. Daily. Paulie's death should have driven me toward the guys; it shouldn't have caused me to run from them.

"And it was just too much," I said.

"So, we shouldn't get close to anyone because we don't know when we'll suddenly lose them?"

I shrugged. I didn't know what else to do, what else to say. The lies were building layer by layer.

His hand touched my shoulder. I imagined him kissing me, caressing me even more. But what I really deserved was for him to take his hand away and never touch me again.

"It should have brought us closer."

# PRISONED

He was right, of course. If only the circumstances had been different.

"We should have been there for each other," he continued. "We needed it. I needed *you*."

I knew he did. I'd heard it in his voice when he stood outside my front door and begged me to come out. I'd seen it in his face when he waited in the hallway outside my classes. I'd felt it in his touch when he cornered me in the alley, gripped my shoulders, and pleaded with me to talk to him.

*"I need time to heal,"* I had said.

More lies.

Lies I wish I could take back.

"I know." It was too painful to meet his eyes, so I kept them on the ground.

"Why did it have to happen *that* night?"

It was a question I had asked myself so many times before.

"The same night I finally got to taste you," he continued. "Had it happened any night after, you wouldn't have slipped away so easily."

Easily?

*Breathe for me.*

He thought my decision to run was an easy one to make? That it was even a decision at all? That it hadn't eaten at me then and every day since? That his eyes didn't remind me of all the years I'd lost, years I'd never get back, years where I could have had everything I wanted?

"I never planned on letting you go, Kyle."

I looked up slowly, my arms squeezing my stomach. My knees were shaking. I knew my chest would be next, that my breathing would only get worse.

"I was going to bring you to Vegas with me, get you into college out there, and take care of you. I was going to love you." He turned me to face him. "Fuck, Kyle, I did love you."

"Stop." I tried to move around him, but he wouldn't let me. I needed to find air. I needed to forget the words he had just spoken. I needed to get the hell out of here. "I can't listen to this."

"Why?"

"It hurts too much."

His hands were on my arms, so I rolled my shoulders to wiggle out of his grip. It didn't work. He only clamped down tighter.

"Tell me why it hurts." I didn't answer, so he lifted my chin until I looked him in the eyes. "Tell me."

"Because I wish I could rewind the past. I wish things had gone down differently. I wish we'd never lost Paulie, and things hadn't changed between the three of us. And..." I was telling him the obvious. What I wasn't telling him was my feelings. There was no reason to hide them anymore. "I cared about you so much. More than you're supposed to care about your best friend. I wanted to be with you. I wanted to give you everything. My heart, my body. All of me. And I threw it all away—our relationship, moving with you, caring for you."

My lips were soaked from the tears that I didn't know had been falling. I tried to move again, but he stopped me. He wasn't going to let me go until I got it all out even though there was so much that would never come out.

"When you kissed me at the bar, all of those memories resurfaced, and the guilt slapped me right in the face."

His bruised eyelids narrowed. His mouth stayed still. His expression hadn't changed at all. I didn't know if I had scared him or given him the answer he'd wanted to hear. The unknown was as terrifying as what was waiting for me outside this cell.

But there was more. The biggest part of all this was resting on my tongue. He had to hear it. He had to know. It was the most honest I would ever be with him.

"I've loved you since I was a kid," I said. "And I still do."

# FOURTEEN

## KYLE

I waited for him to speak; he said nothing. I waited for him to step toward me; he didn't. I waited for his face to give me some sort of reaction; it remained still.

Seconds passed. Then, suddenly, my body was pressed against his. I didn't feel the movement. I didn't see the room flash before me. I didn't even have a chance to take a breath. But, now, I was resting on the far wall of the cell, our mouths locked, his tongue swirling around mine.

The air I inhaled smelled of him. The saliva that ran down my throat tasted of him. That was the way I wanted it. The way I'd always wanted it.

When he lifted me into his arms, my legs wrapped around his waist. He held my face, so I couldn't move, and he devoured my mouth as though it were the only thing he'd eaten in days.

I wanted to be devoured.

I wanted to devour him.

I reached for his cheeks but stopped before I got too close.

As though he could sense it, he pulled his lips away. "Touch me."

I glanced over the spots that had been tortured. "I don't want to hurt you."

"You won't."

"But—"

"You won't," he repeated. "The only thing that will hurt is not having your hands on me."

As our connection deepened, it felt as though our thoughts had mixed in the air, our pasts hanging above us and our fears hanging below. We weren't in this cell. He didn't have bruises and cuts and scabs. We didn't have memories of Breath and Beard. Our mouths didn't taste of plastic.

It was just us.

Our needs.

Our wants.

It was a moment I had been waiting for most of my life, and it was finally here.

And it was either the start of something monumental that would change me permanently, or it was the terrifying conclusion of our story.

I pressed my hand gently against his cheek, brushing my thumb across his coarse whiskers. He closed his eyes and nibbled the side of my palm. That minimal movement, that simple bit of affection, seemed to give him whatever he needed.

But it was softness that *I* needed.

The softness was gone the second his lips touched mine again. He used his weight to hold me against the wall, and he lifted my tank top over my head. He unclasped my bra with one hand. Then, he moved me over to our bed and laid me on it. Before I had time to even take a breath, he had my pants unbuttoned and swept them off my legs. The cold air hit my naked skin, but before I could even shiver, he'd thrown a blanket over me.

"If we weren't in here, I never would have covered you." He looked at me as though he could see through the blanket because no man would ever look at a piece of wool with that much hunger in his eyes.

"Why not?"

Maybe it was the anticipation of him touching me or the dampness in our cell, but I felt something tingle across my neck and over my face.

# PRISONED

*Kyle.*

"I want you naked when you're around me, and I want nothing between us, except air."

"How about when I need…" My voice trailed off the second he started unbuttoning his shirt.

There was something about Garin's skin that was unlike any other man's. Even in the dim light, it looked so shiny and smooth. So overly masculine. Every piece of hair, every freckle, every pore was outrageously sexy.

"When you need to do what?"

My eyes followed his fingers as they worked their way through each button, and he eventually dropped his shirt on the floor.

"I don't remember what I was going to say."

His shoes came off next and then his pants until he was left in just his boxer briefs. I was willing those off with my stare.

"Garin, waiting for you is almost painful."

I suddenly found myself wrapped in his arms, his face inches from mine, his body pressed on top of me.

His hand was circling my throat, squeezing. "Now, you know what it feels like. That pain. That *torture*."

"I didn't do it to hurt you," I said.

*I did it to hurt me.*

As his gaze moved back and forth between my eyes, I could practically taste his tongue. He knew how much I wanted it, and I could feel how much he wanted me. His erection rubbed along my pussy. Every time I shifted my hips to cause more friction, he stilled me.

He nipped my bottom lip, and when he tried to pull away, I wrapped a leg around his waist.

"Don't leave. Stay right here, and give me what I want."

"I'll hurt you."

He was going to make me pay for running away from him. I should have expected that, but maybe if I begged hard enough, he would change his mind.

"I'm hurting enough already. Please, Garin, I want you."

A line appeared between his brow, and his gaze intensified. "I've wanted to fuck you for more than half of my life. Do you know what that kind of want does to you after a while?" There was a grittiness to his voice, and it made me shiver. "It makes you crazy. Violent. Needy to the point where you can't control your roughness." Each description came with a slight shift of his hips, the crown of his dick rubbing over my clit. "If my cock slides inside you, it's going to hurt you, Kyle. It's going to fuck you so hard, you'll bleed. It's going to pound you until the walls of your pussy are completely raw. Until I've come inside you so many times, I've completely filled your cunt." He grabbed my cheeks, the pads of his fingers digging into my skin. "Think about this before you beg me to stay."

It was a warning.

And it was as sexy as foreplay, as his tongue flicking my clit. Wetness dripped down my inner thighs, spreading every time I rubbed them together. My pussy clenched as I thought about him being inside me.

"I'm not scared."

I gasped when I felt his hand move between my legs and push them apart. He didn't ease his way in. He didn't tease my hole or rub my clit. He slid two fingers inside and thrust them in and out.

"You should be."

"Ahh," I moaned, gripping his shoulders, surprised at how quickly my orgasm was building. "I want it rough, Garin."

"I don't know if I'll be able to stop…even if you want me to."

Another warning. One that should have filled me with fear. It did just the opposite. Someone who could make me feel this good with just his fingers would only make me feel better when he finally gave me his dick.

"I don't want you to stop."

He took my lip between his teeth and bit down. It was hard enough to draw blood. While he held my mouth hostage, he growled.

"More," I begged, my voice muffled since he still had ahold of my lip.

He pressed his beard against my chin, roughing up the sensitive skin. "You're going to regret saying that."

"How—" I was cut off when his face disappeared down my body.

His fingers continued to plunge in and out of me, his mouth immediately diving onto my clit. In one long sweep, his tongue flattened against me, giving my clit the friction and heat and wetness it desired. When he reached the top, he flicked it with just the tip of his tongue.

# PRISONED

"Garin!" I screamed, digging my nails into his shoulders, barely able to stop my legs from thrashing, my head from grinding into the scratchy wool.

"This tastes so fucking good." He sucked my clit into his mouth and released it. "I need to feel you on my tongue, Kyle. Your quivering and bucking, your cunt tightening around my fingers. Give it to me."

My legs spread more as his fingers hammered into me, his tongue licking just the right spot. My eyes closed, and my stomach tightened as I let the build ride on.

"Your clit is getting so fucking hard. You're close. I want it."

*Kyle.*

"It's yours," I moaned, knowing it was only going to take a few more seconds.

"Tell me."

"I'm..."

"TELL ME."

"I'm going to—*ah*!" I shouted as his tongue left me, his fingers pulling out. I was almost at the peak, and then the feeling was...gone.

"I told you that you'd regret asking for more."

I leaned up so that I could see his face. "You're punishing me?"

"I'm taking what I want, and that's bringing you so close to the edge until I can feel you almost start to fall."

"Like I said...you're punishing me."

He glanced down at my pussy, a ravenous hunger spreading through his eyes before they met mine again. "Call it what you want."

"And what about what I—*oh God*."

He was licking me again. As he stared at me through his lashes, his tongue swept from side to side, his fingers driving into me. And there was that deliciously intense build. It returned as quickly as it had left, forcing my back to the floor, my hands pinching the blanket. It felt as though his tongue were vibrating on my clit. As though his fingers were filling me as thickly and as wildly as his dick would be.

Maybe if I didn't warn him, he wouldn't know. Maybe if I tried to quiet my moaning, I'd slip an orgasm through. Maybe...

"Mmm," he growled. "So close...I can feel it on my tongue." He stopped, pulling out of me completely. The only thing that hit me was his exhale.

I clawed at the blanket, rocking my hips toward him, waiting for his mouth to return. When he still didn't touch me, I begged, "Garin, give it to me."

*I can't take this.*

*Breathe, Kyle.*

"My tongue..." He gave me just a quick flick, right at the top, the spot that desired the most friction.

Then, there was air, bursts of it, stimulating my clit. My body clung to it, searching for the build.

"*Yes*," I hissed. "More."

"Haven't you learned your lesson about asking for more?"

I leaned up again, bearing my weight down on my forearms, staring through the V between my legs. It was then that I saw the look in his eyes. A look that needed more explanation. "I don't think you're trying to tease me. So, what are you doing to me?"

"I'm making sure your body is ready."

I wouldn't accept his warning, so he was prepping me for the punishment his dick was about to give me. Building me with need, with desire, with so much passion that it would hurt less.

He was protecting me...even when it came to sex.

This man...I would never be able to get enough of him.

"You are..." I paused as his tongue found me again.

"Yes?" His lids turned hooded, his fingers sliding into my snugness.

"Incredible."

"And?"

"Garin, ahh."

His speed had picked up. His tongue used much more pressure. He had sucked my clit into his mouth and was grinding his tongue against the end of it. My hips bucked as I neared that place again.

"Your mouth," I panted, "is dangerously good at this."

I tilted my head back and stared at the light above us. It hummed each time it flickered. And each flicker matched the movement of his tongue. I didn't know if he was going to let me come, but I couldn't hide what was happening inside my body. I couldn't mute my moans. I couldn't keep my legs still or my nails from stabbing whatever they came into contact with.

"You want to come?"

# PRISONED

The sound of him brought me back to the moment and out of this fog of pleasure he had put me in.

"*Yes*," I cried.

He lifted my hips and wrapped his hands around my thighs, and in one swift movement, he was inside me.

"Oh!" I screamed.

He gave me everything I had asked for. Every beautiful inch. Every dominating blast of power. Every bit of wetness that he had created was now coating him as he slammed in and out of me. My breath…it was gone. Stolen. Replaced with his hardness.

"Fuck," he roared. "So fucking tight. So fucking wet." He circled his hips to put pressure on my clit at the same time. "Come on me."

The earlier warning hadn't been a joke. This man had a kind of strength that I hadn't ever experienced before, and my pussy certainly wasn't used to his size. But in between the pain was a pleasure so fierce that it took ahold of me and drove me toward the edge. He showed no restraint, no forgiveness, no mercy, as he relentlessly pumped the orgasm out of me. I was screaming and moaning—more of one than the other, but I wasn't sure which.

"Ahh!" I shouted, my body reaching the peak. This time, I was increasingly more sensitive from all the teasing he'd done with his tongue.

"Give it to me, Kyle."

*Kyle.*

"Give me what I want."

*What I want is…*

"Oh my God!" I yelled.

With each stroke, each churn of his hips, my body convulsed around him. Spasms shot through my stomach. Tingles ricocheted through my breasts. His thumb rubbed my clit, which kept the orgasm coursing through me. Every second that passed, my shouts got louder, my nails dug in harder.

"Again!" he commanded before I had even come down. "I want your cunt milking my fucking cock."

As our mouths touched, I was breathless, unable to imagine how I would fulfill his demand when I had barely recovered from the last one. But as he drove his dick into me, still using a speed and roughness that I'd never thought I would enjoy, I was reminded of how quickly I was able to get there.

My shoulders burned from the wool, the back of my head ached from the hard floor, my legs shook from the strain it took to keep them clung around his waist. Yet I was there. Again. Not just from what he was doing to my body, but also from his scent in my nose, his taste on my tongue, the feel of his skin pressed against mine. He overwhelmed each of my senses.

Just as that familiar build began to resurface, he moved me. I was suddenly on top, straddling his waist, while he leaned his back against the wall.

"Another second on top, and I'm afraid I would have ripped you in half." He gripped my hips and pushed them forward and back. "Ride me."

So, he had been using restraint. I couldn't imagine what full power would have felt like.

In this position, I could take as much of his cock as I wanted. I was finally in control. I lifted all the way to the top, teasing his crown around my hole. He groaned, as though he missed my wetness, causing me to drop back down on his shaft and slowly rise again.

When I felt that twinge of build, sparking at the very lower part of my stomach, I kept his dick buried in me and rocked my hips back and forth. He was so long that his tip reached that extra-sensitive spot inside. Not just reached it. He caressed it over and over, like it was his flicking tongue.

"This body..." His hands were everywhere, squeezing my nipples, rubbing my clit, gripping the side of my cheek. His fingers moved fast, making sure their presence was known, striking the smallest bit of pain before rubbing it out. "How did you keep it away from me for so long?"

There was no way I could answer that question. So, I flattened my palms against his chest, arched my back, and got lost in the movement. The muscles in his chest tightened, and it caused me to tilt my head forward and look at him.

"You're milking my cock."

"I'm close."

His abs contracted, rippling down his stomach, and my fingers followed their trail. The lightest coating of sweat mixed in with the dark hairs. I lifted my hand to my mouth, so I could have his salty taste on my tongue.

His thumb was back on my clit, rubbing circles over the small bead, while his parted lips and hooded eyes took me in. "Fuck, Kyle. You're tightening more."

"Garin…"

"I know…" he hissed. "You're dripping over my cock, and it's begging for my cum."

I moaned so loud that I feared Beard would come in. But, even if he did, there was no way I could stop. Not at this point. I was too far gone to care if he dragged me off Garin's dick and put me on that freezing chair with Breath's nasty tongue on my face.

Some things were worth the punishment. Garin was one.

He angled his hips upward, which gave me even more access to him. I took it all—the rubbing of his thumb and the fullness of his wide, thick cock—and I let my body work through that familiar tingle.

"Even tighter," he moaned. "Suck it right out of me, baby."

I crashed my lips against his. I wanted to feel those filthy words vibrate across my mouth. Then, I tightened one last time, knowing this was the final second I'd be able to hold it in. Garin's sounds told me he felt it. He clamped his hands on my waist and completely took over the movements. Keeping me on top, my fingers holding his shoulders for leverage, he rocked into me as hard as he could. In and out.

In…and deliciously out.

My clit was exploding with pleasure. My stomach was shuddering. My body was numb, except for the spasms that pulsed through each limb and muscle. When I opened my mouth, his tongue filled it.

"You're mine, Kyle. You've always been mine."

*Always yours.*

I was his.

"Yes, Garin, I'm yours."

That must have been what he needed to hear because his abs tightened, his hips rocked against mine, and he moaned my name over and over as he filled me with streams of his hot, thick cum.

When we both finally calmed, he rested my head on top of his shoulder, and I wrapped my arms around him. He was still inside me, my legs still straddled him, and I breathed in his scent. It was warmth. More warmth than I'd had since we'd been put in our cell.

The cell.

It only took seconds before I was brought right back to the cement and the bars and the reason I thought we were in here.

"What if this is the last time?" I whispered.

He tilted my face up, so he could look at me. "Nothing is going to happen to us."

"I'm envious of your optimism." I broke our eye contact and squeezed my thighs over the sides of his stomach. "I hope you're not just saying that because you're still inside me."

He gave my bottom lip a small nibble and moved me to where he'd been sitting. Then, he went over to the sink, dampening a clump of toilet paper. I thought he would hand it to me when he returned, but he rubbed it over my pussy instead. It was an intimate moment. His gentle hand held the wet paper against my opening, cleaning the cum as it dripped out of me. His touch was so fragile, so different than he had been several minutes before. The compassionate side of him was as sexy as the feral one.

After he flushed the clump, he handed my clothes back to me and joined me under the blanket. "I'm going to keep you safe." The clothes stayed where he had set them because he gripped my face, making it impossible for me to move. "If they want to torture someone, they're going to torture me."

He'd kept me so fogged that I'd forgotten about his bruises, cuts, and scrapes. But, now, they all stared at me. Taunted me. Reminded me of Breath and Beard, the power they had, what they were capable of… how badly they could hurt us.

"Garin, no."

His lips were so close to mine, and I breathed in his exhale. It didn't matter how tightly he held my face. He wasn't squeezing a *yes* out of me.

"The decision is up to me," he said. "It's what I choose, and as long as I can help it, nothing is going to happen to you."

"You can't protect me in here. You said it yourself."

He pulled me onto his lap, my naked body straddling his. "Stop," he growled.

I opened my mouth, and his finger pressed between my lips.

"You're going to work yourself up until you can't breathe. Don't do it, Kyle. Let me do the worrying. Let me carry the anxiety. I just want you to take a deep breath, get dressed, and get into bed, so I can hold you until you fall asleep."

Instead of giving me a chance to respond, he lifted me off his lap and set me on my feet. He clasped the bra behind my back and helped me slide into my pants. He even dropped my tank top over my head.

Once he was dressed, he climbed into bed behind me, holding me so close to his body. I felt every inhale. Every exhale. Every beat inside his chest.

"My soul mate," I whispered.

He turned my cheek, so I looked at him over my shoulder. "What did you call me?"

"You're my soul mate, Garin. For some reason, we were put in this cell together and given a second chance."

"You believe in that?"

I nodded. "I believe our soul mate is revealed only once during our life. Maybe it's a glimpse of a stranger. Maybe it's our best friend. The timing may not always be right. But, when they're shown to us, we know it's them. Then, life happens. We grow. We age. We develop scars. And we remember that glimpse. Some are lucky enough to spend the rest of their lives with that person. Some, like me, have only memories."

"Now, you have more than just memories."

He released my face, and I turned around, cozying into his chest.

This was another moment. One that I wanted to hold, that I wanted to live in for as long as I could. One that I'd use to put me in a painless place. There were other moments from my past. All of them included Garin. They shone the brightest in my mind, so I wouldn't ever forget them.

But my past had taught me something. After each of these moments, the moment that followed usually wasn't good. It was tragic. Dark. It had the capability of changing my life for the worse.

I feared that would happen the next time I opened my eyes. That, after this moment, the next would sear us permanently. I needed to prepare myself for that.

So, in my mind, I moved the light. Now, it shone on this. And on us.

# FIFTEEN

## GARIN
## PRESENT DAY

I stared at her face while her eyes were closed. She looked the same as she did all those years ago. So fucking beautiful but healthy. With all her makeup washed off, she had a softness to her skin that women from The Heart didn't usually have. Kyle always had it. Hell, she looked more gorgeous now than she had when she graduated high school.

*Kyle Lang, after all this time, how the hell did you come back into my life?*

And, now, we were here, together, in the most fucked up place. In the most fucked up situation.

When I saw her in the back row at the funeral, I wanted to wrap my hands around her goddamn neck and squeeze every bit of air out of her lungs. But, once I heard all the pain in her voice and saw how much was in her eyes, I knew it wasn't just from Billy's OD. It went deeper than that.

Much deeper.

So, I took her to a place where there wasn't a casket staring her right in the face, where her brother wasn't breathing down her fucking neck. I thought it would help her open up.

It had.

By her second cocktail, some of the old Kyle had started to come out. She was chewing the end of her straw, teasing her tongue around its rim. She had no idea how sexy she was. She didn't when we were kids, and she hadn't been able to handle her booze back then either. One cocktail at Mario's house, and I could get anything I wanted out of her. That was why I'd never let her drink with anyone but me and why I'd put her to bed before she did something she'd regret in the morning.

My plan didn't fail me this time.

Once the liquor began revealing more of her guilt, I sent the text message. Things were set in motion…and they were going to stay in motion.

*Fucking guilt.*

I knew what it looked like; the same shit was rotting inside me. But that had been the first time I'd seen it in Kyle's eyes. I had to give her credit. She hid it well. Too goddamn well. She shouldn't have drunk anything. The booze had broken down her walls and shown me things I should have seen before. Had I seen it, things would have played out differently.

I would have brought her to Vegas. I would have gotten her into school. I would have taken care of her. I would have made her mine.

And I would have protected her.

But now…

Now, we were here.

Having feelings for her hadn't been part of my plan. I didn't know when the fuck that had happened, but I had to keep those feelings separate.

And her body. I tried to only touch her when she stirred, but my hands didn't want to stay off her.

I had to forget I felt anything at all. I had to forget I'd touched her. *Really* touched her.

And I had to focus on getting what I wanted.

Kyle knew something. Whatever that something was…it was going to be mine.

# SIXTEEN

## KYLE

I sat on edge, waiting for Breath to burst into our cell or for Beard to pluck me from Garin's arms. Whenever I opened my eyes, I expected to be on the icy chair again, the ropes burning my wrists, a revolting tongue resting on my earlobe, sticky residue drying somewhere on my body. The only time I'd relaxed was when Garin was inside me.

But as the hours ticked on, Beard eventually returned. He threw down two trays, flashed us his gun, and left with a grunt.

The next day was the same, and so was the one after that.

I knew I wouldn't be kept in the dark forever. There was a reason Garin and I were here, and it would be explained soon. But it felt like the more time I spent in our cell, the further I was from that answer. I began getting a little more comfortable in there. There was someone responsible for that.

Garin.

*Kyle.*

He was doting, caring. He made me laugh so hard that tears streamed from my eyes and my stomach cramped. He made me remember the times we'd shared in The Heart.

He made me feel every emotion.

I didn't know how a cell like ours could feel tolerable, but somehow, Garin made that happen. He made the food taste good by taking my mind to a place where everything was delicious. He made the floor seem less filthy and the sink less rusted. He made the colors less drab and the air not as damp.

He made me feel loved. It had always been there. It had never once weakened. But being here with him brought it back even stronger.

"There's something on your mind, Kyle. Tell me what it is."

My empty dinner tray sat in front of me. My fingers dripped from the buttery sauce the noodles had soaked in and the pineapple juice that I'd searched through to find the chunks.

I tried to stand, but he stopped me.

"Say it." He looked down at my hands and drew one of my fingers into his mouth, sucking off the juice. He didn't rush through the others. He took his time, his tongue swirling around the knuckles and nails.

"That feels better than it should," I said.

He shook his head, like a tiger that had a small animal in its mouth. It showed dominance. And it showed how much he owned me because, even if his teeth were piercing my skin, I wouldn't pull my hand away.

"Everything I do to you is going to feel good." He surrounded my pinkie with his lips, the only finger he hadn't sucked yet. "But you weren't about to tell me how good I made you feel. You were about to say something much more serious than that."

When I looked down at my feet, I felt his hand on my chin, stopping it from dropping any farther.

"No. I want you to look at me."

He wasn't going to let me get out of this. I didn't just have to confess. I had to look at him while I was doing it.

Just a few days ago, I'd told him I'd loved him since I was a kid. I'd told him I still did. But saying *I love you* felt different.

"I need a minute."

"I'm not giving you a minute," he said. "I want the answer now."

I finally met his eyes. "My feelings were coming to the surface."

"Tell me what they are."

"You know already."

"Tell me again."

How could I tell him I loved him when I was lying to him at the same time? Lying about something that really mattered. Lying about something that would change everything between us.

What we had was based on a lie.

The lie was woven into my answers, in my thoughts, in what had happened between us...what would continue happening, I was sure. It would affect the way he felt about me.

It *should* affect the way he felt.

*Breathe, Kyle.*

So, the only thing that made sense was to lie more. I couldn't drag him into this any further. He was already in far enough. He knew he had my body; I couldn't lie about that. But my heart? I could push him away emotionally. I could make sure his feelings didn't deepen, like mine had. It would be too late if that happened.

*Breathe, Kyle.*

Then, he would really hate me once he found out I wasn't who he thought I was.

Then...

*Kyle.*

"I think it was a good thing that I left all those years ago." My stare deepened as I tried to read him, something I hadn't been successful at since we'd been locked in here. "We're too different. Not just our lifestyles, but also our personalities. You were crazy about women back then. From what you've told me, it sounds like that hasn't changed at all."

"What are you saying?"

"I'm saying..." It wasn't true, so it hurt to even think this. It hurt to let the words marinate on my tongue. But because he was able to read me so well, I had to sound believable. "I would never be able to trust you."

"Kyle—"

"You're entertaining. That's all. When your tongue was on my clit and your cock was inside me, I didn't think about being in this cell. I was thankful they had placed me in here with you. But, now that I know how talented you are, I'm even more thankful." I even hated the tone I was using. This wasn't me. Not the words, not the sarcasm. Definitely not the harshness.

He knew that, too.

"You're saying I'm nothing more than a distraction?"

No.

I shrugged. "Your dick is one of the best I've had. So, yes."

"You feel nothing in here?" His hand pressed against my chest. It was a surprisingly forceful move, but it didn't hurt.

My comments had hurt. The way I nodded my head...hurt.

"I don't believe you," he barked.

"It's true."

"Your eyes are telling me a much different story."

I didn't have time to prepare myself before his lips crashed against mine, his tongue filling the space in between. It wasn't just passionate. It was the kind of kiss someone gave before they said good-bye. A kiss that was memorable.

"Your lips are telling me a much different story." His hands moved to my waist, and he lifted my tank over my head. "If this wasn't the only shirt you had, I would have ripped the fucking thing off you."

He knelt on the floor and peeled my pants off. My bra and panties came off shortly after.

I couldn't tell him to stop. I couldn't reach for his hands and still them. I was frozen in pure elation, knowing I would get to be close to him again, knowing I would get to feel his emotions. Knowing mine would only intensify.

It contradicted everything I had just told him. It had the potential of putting my feelings on display. Yet I still didn't stop him. Because having Garin inside me and being released from this prison were the only two things I wanted. And the one I wanted more in that moment... was Garin.

As he shed his clothes, his eyes stayed on mine, his lips parted, determination glaring from his face. "Get over here," was his only warning.

He lifted me off the ground and wrapped my legs around his waist. Then, he carried us to one of the corners and sat down.

Still, I didn't fight him.

# PRISONED

Instead, I basked in the attention. The closeness. The way my pussy rested over his erection, doing everything I could not to grind over the side of it, not to wiggle enough so that the tip would pop in.

Garin didn't move. He just stared at me, as though he were assessing every breath, every blink. When I couldn't take the silence, I let his name slip through my lips.

It took him several seconds to respond. "Your pulse is telling me something very different." He tipped my face upward, holding it steady. "Your pupils are dilated, showing me how strong your need is." He shifted beneath me, his eyes staying on mine. "Your cunt is dripping on me."

My body was failing me. Anything I said would give my lies away even more, so I didn't speak.

"Do you think those reactions are just because I'm entertaining you?" The tips of his fingers ran down my neck and slowly sank between my breasts.

I shivered. A slow, raspy moan came out of me.

"And now? You still think that?" He stared at me through his lashes.

It was an overwhelming stare. Maybe because of the position we were in, by the way his cock was pressing against the most sensitive part of me. The part that couldn't lie.

"You don't have to say anything." His hands moved to my ass, and he lifted until I hovered over his crown. "I'm going to fuck the answer out of you."

I was afraid of that.

"And, once I finish fucking you, I'm going to fuck you again to make one thing very clear."

My wants, my feelings were already so clear.

"Nothing that I'm doing in here is for entertainment. Not the way I touch you, not the way I listen to you, not the way I wrap my arms around you at night. Not the way I watch you sleep to make sure no one but me touches you. If I were looking for entertainment, I'd have you bounce on my cock all fucking day, letting you open your mouth only so I could fill it with my dick." He gripped me harder, his words emphasized even more. "What we have here...it's deep. We both know it."

How was it possible that I wanted him even more than I had just a minute ago? That my emotions for this man were more real than ever?

He lowered me onto our bed. I didn't stop him.

"It's deeper than when we were kids, Kyle."

Yes, it was.

He was on top of me, his body much longer than mine, but our fit was still so snug. His stare was powerful, consuming. Gripping. His hold on me was stronger than the cement that impounded us. That hold didn't waver when his crown pushed straight into me, my opening widening to allow him in.

"It lives right here."

His fist touched the left side of my chest, and I gasped. Not just from his admission, but from the size of him, from the fullness, from the immediate pleasure that spread through me.

"Ahh," I breathed.

His movements were torturously slow. In went the entire length of his shaft; out he pulled until just the very tip of his dick was inserted. I ached for him when he left; I silently begged for more when he was all the way in.

"Tell me the truth."

He kept my hips still, making sure I stayed right where he wanted me, taking me to the place he knew I couldn't return from. There was so much pleasure in everything he was doing—how his exhales warmed my nipples, how the friction caused every nerve to ignite the most erotic pleasure, even how tightly he was gripping me.

"Tell me."

I shimmied my arms out from under him and clamped my hands around his shoulders, my nails finding their way into his skin.

"Your body is telling me so much." He kissed all the way up my neck. After each brush of his lips, he nipped the skin with his teeth. "Now, give me your voice, Kyle."

Just as he reached my face, our eyes connecting, he rocked his hips back and thrust them forward.

"Oh my God!" I screamed. I didn't have a chance to recover. I didn't even have a chance to take a breath before he lifted me off the ground and held me against the wall.

His hands were on my ass, his fingers stabbing my flesh. "That wasn't the answer I wanted."

# PRISONED

"I..."

"Tell me."

With each pump, my back crashed into the wall, and my head rubbed against the cold concrete. I was squeezing my legs around his waist, but I didn't need to. Garin wasn't letting me go. He wasn't going to let me drop. He was dominating my body with his weight, his power, his cock, and I could do nothing but lie against this wall and enjoy it.

"Tell me."

He kept his eyes on me and leaned his head down, so his mouth could flick my nipple. He abused it with just the tip of his tongue until it turned painfully hard. Four, five, six pumps of his dick before he moved to the other nipple. They were achingly desperate to be sucked.

"Garin..."

He looked up at me through his lashes, his teeth hovering around the center of my breast. The look in his eyes told me he knew exactly what he was doing to me. "Tell me."

"Suck it. Please."

His tongue licked just the edge.

"More, Garin. Give me more."

Small pumps in and out of my pussy were all he was giving me. It teased me almost as much as his mouth.

"More," I begged again.

An untamed glare crossed his eyes, and his lips closed around my nipple, his teeth biting down just enough that I shouted out. He let my scream simmer in the air before he quickly soothed out the pain with the swish of his tongue. Then, he did it again.

And again.

"Oh!" I bellowed from the new sensation that throbbed through me.

A foreign sensation.

While his hand was cupping my ass, one of his fingers was caressing it. Not the cheeks but between them, dangerously close to the hole. And then he was there, at the rim, dancing around it, putting pressure on that forbidden entrance, tickling his way into it. It was unexpected. And unexpectedly arousing.

"You like it."

"Mmm," I moaned.

He slowly twisted his finger, which already felt quite wet, until half of it was inside me. I sucked in a deep breath and held it, anticipating a bit of pain. There was no reason to; it didn't hurt. It didn't burn. It only heightened my cravings.

"You want more."

He wasn't asking, and my voice didn't need to give him an answer, but I still gave him one. "Yes."

He slid his dick all the way in, and his hips stilled. The only part of him that moved was his finger. It dipped in as far as his knuckle and back. "When I'm inside your ass, your cunt milks my cock. Without even stroking you, it's squeezing the fuck out of me." He groaned against my lips, and it was the most sensual sound I'd ever heard. "I'm the first person to touch you here, aren't I?"

"Yes."

"I should have been the first man inside your pussy, too."

I didn't disagree.

"Your pussy shouldn't know the feeling of any cock, other than mine," he growled.

I found his possessiveness to be extremely sexy because, in my mind, I had been his for most of my life.

Had things just gone differently…

"I'm going to fuck your ass, Kyle."

"Ah," I hissed as he gave me his whole finger.

"This little tight hole is going to spread just wide enough to let my cock in, and I'm going to take it, just like I should have taken your cunt."

His finger was sliding in and out, moving much faster than before. With this new speed came more power. Fullness. A bursting of sensations that drove me toward the build. And then, unexpectedly, he pulled his finger out, my ass clenching from the void, a feeling I didn't like nearly as much.

"Why did you stop?"

The smirk on his face looked so delicious that I wanted to lick it off.

"You miss it already?"

I nodded.

"I knew you'd like it when I touched your ass, but I didn't think you'd warm to it that fast."

# PRISONED

He rocked his hips back, reminding me that he wasn't done with my pussy, and drove inside it again. "Tell me." The tip of his finger found its way to my ass. "Tell me, and I'll give you whatever you want, Kyle."

"Anything?"

His mouth pressed against mine. I could taste the freshness of his breath. I wanted to suck it into my mouth and swish it around my gums and over my tongue and hold it inside me forever.

"But I want…" My voice died out as he teased the rim of my ass, my whole body shivering.

"You want more than you already have?"

"I'm in a cell."

"You're in a cell…with me."

*You.*

"You," I whispered. "I want you."

"That's what I thought."

He surrounded my lips as his dick plunged in and out of my wetness, his tongue moving in the same speed as his finger, which was now inside me again. I didn't know how many pumps it took. I didn't know if I was screaming or moaning or if there was any breath left in my body.

But I'd lost all sense of reality.

All that was left was pleasure. And it was building in more than one spot.

"Fuck, you just became so tight."

He used more of his weight to hold me against the wall, freeing up his other hand, so he could move it to my clit. He didn't rub it. He pinched it between his fingers, and it was the burst that sent me over the edge.

"Mmm, that's it, baby," he growled. "Come right on me. Let me feel it."

My pussy was clenching his dick, my ass was contracting around his finger, and I was sucking on the end of his tongue while my entire body shuddered. As the spasms inside me came to a staggering peak, I felt a change in his movements. They were sharp, dominant. He bit down on my lip, his hips stilling, before he gave me one last stroke. Then, slowly, warm jets of cum filled me.

I clung to him, still panting, and he moved me to the floor, covering me with a blanket, while he knelt next to me.

Before he spoke, he brushed the hair off my face. "I'm going to wash you, but you need to know something first." He grabbed my wrist, stopping me as I tried to reach out to him. "When I ask you something, I expect an answer. The only thing we have inside this cell is words, Kyle. Don't hold them back from me."

I suddenly felt extremely childish. But my reasoning at the time hadn't been; it was probably one of the maturer decisions I'd ever made. I feared that, at some point, I would have to tell him the truth, and I knew it would destroy anything we had built in here. I was protecting him, his feelings. His heart.

"Get out of your head."

*Breathe, Kyle.*

"But—"

"We're here. Right now. Think about right now. Not then. Not tomorrow. Now."

Now, I loved him.

Now, I wanted him to love me.

"You're right. I'm sorry."

"In the end, I got what I wanted." His hand dipped under the blanket, clasping my clit between his fingers.

I gasped from how sensitive it was.

"This told me everything I wanted to hear."

His hand dipped lower, urging the cum to drip out of me. As it did, I felt him cup his fingers and lift them out of the blanket.

"I need you to make me a promise."

"Anything," I said.

*Did I mean that?*

He lifted his fingers to my lips. The tips were wet, his thick, milky cum coating each one. He rubbed them over my mouth, spreading a thin layer across it. Then, he plunged them onto my tongue. "Suck."

I did as I was told, licking each side and over his nails. He slid them further in until his fingertips were hitting the back of my throat. If I tried to swallow, if I moved my tongue, I would gag. I didn't want that. I wanted to take whatever he was willing to give me. So, I breathed through my nose and tried to relax my throat as I studied his face.

# PRISONED

The face that made everything all right…even though his fingers were threatening to upset the bile in my stomach.

"Don't ever tell me that my cock is for entertainment. Do you understand?"

I couldn't nod. I couldn't speak.

"Answer me, Kyle."

I held my breath and muffled out a response, mentally coaxing my throat to relax again, to put my mind in a space where I wasn't on the verge of gagging.

"I know you're scared," he said, my answer obviously pleasing him. "I know you want the reason we're in here. I know you're trying to picture your life past this cell and see how it all fits together. I'm trying to do that, too. But, right now, it's just us. And there's no then; there's only now. Focus on that."

In one swift movement, his fingers were out. While I sucked in a gasp of air, trying to find that calm again, his hand moved to my chest. He gently traced shapes over my sensitive skin. There was no pain, no roughness. No dominance. This was all pleasure and goose bumps.

"Garin—"

"I'm not done."

He slowly traced down to my clit. This was different than just moments before when he had clamped it between his fingers. This was a rubbing, circling at the very top, that caused my back to arch, my stomach to quiver.

He knew my body better than I did.

"If I tell you I want you, that means I only want you. I won't touch anyone else. If I ask for your body, I expect you to give it to me. Your throat, your pussy, your fucking ass…all of it. If I tell you to never lie to me, I expect only the truth to come from your lips. You'll only hear the truth come from mine."

Maybe honesty was easy for him, but it wasn't for me, not when I had this lie weighing on me. Not when I was the reason we were in here in the first place.

He'd said so much. But they were just words. Not promises.

"You haven't told me, Garin."

"You want to hear it?"

There would be no coming back from this. Once he gave me his answer, I couldn't forget it. I couldn't rewind. This would be us—the *new* us.

Why was I so torn? This was what I'd wanted since the moment all those years ago when I realized Garin was more than just a friend. There would be regret either way. But he had told me to focus on now.

Now, this was what I wanted.

I nodded.

"You want me to make those promises to you? Tell you I only want you? Tell you I'll never lie to you? Never hurt you? Then, I'm going to need your voice, Kyle." He took my hand and placed it on his erection. It felt painfully hard. His breathing hitched as I ran my fingers over the length of it. "Say it, so I can fuck you again."

My thumb ran over the wide crown and the hole right in the middle of the tip. A small bead of pre-cum leaked out. I wanted to taste it. I wanted more of the cum he had fed me earlier.

I scooped up the bead and sucked it off my thumb. He needed to know that I would drink it even if he hadn't forced me to.

As his gaze deepened, watching me swirl my tongue around my nail, the desire between us grew. I had felt his need. Now, I tasted it.

Now, I needed more.

"You're hungry?"

"Yes," I mumbled with my thumb still in my mouth.

"You want me to feed you."

I nodded, and his stare turned ravenous.

"Now. Please."

"Why should I feed you, Kyle?"

Even though the answer was so obvious and I was sure he already knew, he was making me say it. I owed him that. At least this part was truthful.

I lifted his hand off my pussy and placed it on my chest. My heart was pounding so hard that I needed the pressure, so it wouldn't tear through. "I want you to promise because…I'm promising you. I only want you. I won't touch anyone else. My body is yours. All of it."

I couldn't promise the last part. There were lies.

Maybe there would always be lies.

## PRISONED

Just as I worried he had picked up on it, he moved on top of me. And, just as I thought he was going to bring it up, he plunged his dick straight into me.

# SEVENTEEN

## KYLE

"Wake. The. Fuck. Up." Following each of Breath's syllables was a lick across the outer edge of my ear.

The odor from his mouth was enough to wake me up. Definitely enough to pop my eyelids open. Undoubtedly enough to cause my entire body to shake. His tongue was sharp and putrid. It felt like a razor slicing my earring hole through the bottom of my lobe. When I tried to move away from him, his palm drove into my cheek, which slammed the back of my head into whatever was behind it.

I tried lifting my hands. I tried kicking my legs.

I was tied up.

Again.

"Have you missed me, Kyle?"

Through the pitch-black that surrounded me, I saw stars. Sparkling little bursts of silver from hitting my head so hard. Then, there was the *drip, drip, drip* of my wet hair onto my naked back. The soaked strands clung to my cheeks and lashes. Every time I blinked, it felt like sand was scratching across my eyes. With my hands tied behind my back, I couldn't pull the hairs out of them. I couldn't rub them to make them feel better. I couldn't even shake my head with his hand gripping my throat.

He'd taken my clothes off again. He'd bathed me.

*"I'm just going to use you as a landing pad for my cum."*

My stomach churned as I thought about what else might be on my skin.

"No," I finally said. "I haven't—*ow!*"

Something clamped down on my nipple. It wasn't sexual, like Garin's fingers, or titillating, like his teeth. This was spiked like a barbed wire, and the points were piercing my skin.

"Why are you hurting me?" I cried.

"Wrong question."

"What—"

He slapped my face so hard that my front teeth bit through the end of my tongue, and my mouth filled with blood. The copper taste didn't mix well with my stomach, and I gagged. It was just enough of a heave to stir the acid in my stomach, and as it rose to my throat, he pushed my face to the side, so it wouldn't get on him.

The heartless fucker didn't even give me a break while I purged. He slapped the back of my head, like it would make the vomit come out faster.

"I'm done!" I yelled, my stomach empty, the back of my throat feeling as though he were holding a butane lighter to it. I licked the wetness off my lips and spit it out.

"I should make you swallow that."

I wouldn't taste it. My throat burned too badly, the fire masking all the flavors that were in my mouth.

He clasped something around my throat. It was as cold as ice, and it felt as though it had teeth, taking small little bites of my skin.

"Do you want me to make you swallow it? Scoop up everything you just puked on my floor and shove it down your fucking throat?"

I wasn't sure I could give him an answer. Whatever was around my neck was squeezing tighter, wringing all the air out. Biting. Pinching.

Freezing me to death.

"*Puta*, do you want me to make you—"

"No!"

# PRISONED

He laughed.

The sound made me never want to laugh again.

"It's time."

There was no warning. No flash of movement. Just his breath swishing through the air, past my face, and suddenly, I was in the air. He'd lifted the chair by the legs—this one obviously not bolted to the ground, like the other one had been—and as he roared, he threw me. I couldn't scream, the vise on my throat was too tight. I couldn't reach out to stop my face from hitting anything, as my hands were tied. I couldn't see what I was headed for; it was too dark. So, I closed my eyes and tried to prepare myself for the fall.

*Bang, bang...bang.*

The chair banged against the floor. Each time it hit, the landing shook my body, made my muscles throb, sucked even more air out of me.

*Kyle, breathe.*

"Just how I want you—on your back with your legs spread." He straddled my waist and sat on my stomach. "*Puta, puta, puta*, it's time you ask the right question."

My nostrils flared as I tried to breathe. With all of his weight on my belly, he was constricting even more of my air.

"Prove to me that you're more than just a pretty face."

"What do you want from me?"

I cried out as his fingernails stabbed my cheeks. They pushed in so far that my mouth opened, my tongue hanging past my bottom lip.

"Before you say another word, I want you to think. Stop fucking rambling, and think."

He tightened the clamp on my nipple, but because of the way he was holding my mouth, I couldn't scream. So, I whimpered and groaned and dripped tears down his fingers. None of it helped.

"You know why you're here. You know why I put you in a cell with Garin." He leaned forward and bit the end of my tongue. It was already so sore from when my teeth had stabbed it earlier.

The smell. The sensation. The pain.

I couldn't take it.

I couldn't breathe.

Just as the silvery stars started to return, he let up. But he didn't release it. He wrapped his lips around my tongue and sucked it back and forth, like he was giving it head.

"Mmm," he moaned, filling the air with a stench that made everything hurt even more. "This is what your cunt is going to do to my dick. It's going to squeeze the fuck out of it just like this…" His suction tightened. "And its hotness and wetness and tightness is going to drain every bit of cum out of me." He laughed again, his lips moving to my ear. "And then I'm going to give you to my boys. Do you know what my boys do to pretty girls like you?"

I grunted even though I knew the answer would make me feel worse.

"They're going to gang-bang the living fuck out of you. And when you're covered in all their cum, they're going to cut you." He moved to my other ear, pressing his lips so close that they touched the inside hole. "Like throwing a piece of meat inside a cage full of dogs. But these dogs have knives, and they like to butcher."

Silence.

I was sure he was letting me ponder the terrifying reality of what was to become of me, and that was…I had no chance of getting out of here. I had no chance of surviving this. I was going to die in this prison, raped by however many men Breath employed. Filled with their cum.

And…

I couldn't even wrap my head around the rest.

"You're making me wait, Kyle, and I fucking hate it when people make me wait." He stood and lifted the chair, so I was back to a seated position. "I'm going to show you just how much I hate it."

His hands weren't on my body anymore, his smell no longer in the air. But I heard him. Steps on the concrete, clothes swishing as he moved.

"Come here, babies. Come to daddy."

What were his babies?

There were high-pitched sounds. Lots of them. I couldn't place it, but it was all I heard, and the noises continued to get louder as each second passed.

"Come meet my friend."

"No," I cried.

## PRISONED

I didn't want to meet the source of the noise. I didn't want more pain. I didn't want—

"Ahh!" I screamed as the most intense burning seared through the ends of my toes.

I didn't know what his babies were doing, what they were using, what the hell they were, but it felt like the skin was being sliced off. I couldn't kick them away. I couldn't move my legs. I couldn't...

"What do you want?" I sobbed.

"Shut up." The back of his hand slapped my mouth. Then, he squeezed my lips and pulled them until it felt like he was going to rip them off my face. "Don't make another sound."

The tears fell even faster—not just from the pain and the fear, but also from the question I already knew he wanted the answer to. What didn't make any sense was why he wanted this information. I couldn't piece that part together. Everyone was dead.

*Oh God...*

The babies had moved up to my ankles. I wasn't sure if I had any feet left. It felt like they had finished off the skin and were on to my muscles and bones.

"I'm losing my patience with you, Kyle."

I shook my head, snot and drool flying off my face.

"When I release your lips, you're going to ask the right question."

*The right question.*

"Babies, stop!"

After his command, the gnawing on my toes immediately halted. The noises quieted. Then, his fingers left my mouth, my lips smacking back into place. But the hurt...the hurt stayed. I knew, if he flicked on the light, I'd see I was a bloody mess with wounds that may never heal.

"Don't keep me waiting, Kyle." A warning that he could make the babies start up again as quickly as he had made them stop.

My lips parted, spit dripping down both sides. My tongue burned as it hit the inside of my teeth. I swallowed. Whatever was wrapped around my neck hadn't let up one bit.

"You want to know who killed Paulie."

"Finally. The right fucking question." His voice was more sexual than it was commanding. "You just made my dick hard." He straddled me again, but this time, he didn't sit.

I heard a zipper. A button popped open. The stench...if I had anything left in my stomach, it would have come out. It was so much worse than his breath. Molded cheese and decayed meat.

He pressed his dick against my cheek, running it up and down my skin, as though he were wiping off the drool. I wanted to turn my face and bite the fucker off. But I couldn't do that. If there was even the slightest chance of me getting out of here, I would ruin it.

"*Yes*. I love how your tears feel against my dick." He pressed his weak erection against my other cheek. "Say those words again, Kyle. My dick wants to feel them."

I only opened my lips a tiny bit, fearing that he would stick his cock between them. "You want to know who killed Paulie."

"Fuck," he moaned. "That sounded so fucking hot. Now, make me harder, and tell me who did it."

I didn't know where the courage came from. I hadn't felt it when I woke up in the darkness or when he was hurting me or when the babies had been eating me. But it was raging inside me, and it stirred on my tongue before I could stop it. "You might as well kill me because I'll never tell you that."

"You fucking cunt."

His dick stopped rubbing against my cheek. All noise in the room was silenced. There was only breathing and his odor.

And pain.

So much of it. And so much blackness. Blackness that didn't just come from the room.

Blackness that came from...

*Thump. Thump. Thump.*

# EIGHTEEN

## GARIN
## ONE MONTH AGO

My cell vibrated from the inside of my jacket pocket as I walked down the hallway to my bedroom. Shitty fucking timing. Had it been one minute later, my cock would have been in the ass of one of the twins. They weren't identical. I wasn't even sure they were sisters. But, hell, they both had blonde hair and light eyes, and they responded to the nickname. That was easier than remembering their names.

I'd left them in my bedroom a few minutes ago to get us some drinks. They were naked, kneeling on the bed. I was sure they were still in the same position, just waiting to suck the cum out of me. Those filthy mouths couldn't get enough of my cock. They pumped that fucker with every part of their body until they got what they wanted—every goddamn squirt of it. Then, they ate it off me. They swapped it between their mouths. And they swallowed that shit down.

I fucking loved it when they came to my place.

But Billy's name was on the screen of my phone, so they were going to have to wait a few more minutes before I joined them.

I walked to the doorway of my bedroom, set the glasses down on the floor, and held up a finger to let them know I'd be back. Then, I went into my home office and shut the door behind me. "What's going on, Billy?"

"I met someone that said she used to do side work for my brother."

I took a seat in the chair, shifting my pants to make room for my hard-on. Seeing those two bare pussies again had made my dick throb. "I thought you were going to take a break from this shit?"

"I was." He exhaled a mouthful of smoke. "But then I came across this chick, and my search picked right back up. She said Paulie owed her money when he died."

"That tells me nothing."

"She's a hooker, Garin."

I shook my head, knowing this was just going to lead to more needles and black tar. "So, Paulie liked to get his dick wet with hookers. How the fuck is that going to help us find out who killed him?"

"Because he didn't fuck her. This chick worked for him, and the money was for some tricks that he never paid her for."

I pushed the chair back and leaned on the desk. "What are you talking about?"

"She said she wasn't his only hooker. He had others, and none of them got paid."

"Paulie wasn't running a prostitution ring. We would have known."

"Maybe we were wrong."

Nah. I wasn't fucking wrong.

Paulie ran drugs for the bosses. He didn't work in prostitution. Prostitution was street level, and the bosses didn't mess with it. The profits were risky because the girls OD'd faster than the guys could hire them.

When you worked for Mario and his crew, you didn't have a side job or another source of income. The bosses owned you, and they gave you a small piece of your total earnings. If you tried to hide money, they found you…and they killed you.

The bosses hadn't killed Paulie. We'd determined it was an outside job back when the murder happened, and the bosses knew nothing about the killer. But, if information was just now surfacing, there was a chance they'd heard about it.

"I'll talk to the bosses," I said. "But don't expect this to lead to anything. If anyone knew what Paulie was up to, they were smart enough to keep their mouth shut. Do me a favor; keep yours shut, too—at least until I talk to the guys and get a better idea of what's going on here."

"Too late."

*Fuck.*

"Who'd you talk to?"

"Guys on the street. You know, the dealers who worked in the area at that time."

Those dealers still worked for the bosses, so I was sure word had spread. I was surprised Mario hadn't said anything to me about it.

"Did they know anything?" I asked.

"Nothing. Not even one of 'em had a clue on what Paulie was up to."

He sounded deflated. I knew it wasn't just from searching for Paulie's killer.

"All right," I said, "I'll take it from here, but I want you laying low. If rumors start flying that Paulie had a side gig, the bosses are going to be pissed, and it's not going to look good if you're the one spreading them."

"Yeah, yeah."

"While you're laying low, how about you get some sleep? You sound like shit."

I checked the screen of my phone. I'd been talking to Billy for almost ten minutes, and the girls hadn't made a noise. I hoped one of them was still on her knees, her tongue running over the other's cunt. I fucking loved watching them eat pussy.

"I'm fine."

It made me crazy whenever he said that. He wasn't healthy. He wasn't rested. He wasn't eating. He definitely wasn't sleeping. He was shooting as much heroin as his body could handle. Every time I spoke to him, he sounded worse than the last time.

"You're not fine. We both know it."

"Don't fucking worry about me. If you lecture me every time we talk, I'm going to stop calling you."

If he stopped calling me, I'd have one of the guys track him down and shadow him, sitting with him every minute of the goddamn day. Telling him that would only start a fight. And fighting with Billy meant he'd only use more.

I couldn't be the reason he cooked up more dope...considering I was the reason he'd started using in the first place.

"I'll call you when I know something."

He chuckled. "I'll talk to you tomorrow then."

"Yeah, tomorrow."

I hung up and set the phone on my desk, knowing I'd call him whether I knew something or not. Maybe if I could get some answers or at least a little resolution, Billy would go to rehab for me.

I shook the mouse beside my computer, and the monitor lit up. I clicked on the feed for the master bedroom security camera, and a full-angle shot of my room popped up. I zoomed in on the bed. One of the twins was on her back, her head on my pillows, her knees bent. The other was buried, face-deep, in her cunt.

Just how I wanted them.

I exited the feed, left my phone on the desk, and walked to my bedroom.

# NINETEEN

## KYLE

The lights flipped on. I could almost feel the electricity running through the wires and into the bulbs. It was like the current was running through me. It drove my eyes open, made my head thrash back and forth; it forced me to scream. It felt like I'd been electrocuted—not just pain, but an excruciating amount of agony pounded in every part of me.

And I was still here...in the torture chamber. Still tied to the chair. Still naked.

When I tried to speak, my tongue ached from where I had bitten into it, where Breath had chomped on it. My cheeks hurt from where he had squeezed and slapped. My toes...

I looked down, and the ends of my toes were raw. The tops of my feet looked like a dog's chew toy. My ankles looked like they had been painted red. The babies hadn't just bitten me; they had fed on me. And the blood wasn't just on my body; it was all over the floor.

It reminded me so much of...

"I thought you'd find this scene familiar."

I jumped at the sound of Breath's voice, which came from behind me. I didn't know how, but he'd read my thoughts without even seeing my face. There was only one other time I'd seen so much blood. Breath knew that. He'd done this on purpose.

He wanted me to relive it.

He moved in front of me and knelt in the red puddle. This was the first time I'd seen him in the light. He was thinner than I'd imagined. Not scrawny, but not fit. He had a patchy beard and small eyes and an evil dimple on his left cheek.

"All this blood came from your feet," he said. "There'd be so much more if I put a bullet in your chest."

I could picture it because I'd seen all the blood that surrounded Paulie when he'd been shot in the chest.

Breath wanted me to picture it.

He stared at me as he dragged his hand through the pool of blood. "Was it hard lying to Garin? Pushing him away because you couldn't stand yourself? Or watching Billy shoot up, knowing you could help him, but you were too selfish to tell him the truth?"

How did he know? How had he gotten inside my head?

"The truth hurts worse than your feet do right now, doesn't it?"

I didn't have to tell him; he knew. He seemed to know almost everything already...everything but the identity of the killer. His accuracy was as terrifying as the torture.

"You saw Paulie's murderer..." He pressed his finger into the blood and used it to draw over the cement.

It took a minute before I realized he was drawing the outline of a body. Paulie's body.

"I want to know who it is."

*Paulie*...his arm had been bent slightly inward. His face fully pressed into the pavement. His right leg was straight, his left turned outward at the knee.

I saw it in my head. Over and over.

And Breath captured it all perfectly.

Too perfectly.

"Let me out!" I cried.

"You want out? Then, start talking. I'll even let Garin out. I'll put you both in a boat and ship you back to the mainland where Garin's plane can take you to the States."

# PRISONED

My eyes were burning from the light. Our cell had been so dimly lit that it felt like I'd been in the dark for...weeks? Months? My hair dripped down my back, keeping me constantly freezing. The temperature in here didn't help. And the cold seemed to make my wounds hurt even more. Even my brain ached, making it hard to process what he was saying.

"What do you mean, take us back to the States?"

"Where do you think you are, *puta*? Fucking Miami? Rhode Island? West Virginia?"

I looked around the chamber, as if the answer were somewhere inside here. But there were no windows, no maps, no signs telling me anything. "Where are we?"

"Margarita Island." His accent suddenly became thicker, rolling the Rs, something he hadn't done before.

"Where is that?"

"Venezuela, baby. So, if you're a good girl, I'll have the boat take you to Caracas where Garin's plane will be. You'll never have to return, never have to see this cell again. Never have to get any more love from my little babies." He got up and leaned into my ear. "Never get gang-raped by my boys." His tongue wiggled around my earlobe, and I could smell the coppery tang of blood. "Never get to feel more of my cum on you."

I shook my head, but his tongue didn't move. He didn't move.

"I can't."

"It's simple."

"It's not fucking *simple*!" I gasped as I felt something solid against the bottom of my throat. It was freezing, sharp.

He held it in place but pushed it deeper into my skin. When I felt the slice, I knew it was a knife.

"Like I said, it's simple. You tell me what I want to know, or I'll slit your throat."

I tried to calm my mind, my breathing, my heart that throbbed out of my chest. Every time I filled my lungs, the knife pushed deeper into me. I didn't know how I was going to stay calm, but I needed to.

*Garin.*

I had to pull out one of those memories that I had saved. His face, his touch. The way he made me feel. Garin would tell me not to panic. He would tell me to breathe. He would get my mind off the knife, off this chamber, off all the pain in my body. Garin would tell me Breath couldn't kill me because I was the only person who knew the truth.

If I died, the secret died with me.

"What's happening on the first?" Breath asked.

*The first*, I repeated in my head.

He'd heard my conversation with Garin.

*"They have until the first. Then, things will get interesting."*

At least that was a question I could answer. But, now, I knew he could hear everything that had been said inside our cell...everything that had been moaned.

Or had Garin told Breath what I had said?

The thought left as quickly as it came. Garin wouldn't have told him anything. Garin wouldn't do that to me. He'd take torture before he betrayed my trust.

"My brother," I said. "He's coming on the first."

"Why?"

"He comes to Florida once a month...to visit my mother."

"That's a long trip from New Jersey. Why does he come so often?"

"They're really close, like best friends. Mom doesn't like to travel, so he comes to her."

They were close, but that wasn't the reason he came to Florida every month.

"Tell me why things will get interesting."

The blood oozed out of the cut on my throat and dripped between my breasts. My chest was covered.

More red. More...

*Breathe, Kyle.*

"He'll come to my house," I finally said, "and when he realizes I'm not home and I haven't been to work, he'll come looking for me."

As Breath laughed, the knife wiggled on my neck. "*Puta*, your brother isn't going to find you. We left no trace of your kidnapping. He can dig and search every fucking crevice of North America, but you and Garin simply"—he breathed a puff of air into my ear—"vanished." He walked around to the front of me and straddled my legs. "Do you know what my boys do to punks like your brother?"

"He'll know I'm missing. That was all I was trying to say—"

"We gut them." He pointed the knife to the middle of my forehead. "We start here, stabbing right through the sinuses. Not hard enough to kill, but hard enough to paralyze with pain. Then, we use a chainsaw and run it down the middle of his face and cut off his nose." He smiled, showing me his rotted teeth. "Who needs a nose anyway, right?" He licked mine, slowly rimming and flicking each nostril. "We skip down to the legs, tearing through the muscle, shredding the tendons, snapping the bones. Do you know why we skip the chest?"

I shook my head as his erection pushed against my stomach. Death got him hard; gutting innocent victims turned him on. He was a monster—much worse than I'd thought.

And I was at his mercy.

"Because slashing through his chest would kill him right away," Breath said, unbuttoning his pants, his dick falling through the hole of his boxers. "We want him to feel the sharpness of the blade as it rips him apart. Then, we let him scream until he dies. Once his heart finally stops beating, we slice open his chest." He shifted on top of me, pushing his dick up toward my ribs, holding the back of my neck so that I couldn't move. "Maybe I'll have one of my boys go to Florida on the first and bring your brother here." He moaned as he rubbed his dick over my stomach, pushing hard enough that my skin gave him friction. "Because I want to gut him. I want to gut anyone that tries to save you. And I want you to watch while I do it." The way he rocked his hips and groaned reminded me of a rabid raccoon. Spit shone across his blackened smile. His eyes spread wide and his pupils dilated. "Look down, *puta*. I want you to see what you do to me."

I didn't want to look down. I knew what would happen if I did… and I knew what would happen if I didn't. Just as I glanced at my lap, thick streams of cum shot over my stomach, reaching as high as my breasts.

He grunted my name, "Kyle, Kyle, Kyle," with every pump of his hips. His seed smelled worse than his breath.

"You're sick, you know that? You're fucking sick and twisted, and I—"

"And you love it. That's why you're not telling me the killer's name. You want more of my sickness. More of my cum. And I'm going to give it to you…"

"No!" My eyes caught the white glob that was slowly running down the top of my breast. I couldn't take any more of his cum. His

breath. I had to get out of here. I had to grab Garin and flee somehow.
"I don't want this—"

The knife was back. He belted me across the face with the handle. I screamed as blood squirted from my nose and sprayed across his chest. It dripped to my lips. When I opened my mouth to take a breath, I tasted the coppery flavor. And plastic.

There was always plastic.

He wiped the blood off my cheek and smeared it all over his. Then, he scooped up more and smiled as he painted it across his neck. "I'm going to cover myself in your blood as I cover you in my cum."

"No!" I screamed as he shoved the tip of the knife into my bicep. "You just stabbed me."

As blood poured from the hole, he leaned forward and rubbed his face in it. "Mmm," he moaned. "And I'm going to stab you again."

The roughness of his whiskers scraped across the wound, and I shouted from all the pain. I shouted as his tongue lapped my skin. I shouted from the burning I still felt in my feet. And I shouted from the look in his eyes. It was one I'd seen only once before, but it hadn't been this intense…this delusional.

"Blood gets me all"—he glanced down as he jerked his erection against my stomach—"hard and fucking horny."

When he smiled again, I shivered.

"Stick out your tongue."

I knew this was only going to cause more pain since he'd grabbed ahold of my tongue before, but I didn't think I had another choice. There was a knife in his hand, and he got off on the sound of my cries.

I slowly parted my lips, and as my tongue came through, he clamped his fingers around it. My eyes watered, and my stomach churned from the gagging.

"I want you to ask yourself how much your tongue means to you. Because there's a good chance you're going to wake up, and it's going to be gone. I'm going to rip it from your mouth and use it to paint your blood all over my body, and then I'm going to use it to jerk off."

He finally released my tongue, and I sucked in as much air as I could.

"You must be hungry by now. I could feed it to you." He bit into my cheek so hard that I thought he was going to take a chunk out of it. "Your cum-covered tongue, piece by piece. I'll even cut it up for you, so you don't have to swallow it all at once. You can take your time with it. Really chew it."

I couldn't hide the emotion on my face, the anxiety that caused my whole body to shake, the fear that was gnawing as deeply as the babies had chewed my feet. He was getting what he wanted, and I was sure he could see it all over me.

How long could I endure this?

Was it even worth it?

Not if I didn't get out of here alive.

"I have work to do." He reached behind him, his hand returning with a syringe.

"What kind of work? What are you going to do to me? Are you going to take my tongue..." My voice drifted off as he shot the liquid into my body. I no longer felt my mouth. Or my tongue.

I felt heat.

I felt each ray wrap its toasty light around me.

And then all I saw was black.

# TWENTY

## KYLE

"Kyle."

The sound of Garin's voice started to break through the fog. I couldn't decipher his words; I could just hear the different tones that came out of him. And I could feel him—the warmth of his skin on mine, the smell of his air. His presence.

*Kyle.*

It took several blinks until I finally heard what he was asking.

*Wake up, Kyle.*

He wanted me to wake up. So, I tried to liven my body, wiggling my toes, pressing my knees closer together. They hurt, much more than I was prepared for. I stretched out my fingers and my arms and my shoulders, and those were really sore, too. I opened my eyes last.

"Hi."

I was greeted by green. Garin's green. So deep, so perfect, so gemlike that it almost made me squint. They stared into mine and didn't move. Neither did his face as it hovered over me. Close. So close

I could smell him…so I knew. I knew it really was Garin. Not Breath. No torture chamber. Just Garin and me.

And our cell.

"Hi," I whispered back, groaning into my palm as the hurt started to really spike. My tongue ached like it had been sucked through the hose of a vacuum for hours. But it was still attached; that was the important part. I did a quick shimmy to make sure all of me was still attached. I was naked, but I was all there.

"I'm going to lift your head, so I can stand, but I don't want you to get up, and I don't want you to move."

I looked at his face again. "Where am I?"

"On my thigh. That's where you've been sleeping."

He moved gingerly, sliding out from under my head, gently resting a blanket in its place. He was treating me as though I were broken. Foggy, stabbed, achy, yes. But I wasn't broken. At least not yet.

The way he had me faced didn't have a view of the toilet or sink, so I wasn't able to see what he was doing. But I heard the water running and the toilet flush. I smelled the sweet scent of the soap. Then, there were footsteps and a rush of air as he knelt down beside me.

"The water is as hot as I could make it." He lifted the blanket and tucked it up to my knees. "Tell me if it hurts, and I'll stop."

He dropped the soapy toilet paper onto my toes, and I jumped. "It's okay. Put it back," I said when he lifted the paper off me. "It was just hotter than I thought it would be."

"Your toes are in pretty rough shape."

I didn't want to tell him about the babies. The less I talked about it, the easier it would be to get it out of my mind. I hoped.

"You're making them feel more comfortable," I said.

He left the clump soaking over my feet and moved up to my face, holding another clump of heat against my cheek. "Did someone bite you?" He ran his thumb over the mark on my bicep. "And stab you?"

"I…don't know. I think I blacked out."

A lie.

Another one to add to the growing list. I just didn't want him to worry or to get violent the next time Beard came in to give us food. The gun Beard continued to flash at us every time he came into our cell made it impossible for us to try and escape or to win a fight if we tried to start one.

## PRISONED

"Tell me what happened to you, Kyle." His stare was so healing, so nurturing. But so helpless in this horrible place.

"It looks much worse than it feels. Like I said, I blacked out. I don't remember much, besides waking up a few minutes ago."

*You lied. Again.*

As he tended to my wounds, I relived it. There was no hope of forgetting it. Snapshots of how each mark was born—the torture, the threats, the promises. How every part of Breath's body had been used to abuse me.

Every time I was taken from this cell, I returned in worse shape. I had to come up with a plan before there was nothing left of me.

"How long was I asleep?" I asked.

I didn't know how many clumps of toilet paper he'd brought over, but there were now several on the ground. All of them were tinted a dark brown, but at least my skin was clean.

"You were gone for three days, I think. I counted how many times the window turned light and dark. And you've been back for at least one. You've been asleep since Beard dropped you off."

All of that pain because I was unable to answer Breath's *simple* question.

"I'm not going to let it go, Kyle. I want to know what he did to you."

I lifted my hand to his face. The bruises were almost gone. The scrapes had all but healed. "Did they take you?"

"No." His hand circled around my fingers and squeezed. "Answer me. I *know* you remember."

Everyone wanted answers.

"Garin—" My voice was cut off by the look in his eyes. There was so much anger in them. I was worried about his fists, and what he was going to do to the cement walls. "I survived. That's what matters. Recounting the details isn't going to help my breathing. It isn't going to help you. And it certainly isn't going to help us."

"I want to kill them."

"Shh." I stuck my finger in the air, signaling him to come closer.

He wanted to protect me, and I loved that about him. He wanted revenge, and I loved that even more.

When he gave me his ear, I whispered, "They can hear you. There's a microphone somewhere in here."

It wasn't on any of the walls or the ceiling. I'd looked at both of them so many times. I'd memorized them. Every bump, every rock, every dent in the concrete. It had to be somewhere I couldn't see.

I pointed at the windowsill.

He moved over to it, gripping the ledge to pull himself up. He was only up there for a second before he lowered himself back down.

*Camera?* I mouthed.

*Microphone*, he mouthed back.

He returned to the wall that I was now leaning against, and he sat next to me. He wrapped his arms around me, and when he pulled me into his lap, I winced. I regretted the sound the second it came out of my mouth.

"Fuck." His arms dropped. "I'm sorry; I wasn't even thinking."

"No, Garin, don't stop touching me." I wiggled in between his legs, pushed my back into his chest, and locked his hands over my stomach. "I'm fine. I may not look it, but I am."

He tucked his face into my neck. I could tell by his breathing that something wasn't right.

"Tell me what's on your mind before I take control of your lips and don't release them for a very long time."

"Jesus, Kyle, I thought they killed you." There wasn't anger in his exhale. It was pain. "I heard you scream. For two days, I heard it, and I just sat in this goddamn cell. Beard didn't bring any food, so I couldn't even attempt to get out. Your screams...they fucking destroyed me."

I had to see his face, so I pulled my body off his and turned around. I held in the gasp, but it wasn't easy.

This whole time, I hadn't even considered that Breath would out me. If Garin had any idea that I knew who Paulie's killer was...

"Did you hear anything else?"

"No." His eyes narrowed. "But I was going to murder the next person who came into this cell. The next person ended up being you."

I should have felt relief. I should have turned back around and snuggled into his chest again. But I couldn't move. Something inside me was making my chin quiver. Was making my lips shake. Was making tears well in my eyes.

My body was paralyzed with guilt, and it showed all over my face. I had to try hide it. He couldn't know. He couldn't...

"You saved me," I blurted out.

"No, I didn't, Kyle. I couldn't get my hands on them."

"But, in my mind, you did. You were the happiness I felt when he was torturing me. Your face and presence. You got me through it. You told me to breathe."

"You stopped screaming after the second day. A whole day went by, and you still hadn't returned. I had nothing, not even whispers to hold on to." He ground his teeth together. "Do you know what that did to me? What it made me think?"

"I'm here now."

He nodded, as though he were reminding himself of the same thing. "Come here." He tapped his leg with the back of his hand. "Lie down right here."

"I don't want to lie down."

I watched him tug at the corner of his mouth, and I was jealous of his teeth. Jealous that they got to bite into the flesh that I wanted to sink into.

"You need—"

"I need you, Garin. I need you to make me forget about those three days."

He shook his head. "No fucking way."

He had washed everything off me, but he hadn't cleansed the memories.

"I need you to take my mind to a different place. My body…take my body, too."

"You're too sore. You're cut."

"I'm fine. Please." I dug my nails into his thighs and looked at him through my lashes. "I need this. I'm begging you."

It took him a few seconds before he responded, and then I slowly started to see the change in his eyes. The dominance was back. The control. The need.

"You don't want it soft."

He didn't phrase it as a question. I loved that.

"Or slow," he continued.

"No. I don't want either."

His growl tore through the entire cell as he moved on top of me. He stripped his clothes so fast that I was sure they had ripped. I expected him to slide between my legs, for his lips to be somewhere on my body, his hand on my clit. I expected the memories to sink into the cement below me.

But all I got was a stare. A lick across his bottom lip. His fingers giving his erection a few pumps. I was thankful there wasn't a video camera inside our cell. Breath probably would have punished me for his insecurities when he compared his pathetic hard-on to the length and girth of Garin's.

"How far can I take it?"

He had all of me. He had to know that by now.

"There are no limits."

"You're sure?"

I spread my legs wider, so my feet pressed against the outside of his thighs, and I dipped my hand between them. As I found my clit, I gently rubbed it. "I'm definitely sure."

"Fuck," he moaned. "Do you know how sexy you look, touching your clit the way my tongue would?"

*Touch me.*

After three days in the torture chamber and another day fully asleep, I had an idea of how I looked, how I smelled, how desperately my body needed a very long soak in an extremely hot tub. But I wouldn't have known that by the way he was staring at me.

"How does it feel, Kyle?"

"Ahh," seeped through my lips. "Not as good as you."

"Do you want my fingers?"

I nodded, lifting my hand off my pussy.

He licked his pointer and middle finger and dropped them between my legs. I felt one on my clit, rubbing much rougher, much faster, than I had and it caused me to buck against his palm. But I really started to scream when his other finger moved to my ass. He didn't tease the hole, like he had last time, or tickle between my cheeks. He drove straight inside. It took a second for my body to adjust, for the invasion to turn to pleasure, but I was quickly reminded of how good this could feel.

"You look like you're about to ask for something. What aren't I giving you, Kyle?"

"You." I reached out, but his dick was still too far away. "Come closer, so I can touch you."

*Touch me.*

# PRISONED

"You're going to get plenty of that in a second." His hand slowed, but his power increased, pulling out to the ends of his fingers and driving back in. He did it several more times and then flipped me onto my stomach. "You want more?" He leaned into my back, his erection pressed against my cheeks.

"Yes."

"No limits?"

"No limits."

He parted my cheeks, his dick pressing against my hole. "I want your fucking ass."

I could feel the bead of cum on his tip that was soon going to mix with my wetness. In anticipation, I reached over my head and gripped the blanket, digging it between my nails to prepare myself for how this was going to feel.

"Damn," he hissed as he pushed inside me. "You were tight around my fingers but not like this. You're squeezing the fuck out of my cock."

I breathed through the pain as he got the tip in. He kept it still, allowing me to adjust to him.

Then, he leaned over my back and whispered in my ear, "Don't try to crawl away from me, Kyle. Now that I've started, there's no way I can stop."

"I won't."

"This ass"—he moved inside a little more—"is going to be mine."

I opened my mouth, but nothing came out. I didn't have words... not yet. All I had were sounds as my body adjusted to his size. He'd prepped me with his finger, so it wasn't a complete invasion, and he had stayed still long enough for my hole to spread. But I worried it would be a while before I'd be able to sit again.

As he slid in a bit more, that worry was confirmed.

"I can tell I'm your first because I've never felt anything this tight." He reached underneath me and began to rub my clit. "A virgin ass... that I'm going to destroy."

"Ahh," I moaned as he slid in a little more.

"Your cunt is so wet." He dipped down to my other hole, spreading the juices between that and my clit. "You're wet because you like having my cock in your ass."

He finally moved all the way in, and I moaned out a response.

"I don't think I can be gentle for much longer, Kyle. Tell me you're ready for me."

"I'm"—I gasped as he slowly pulled out and drove back in—"ready."

"You're pulsing around my cock. Your pussy's tightening, and your clit's getting hard." He gripped my clit between his fingers and held it tightly. "A few more squeezes, and I'll have you coming."

"Yes," I groaned. "I want that."

My body had quickly accepted him, using all the fullness to build. But I wasn't sure where the build was coming from because the sensations in my ass, my pussy, my clit were all so strong that they were competing against each other.

"Oh my God."

"That's it, baby. Push into me, so I can give you all of it."

Each pump drove my face into the scratchy blanket. It caused my fingers to clench the wool. I was trying to keep my voice down, knowing Beard and Breath could hear me, but I couldn't. Screams poured out during each exhale, and moans released during the inhales. This fullness was too much, too overwhelming…I couldn't keep it contained.

"Jesus," he hissed. "You're milking the hell out of me. Squeeze the blanket, and hold on. I'm going to fuck you so hard."

I gripped the blanket and tried to hang on. All of my strength was consumed by this orgasm. It felt like it was sucking everything out of me and throwing it back at the same time. Between the explosion happening inside me and his powerful strokes slapping against my skin, I completely lost myself.

There was an eruption in my clit, a bursting euphoria in my ass. Then came the tingles. Everywhere. To the point where I wasn't sure they would ever stop, ever lighten. Garin pumped me through the peak and slowed during my final shudders, and the numbness gradually started to leave my body.

"I need your fucking mouth."

I was suddenly on my back again, and Garin was kneeling between my legs, his fingers rubbing circles over my clit. He was no longer inside me, and my body missed him. Clenched for him. Begged for him.

# PRISONED

I looked between my thighs and saw his dick. It was so hard, pointing straight at me, my slickness shining from his skin. The capabilities of that organ were endless, the places it could bring me, the sensations it could make me feel.

"You want more of it?" The slight grin on his face told me he saw what I was staring at.

"Yes."

"Give me that mouth then."

I leaned up and met him halfway, his lips pounding into mine, his tongue swiveling through my opening. As he gripped my face, I smelled myself on his fingers. My scent was like a marking. Whether we stayed in this prison or we were eventually released, I didn't want any other scent on him. I wanted my pussy to be the only one he was ever inside of, my ass to be the last one that milked him.

"Garin," I moaned.

He inched closer, his hand rubbing my clit again, while he pressed the tip of his dick against me. "I'm not done with this yet."

*This* wasn't my pussy.

Before I was able to take a breath, his crown was back in my ass, thrusting his full length straight into it. I didn't think my body would respond so quickly, but the intense strokes and the rubbing on my clit was all I needed. So was his face—that gorgeous, hairy, deliciously handsome face that gazed at me as though he couldn't get enough of me.

"That didn't take long."

He knew my body. He always knew.

"I can't stop it," I said.

"I don't want you to stop, but I want you closer." His hands moved to my lower back, and he lifted me until I was straddling his waist and wrapping my arms around his neck. "Hold on to me, Kyle."

"I am."

"No. I need you to really hold on to me. I'm about to pound the fuck out of you."

I locked my hands together.

"I can't promise this isn't going to hurt."

"Hurt me then."

I stayed on my knees, several inches above his waist, the tip of him barely inside me, and I waited for whatever beating he was about to give.

He held my hips and slowly brought me down to the base and back up to the crown. "I've been inside you all this time, and you're still so fucking tight."

As he drove into me, his short coarse hairs rubbed against my clit, and I cried out. The friction caused a burn, and the burn caused the most intense tingling.

He grabbed my bottom lip between his teeth and growled. "You keep giving me those sounds, and I'm going to come."

"It feels...so good."

"This is going to feel even better."

He lifted me in the air and walked us over to the sink, spreading my legs across the chilly bowl, pressing my back against the rough concrete. With the sink holding my weight, keeping me at waist height, Garin no longer had to carry me. He could stand in front of me and use all his power to fuck me. And that was just what he did, rubbing my clit and stroking my ass with more intensity than he had before.

"You're clenching my cock like you're going to come."

The sink was too slippery to hold on to, so I wrapped my fingers around the back of his neck and yanked on his hair. "It's what you do to me." I pressed my lips on his, our connection helping me build. "I can't...hold it off for much longer."

He stuck a finger inside my pussy. The probing matched the speed in which his hips thrust into me. "So fucking wet, and...mmm, you're tightening even more."

"Come with me," I begged.

"Look at me."

I didn't know at what point I had closed my eyes, but I opened them on his command and stared into his.

"You want me to come in your ass, Kyle?"

"Yes."

"Tell me."

I tugged on his hair to drag his face closer to mine. "I want you to come in my ass."

"Say it again."

# PRISONED

He was rocking into me so hard. I didn't know what sensation was taking me to the edge. But I knew there was pain, I knew there was plenty of pleasure, and I knew there were only seconds left before my own orgasm exploded.

"Come. In. Me."

He growled against my lips. "Begging me to fill that tight little ass with my cum?"

"Yes. I want it."

"You're going to get it. Right now."

I didn't think he had any more speed and power left, but he did, and he used it to drive into me. His thrusts were long, deep, fast, sharp. Raw. His mouth hungrily devoured mine. His fingers continued their assault on my pussy, and I completely unraveled.

"Kyle," he moaned, "you're milking it right out of me."

I couldn't respond. All I could do was hold on to his neck and let the orgasm blast through me. His abs tightened, his groaning deepened, his hips bucked—all of it telling me we were coming at the same time.

When he finally stilled and slowly pulled out of me, he said, "I'm not going to clean you."

"You don't have to. I'll do it."

As he looked down, a thick warmness began to seep out of me. It dripped into the bowl of the sink and clogged around the drain.

"No, you're not." He reached under me and pushed my cheeks together. "There's more in your ass. I want it to stay in there. Don't let it out, Kyle. I want only my cum on you."

He didn't say it. I didn't dare bring it up. But it was as though he knew what Breath had put on my body. And like the feral animal that Garin was, he only wanted his scent on me. His scent to replace Breath's.

"Okay," I agreed.

"You need to get some sleep and heal this body." His palms grazed over my thighs. "I wasn't easy on you. You're going to be sore."

"I asked for it."

"I fucking love that about you."

He carried me off the sink and brought me to our bed. We lay on our backs on the scratchy wool blanket, air pounding in and out of our lungs. The light flickered above us, showing the dark window on the nearby wall. Another night was passing.

Another night I was still alive with the only man I would ever love.

"They must think you have the answer." I felt his face turn toward me. "Why else would they take you for three days and leave me here?"

A part of me wanted to turn my head and blurt it all out. If anyone in this place deserved to kill me, it was Garin. But that wouldn't help us get out of here.

"What's stopping you from giving them what they want?" he asked.

He didn't know our reason for being here had anything to do with Paulie because Breath and Beard hadn't told him anything. He didn't know the question Breath wanted me to answer. And he didn't know I'd been holding in a secret. He just knew we were in here. Together. And he knew he didn't have the answer.

Therefore, it had to be me.

I tilted my face toward him and mouthed, *My brother.*

# TWENTY-ONE

## KYLE
## TWELVE YEARS AGO

Garin had kicked me out. He hadn't escorted me to his front steps and slammed the door in my face. But he'd pulled away from me when we were in his bedroom and made me leave because he wanted to take things slow.

*"I'm out of self-control. I've been trying real hard, but I want you so bad, it hurts. If I don't stop now, I'm going to take things much further, and you don't want that yet."*

But I did want that. I wanted further. I wanted more.

I knew the girls he'd been with in the past. He hadn't pulled away from them, and he definitely hadn't taken things slow. So, why was I different?

Maybe he was trying to be a gentleman even though I knew he wasn't one. Sending me home before I was naked and stripped of my virginity—before his sheets could be covered in my blood and who-knew-what kind of words would have been flying out of my mouth—was the respectable thing to do.

But so many years had built up to that moment.

I expected more, and...he'd just pulled away.

My feelings weren't going to change. They hadn't changed in the years since I realized what I really wanted from him. But I wasn't going to fight with him tonight, and I didn't want to beg.

Tomorrow night though?

Tomorrow night would be different. I wasn't going to leave so easily. In fact, I wasn't going to leave at all. I was going to sleep in his bed. With him...for the whole night.

Go slowly? Screw that. We'd gone slowly enough.

As I walked down Garin's front steps, I opened the package of sugary doughnuts that he'd given me. He was always so worried about what I ate and how much. He knew these doughnuts were my favorite. He gave them to me for breakfast every morning; he would never let me go to school on an empty stomach. He just didn't understand that I required less food than him. Over the years, my body had gotten used to the emptiness, the cramps, and the growling. There had been plenty of both tonight, but I was too worked up to be hungry. I was only going to eat these because he wanted me to.

I reached the sidewalk just as Paulie was walking out of his apartment. It was dark out. The light from his phone, held so close to his face, showed that he was scowling. His movements were exaggerated and as dramatic as mine.

"You okay, Paulie?" I asked.

When he saw me, he shoved his phone into his pocket and dug around until he finally found his keys. "Yeah, I'm good."

I waved. "Okay. I'll see you later."

I walked past his front steps on the way to my place and bit into a doughnut. The powder soaked into my tongue and tickled the back of my throat. I almost coughed. I loved when it did that—when clouds of white came out of my mouth because something tasted so good.

The clouds always made me and Garin laugh.

"Hey, Kyle?"

I turned around.

Paulie was standing at his car door. "Has your brother been around?"

# PRISONED

Paulie and Anthony were best friends. They talked to each other as much as I spoke to Garin and Billy, which was certainly more than I chatted with my brother. If Anthony was around, Paulie would have already known.

"No," I said. "I haven't seen him." I scanned the cars that were parked in front of my apartment.

Anthony hadn't been home when I'd left for Garin's, and even though it was hard to see, it didn't look like he had returned.

"You talked to him though?"

I tried to think of the last time.

"Nope. Not today."

I watched as a car took a left onto our street and started driving toward us. It was hard to see the make and color; The Heart wasn't well lit. Most of the streetlamps were out along with the lights outside our front doors. When the city replaced one of the bulbs, it would be stolen within a few hours. Lights showed faces; they showed dealings, they showed illegal things being exchanged between hands… they showed evidence. The Heart didn't like that. The things that happened here needed to stay in the dark.

"Have you tried calling him?" I asked. "Maybe he just lost his phone or something."

"He didn't lose his phone. He…" His voice trailed off as the car got closer, and Paulie started walking toward the road.

The parked cars were blocking most of my view. But I was able to see Paulie's profile and how the headlights were lighting up his legs and jacket and face.

I didn't know why, but I couldn't drag my eyes away from him.

Something felt off—in the scowl on his mouth, in the questions he'd asked, in the way he moved farther into the street. In the way the car was coming toward him, driving so slowly.

Whatever that something was, it told me not to move. It told me to keep watching Paulie. It made everything inside me shake.

I'd lived in The Heart all my life. I knew how dangerous it could be. I'd learned at an early age to trust my gut. So, why the hell wasn't I listening to it? Why were my feet moving me toward Paulie?

I felt the packet of doughnuts fall out of my hand just before I jumped over the curb. "Hey!" I yelled to get his attention. It didn't work; he stayed facing the car. "Paulie, come here!"

Didn't he see how slowly the car was moving? Didn't he feel what I felt?

I had to reach him. Warn him. Grab his hand and pull him back inside his apartment.

The headlights turned off. The light was suddenly gone.

Another warning.

I was running out of time.

"Paulie," I gasped, trying to find my footing, my legs not wanting to move as fast as the rest of me. My breath came out in huffs. "Come back here. Come back—"

There was noise. More than just the sound of the engine. This was a grinding, like the window was rolling down and the tracks needed to be greased.

*Oh God.*

Something poked out of the open window. It was thin. Circular. Dark. It got longer and longer.

The barrel of a gun.

"Paulie...no!"

Why wasn't I moving faster? Why couldn't I find his hand?

"Kyle, get back."

I heard him so clearly. I knew how close I was to him.

Just a few more steps.

I finally saw his hand, close enough to reach. I clasped my fingers around his thumb. "Come on, we have to go."

He turned a bit and then pushed me back with both hands. "Get out of here, Kyle."

I stumbled. I tried to catch my balance, but I slammed into one of the cars along the curb. "Paulie—"

The car with the gun had almost reached him.

"Paulie, *get down!*" My shoulder ricocheted off the door, and I fell to the ground.

Paulie didn't listen. He stayed right where he was, his body facing the car. The gun was pointed directly at him.

He didn't say another word. He didn't duck; he didn't try to hide. He didn't reach for his own gun, the one I knew was tucked in the back of his jeans. He just walked toward the car. And then he went completely still.

He knew.

# PRISONED

Somehow, Paulie knew...and he did nothing.

My arms wrapped around my stomach as I cowered against the side of the tire. My whole body tightened. I held my breath, and I waited for the sound. I waited for the explosion. Whoever was about to hurt Paulie was going to come for me next.

No witnesses. Not ever.

Not in The Heart.

This was the end...for both of us.

*BANG.*

Paulie fell to the ground. It felt like the pavement vibrated underneath me, but I knew it hadn't. I covered my head with my arms. No breath. No air. Through the small space between my forearms, I saw the blood start to pool out of the side of his body.

Where was the second shot? Where was the pain in my chest?

"Paulie," I cried. "*No.*" It came out as a whisper. "Paulie. Paulie, stand up. Paulie..."

He didn't move. Didn't twitch. Didn't cry out. There was silence, except for the sound of the engine idling, and stillness, other than the growing puddle of blood.

"Get up, and get in this car, Kyle."

That voice...I knew it.

Why wasn't I dead? I should have been. I should have been slumped against the car that I was leaning against, my blood flowing into the street to meet Paulie's.

The window rolled down even more, and the set of eyes that stared back...

*No.* This wasn't happening.

Not with that voice...not with those eyes.

"Kyle, get in this car right fucking now."

"I...can't. I ca-can't mo-move."

I couldn't leave. Paulie needed me. He needed me to call the police. No one else around here would do it. If they had heard the sound of the gun, they would back away from their windows. They wouldn't come outside. They wouldn't check to see who'd been shot. And if they happened to see something, they wouldn't tell the police. They wouldn't tell *anyone*. That was how it worked around here. So, I needed to stay. I needed to pound my hands on his chest and breathe into his mouth and do something to get him moving.

"I'm not going to ask you again. Get in the goddamn car."

"No—"

"Don't make me come out there and get you."

I'd heard his threats before. I'd seen the results of the people who didn't listen to him. But until now, I didn't know that The Heart had sliced open his chest, ripped his heart out, and left him soulless.

It sounded like, if I didn't get off this pavement and get into his car, I'd be joining Paulie.

I pushed myself off the ground, my knees wobbly, my feet unsteady, as I ran to the passenger door. He opened it from the inside, and as soon as I reached the doorway, he pulled me in. My shoulder smashed into the console; my head banged into the middle armrest. He didn't wait for me to be seated before he shut the door and took off.

"Stop fucking crying," he snapped. "Paulie doesn't deserve your tears. He deserves to be dead, so wipe your goddamn face, and get it together."

Get it together?

I still hadn't processed that I hadn't been shot, too, and I definitely hadn't processed Paulie's murder. But every second of it, every bit of detail, was flashing in my head.

Paulie was practically family. I'd seen him almost every day since I was a kid. He'd walked me to the bus stop whenever Garin and Billy skipped school. He'd given me rides, gotten me food. He'd even kicked a kid's ass when the kid had tried to rob me on my front steps.

Paulie was nicer to me than my own brother.

And I was supposed to stop crying and get it together and act like it had never happened?

Impossible.

This was so deep, deeper than I could even wrap my head around.

Billy. Oh God, what was this going to do to Billy? And to Garin? And to all of us?

It hurt. It hurt and it stung and it made my stomach churn, and whatever was inside of it was now rising to the back of my throat.

"I have to get out of this car," I moaned, wrapping my arms around my belly.

"Not a fucking chance."

"Pull over, or I'm going to puke on your floor."

"You're kidding."

# PRISONED

I rocked back and forth, my mouth watering more as each second passed. "No, I'm definitely not."

He weaved between lanes, already several blocks outside The Heart. "You can puke out the window. I'm not pulling over."

I hit the button, waiting for the glass to roll down.

There was grinding. This side made the same noise.

*Grinding…window…gun…BANG.*

It all came back so quickly.

I leaned my face out the window and opened my mouth. Vodka poured out. I'd taken a few sips before I had gone to Garin's. It was supposed to help take the edge off, so I'd finally have the courage to tell him how I felt.

But nothing could take the edge off of this.

"Don't get any puke on the fucking car!" he yelled.

I hardly heard him.

All I could think about was that Paulie was dead.

# TWENTY-TWO

## KYLE

"Ahh!" I screamed as something freezing and sour-smelling splashed onto my face.

My eyes snapped open and immediately closed again. The mysterious liquid stung my eyes something fierce and burned the hell out of my tongue. It was inside my nose, running down the back of my throat, so potent that I gagged.

"Air," I gasped. "I...can't...breathe..."

Something was squeezing my chest, constricting my airflow. I opened my eyes to see what it was, and tears poured from my lids. I tried to blink out whatever was burning them; it only got worse. My vision was blurry, and the light in here was dim, but I was able to see the ropes. They weren't just on my wrists and ankles. They were circled around each breast, meeting in the middle and weaving into a braid that traveled down my stomach, under my pussy, through the slit of my ass, up my shoulders, and met again at my breasts.

It was a jumpsuit of rope. Tight, scratchy, unforgiving rope. And, every time I moved, the rope tugged against my clit, squeezed my breasts…and prevented me from taking in any air.

"I've missed you," Breath whispered from behind me, his lips pressing against the back of my ear. He tugged my hair, so my neck flew back, my face now pointed toward the ceiling. "I heard you while you two were fucking. You sounded so good; you made my dick hard."

He rubbed his erection across the back of my head. It was a pathetic hard-on. Disgusting. And it smelled revolting.

"I hoped you were using your fingers. Sticking them into that sweet cunt of yours. Balling them together, so you were giving yourself your whole fist. That's what it sounded like, so I had to see it for myself. I had to see if I could fit my entire fist in you." He wrapped his hand around my hair and pulled down even harder. "You know what I found, *puta*? I found Garin's cum in your ass…and I didn't fucking like it."

His nails dug into the backs of my ears, and it felt like he was piercing my lobes.

"Did you hear me? I didn't fucking like it. I'm going to make sure my cock is the only one that will ever be inside your ass again."

He was going to make sure?

"Did you do something to Garin? Where's Garin? Don't—"

He yanked the rope until it tightened against my pussy and around my breasts. I felt my skin start to split. When I opened my mouth to scream, he slapped his hand over it.

"I'm going to give you the biggest load your ass has ever gotten. And, while I'm coming in your ass, you're going to get my fist in your pussy. How would you like that?" He moved to the front of me and straddled my waist, blocking me from looking at anything but him.

The pressure on my thighs tightened the rope. My clit was about to burst.

"Don't you dare scream," he warned. "If you want the pain to stop, then you'd better start obeying me."

I shut my mouth and screamed on the inside instead. I blinked away the tears. I tried to find the tiniest bit of air to fill my lungs. And I searched for the memories of Garin—his face, his eyes, his presence, whatever would get me through this.

Breath leaned forward, his rancid tongue tracing the outer edge of my mouth. When he finished the second lap, his scent stayed on me. It was the only thing I could smell. It felt like I was stuck inside a toilet. No air, just his tongue and the foulest stench.

He grabbed his dick through his pants and rubbed it. "Are you ready for me, Kyle? Ready for me to be inside your ass?"

I shook my head.

"No?" He laughed. "Then, tell me what I want to hear."

Telling him the truth would only get more people killed. I was sure he was going to kill me, so why not just take the punishment and die with the secret? Why get more people involved? I was as guilty as the murderer anyway because I hadn't told anyone what he had done.

"No." I knew the consequences of giving Breath that answer. I knew things could probably get much worse. But as long as he was only hurting me, then I'd take it. I'd take it to my grave, and I'd save Garin. I'd die without anyone else having to die, too.

"Wrong answer."

His nails stabbed the top of my nipple. I felt him go through the skin. I felt the skin snap open. I felt the blood seep out.

"No!" I yelled. "I still won't tell you."

Garin was there, behind my lids. That scruffy beard that tickled my cheeks as he kissed me. Those hands that gripped my face, not allowing me to look at anything but him. Those beautiful eyes that held me with a type of strength I'd never felt before. I didn't know where the air came from, but it huffed through my nostrils as I breathed through the pain. And the scream stayed inside me. It simmered, it festered, but it didn't come through my lips.

Paulie hadn't screamed. In those seconds it took him to die, he had held it in.

I'd hold it in, too.

"Tough girl, huh?" Breath hissed.

His hand dipped to my pussy. I didn't think it could do any more damage, and I didn't think the rope could squeeze my clit any tighter.

I was so wrong.

"Oh, *puta*, this is going to feel really good."

He pushed the lips of my pussy against the nylon, so the sensitive skin on the inside ground into the roughness of the rope. I was raw. My clit felt like it had been chewed off. And just when I thought it couldn't hurt any worse, he shimmied the rope back and forth as though he were trying to start a fire.

The memories of Garin were gone. The air...gone.

I couldn't keep the screams in. They shot up my throat and shouted from my lips, spit pooling in the corners, tears falling in my open mouth.

"I knew it would feel good." He stopped and looked down at my lap. "You're bleeding. But you're not bleeding enough. I want more of your blood. I want to know you'll never feel pleasure again. And anytime something touches you down there, I want it to hurt. I want it to *always* hurt."

"Do-don't do this to me-me."

"Why? Because you've been such a good girl? Because you've given me everything I've wanted? Because you've answered every question I've asked?" His hand disappeared behind his back and returned with a knife. "You haven't done any of those things. So, *puta*, I'm going to make you my own personal coloring book." The tip of the knife stabbed into my breast. "I'm going to try real hard to stay inside the rope."

As the knife pierced the skin at the top of my breast, blood squirted from the small hole and sprayed him in the face.

"Stop," I begged. "Please...stop."

He stuck his tongue out and caught the drops as they fell from his lip. "I'm just getting started." His eyes were demonic as he dragged the blade across my skin. Sick and beyond demented.

"I can't..." It hurt so badly. My tongue didn't want to work. My voice was gone. My courage and my hope were slipping with each drop of blood that poured out.

When he reached the bottom of my breast, half of it now cut, he smiled from his handiwork. "I'm headed for your pussy next. Do you want to know what I'm going to do to it?" He moved to the side, so I could finally see what was across from my chair. "I'm going to make your pussy look like this," he said.

When I realized what I was looking at—*who* I was looking at—I screamed with every bit of strength that was left in my body.

# TWENTY-THREE

## GARIN
## FIFTEEN DAYS AGO

I was stepping into my private elevator when my cell phone rang. I knew it was Billy. He usually called around this time, right before I was about to get my dick wet. Tonight was no different. The slut on my arm was some chick who worked at the club downstairs. I wasn't sure if I'd fucked her before, but she met all the requirements—thick ass, decent rack, eyes that told me she'd take whatever I gave her.

What I was about to give would tear her the hell apart. I wanted her screaming as loud as she was moaning. And when she walked out of my condo, I wanted it to hurt.

I reached into my pocket and put the phone up to my ear. "Billy, I'm going to have to—"

"It's Mario. Not Billy."

I looked at the slut next to me. "Hold on a second," I said into the phone.

I hit Mute on the screen and held the phone against my chest while the elevator climbed to the penthouse. When the door slid open to the entryway of my condo, I walked her inside and pointed at the living room. "Sit there. Don't move. I'll be back as soon as I can."

I headed toward my office without waiting for her to respond. I knew she'd sit there and wait for me. She'd wait until morning if that was how long it took me to get back. The girls I brought up here obeyed all of my commands. When they were anywhere inside this building, even on the top floor where I lived, I was their boss. And, if they didn't comply, they knew there were consequences.

When the door to my office was shut, I brought the phone up to my ear. "Sorry. I wasn't alone."

"Pour yourself something stiff to drink, and sit down."

I pushed my back against the door and looked around the room. There was plenty of booze in here. None of it appealed to me. Whatever Mario had to tell me, I needed to hear it sober. Because the sound of his voice and the sharpness of his demand told me his news was personal.

"Spit it out, Mario."

He sighed into the phone.

A sound I fucking hated.

"Billy was found about an hour ago in an alley not far from the boardwalk."

I gritted my teeth together and slammed my fist against the back of the door. "Say it."

"He's dead, Garin."

My heart was beating so goddamn hard that I felt it in my stomach. I reached my fist forward and slammed it back into the door. The wood splintered under my knuckles; pieces of it stuck into my flesh. I didn't care. I didn't give a fuck about anything besides Mario's words that repeated in my head.

*"He's dead, Garin."*

*"He's dead, Garin."*

*"He's dead, Garin."*

Billy Ashe. My best friend.

Dead.

I pulled my hand out of the door and walked to the other side of the room. "How?"

"The needle was still in him."

"HOW?" I yelled.

"My boys are looking into it right now. I got the call and wanted to tell you before you heard it from anyone else."

I knew the procedure. When one of us died, Mario's boys got to the scene first. They'd take what they needed and leave what evidence they wanted the police to find. Billy wasn't one of us, but Paulie was. Because no one had been blamed for Paulie's murder, I was sure Mario wanted to see if the deaths were somehow related.

"Send me the pictures," I said.

I knew he had them. Snapshots of the body, the weapon, the scene, the evidence—it all was part of the procedure. They were immediately sent to Mario along with a detailed report. He usually had it in his inbox before the police even arrived.

There was that sigh again. "I'll send them over in the morning."

"Send. Them. Now."

"He was family to you. You should wait until the morning to look at them. You need a second. Trust me on this, Garin. I've lost enough people to know."

"Send them."

"Fine...but I warned you."

I grabbed the picture frame off the back wall and walked it over to my desk. It now sat on top of a stack of folders and stared at me while I took a seat. It was of the three of us—Billy, Kyle, and me. We were in Mario's basement. We were laughing. We were high.

We were so fucking happy.

"Have the cops filed anything yet?" I asked.

"I hear they're going to rule it an overdose because of where he was found and since the needle was still in him."

So, the police weren't going to look into it. I wasn't surprised. It was less work for them that way than pulling together an investigation. One less junkie on the street, they thought.

Billy wasn't just some junkie. He was my goddamn family. But having the police investigate wouldn't help me. If there was something to be found, I'd find it on my own.

"Who sold him the junk? Was it us?"

"I'll have that answer tomorrow. If it wasn't us—"

"I'll want his name, Mario, and I'll want to know who he works for."

"You'll have everything you need."

I flipped the picture over. I couldn't look at it for another second.

Billy should have been in rehab, sober living, or clean and living with me in Vegas. But dead? Fuck no. My best friend shouldn't be dead.

He should have been saved.

And I should have been the one who saved him.

"You know we'll take care of everything—the funeral, any other costs," Mario said. "Whatever you need, you just tell me."

"Thanks."

I wasn't looking forward to the call I needed to make. Billy's ma rarely answered her phone. Hell, she wouldn't have one if I didn't pay the bill. I just hoped I could reach her before she heard the news from someone in The Heart. She needed to hear it from me.

"I'll see you tomorrow?"

"Yeah," I said. "I'll be in Atlantic City by the morning."

"I'm sorry, brother."

"Me, too."

Seconds after I hung up, Mario's texts came across my screen.

Leaving my phone on the desk, I went to the other side of the room and poured myself a few fingers of whiskey. I'd heard the news. Now, I needed to numb it. I swallowed down the dark liquid and poured more.

I knew where Billy should have been right now, but that didn't mean I hadn't thought about this moment. I'd told myself plenty of times that the day I saw my best friend sober would be the day he was lying in his casket. Still, that didn't mean it didn't fucking hurt.

I carried my third glass of whiskey over to the desk and picked up my phone, finally pulling up the snapshots. The first picture showed his face. The shot was zoomed in, his lips dull blue.

The color, *that* blue, I couldn't get it out of my fucking head.

The second shot showed his whole body, his back slumped against a brick wall. His feet were out in front of him. His shirt was pulled up to his neck, and there was an empty needle sticking into his heart.

His goddamn heart.

I shook my head, my fist balling again. The only thing close enough to hit was the desk. The desk was going to get hit. So were the walls and the door and someone's fucking face once I got my hands on them.

# PRISONED

Mario knew.

I guaranteed that was one of the reasons he didn't want to send me the pictures. He didn't say anything because he probably figured I couldn't handle it right now.

Anyone who had been around drugs as much as we had would know.

Billy had OD'd. There was no question about that. The heroin had been too potent, the dose too lethal for his body. That had ultimately caused his death.

But Billy wasn't the one who had stuck in the needle.

A junkie hit up a vein. They shot straight into their bloodstream. They sure as hell didn't stick a needle into their fucking heart.

Someone found out that Billy had been looking into Paulie's death. Someone wanted that secret to be kept buried. Someone thought that killing Billy would ensure that. So, someone filled that syringe with a dose strong enough to take Billy's life and had tried to make it look like an accidental overdose. That someone had stuck the needle into Billy's heart.

They had murdered Billy.

Whoever that motherfucker was…I was going to murder him for it.

# TWENTY-FOUR

## KYLE

*"No!"* I shouted as I stared at what was left of Garin, slamming my back into the chair, trying to thrash my arms and legs, even though they were bound. "How could you do this? How could you take him from me?" I dragged my gaze over to the man who was responsible for this. "I hope you die. I hope your babies come out here and eat your flesh and chew off your fucking face and—"

Breath grabbed my lips and twisted them. "And what, *puta*? If I'm gone, there's no one here to take care of you. And do you know what would happen then?"

He may have been holding on to my lips, but I kept on screaming. I screamed because they had put us in this prison and had done horrible, sadistic things to us. I screamed because we were still in here, and I knew I was never getting out. I screamed because Breath had tortured Garin to death and taken away the one man I loved.

And I screamed, *"Garin,"* again and again because I just wanted him to lift his head and look at me, but I knew he wouldn't. "Open your eyes, Garin." My words were so muffled, but that didn't stop me. "Come back to me. You can't leave me, not after all this. Garin…"

"Do you see his flesh?" Breath spoke close to my ear and held me so tightly I couldn't move. "That's what your pussy is going to look like. Torn up and bloody in a way that can't be fixed."

His flesh…or what was left of it.

Breath had placed Garin in a chair, two ropes crisscrossed over his chest and tied around the metal spine of the chair. His hands and ankles were shackled. His skin had been chopped, as though a butcher had been sharpening his knife across Garin's entire body. All of him dripped blood. I couldn't see a piece that hadn't been slashed. His wounds were spread open; some so deep, there was raw muscle sticking out. The blood dripped, dripped, dripped down his body, forming a pool beneath him.

A pool like the one that had gathered around Paulie.

"Why did you do this?" I seethed, glaring at the man I hated more than anything in this world. "Why did you kill him?" Killing Garin killed me. Emptied me. Destroyed me. There was no reason for me to be here anymore. "Garin didn't know about Paulie's murderer. Only I did. You should have killed me, not him." I looked down at the knife that was in Breath's hand. "Slit my throat. Do it. Get it over with. I can't live another second."

"I'm getting real tired of your screams, *puta*." Two of his fingers slipped inside my mouth and clamped around my tongue. "If you look close enough, you'll see his chest rising and falling." He turned my head, so I faced Garin, and then he squeezed my tongue even harder. "Your boyfriend isn't dead…yet," he snarled.

*He's alive?*

The tears, the screams, the anxiety, the guilt, the dread, the weight—it all lightened.

Garin…was really alive?

The sobs I wept were out of happiness as I finally saw the movement in Garin's chest. His inhales were shallow, but he was breathing. And, suddenly, I was breathing, too. I was breathing for the both of us. I was breathing because, despite how terribly mangled he looked, my Garin was still with me.

"*Levanta la cara del prisionero,*" Breath barked at Beard, who I now noticed was standing in the front of the room.

# PRISONED

Beard moved over to Garin and grabbed his hair, lifting Garin's head so that I could finally see his face. There were slashes across his cheeks, his forehead, his nose. His lips were so beaten; they looked like hamburger meat.

"Kyle," Garin moaned.

His voice was so soft. I almost didn't hear him.

"I'm here, Garin."

I tasted the tears on my lips. I tasted bile. I tasted plastic.

I tasted guilt.

Garin opened his eyes, stopping when they were just tiny slits of white. "Kyle," he groaned. "Kyle…Kyle."

It sounded like when he was being beaten, when Breath had made me listen to Garin whispering my name over and over. I had thought those were going to be his last words. Now, I feared they truly would be.

"He needs to go to the hospital," I snapped at Breath. "He needs surgery and blood. He needs to be fixed."

"He'll have all that," Breath spit in my ear.

"Then, take him."

Breath didn't move. Beard didn't either.

"Take him right fucking now!"

Breath walked around to my side, gently resting his hand on my shoulder. It was too late for gentle. Gentle wasn't a language Breath spoke. I didn't like it. And I didn't know what it meant.

"He's not going anywhere until you give me what I want," Breath said. "Then, *puta*, I'll take him to the hospital, and he'll get all the care he needs."

"And me?"

He smiled, like I had just told him I loved him. "You'll get the punishment you deserve."

I knew what it all meant now.

"Confess and save Garin, or I'm going to kill you both. The choice is yours," he said.

I'd known all along I was going to die in this prison. Life beyond this cell was simply a fantasy. The two of us walking out of here, Garin's hand clasped in mine, living the life I'd always wanted—that was fiction.

It wasn't what I deserved.

Not after what I'd done.

"Do you promise me?" My voice was loud and stern. "Do you promise that, if I tell you what you want, you'll take Garin to the hospital?"

I didn't know if I could trust Breath, but I had no other choice. Garin was getting weaker by the second. He was losing more blood. He was slipping further away from me.

I couldn't drag this out any longer.

"I promise you, *puta*."

This was the confession I should have made back then. This was what I should have voiced every time Garin and Billy had banged on my front door, when they'd waited for me in the hallway outside my classes, when Garin had cornered me in the alley.

This was my second chance.

"Garin, I'm so sorry."

His eyes opened again, looking at me through those tiny slits.

"I could tell you why I lied to you and Billy, but it doesn't matter anymore. There's no excuse for what I did. I was wrong. I know that. I've paid for it every day since. It's eaten me up, and the guilt has never once let me go. I don't deserve forgiveness. Just know that I love you. I've always loved you."

Breath stuck something sharp in the side of my neck. "Spit it out. I'm tired of listening to this bullshit. You've tested my patience long enough."

"I'm sorry," I whispered again.

I watched Garin's face as the name of the murderer slipped through my lips. Even in his state, even with all the blood and all his wounds, I saw it—the anger, the resentment.

The hatred.

And then all I saw was black.

# TWENTY-FIVE

## KYLE
## TWELVE YEARS AGO

"Roll up the fucking window," the murderer hissed. "You have to be done puking by now."

It had been at least a minute since I heaved. My stomach was empty, my body still shaking. But the cool night air felt good against my burning skin, and the wind that blew past my face seemed to pause the nightmare that kept replaying in my mind. It was the nightmare that had made me throw up in the first place.

Unfortunately, the pause was short-lived.

He rolled up the window, and he yanked my face back in the car.

"You're a monster," I spit. "Why don't you let me out, so I can get the hell away from you?"

He slammed his fist into the steering wheel. "You weren't supposed to be outside. Why the fuck weren't you home? Asleep? What were you doing out there?"

"I was walking home from Garin's."

"Why didn't you just stay the night there?"

I wanted to.

I should have fought Garin. I should have begged him to let me stay. Then, I wouldn't have seen Paulie or the gun or the shot that took him to the ground. Or the blood.

But I wasn't going to say that to him. I doubted he was looking for an answer anyway.

"Jesus fucking Christ, Kyle...I almost killed you."

I'd heard him say something similar to that before. But, back then, we were just kids, and I was teasing him about something stupid, like the ridiculous porn he liked to watch in his room, and he would rant about how he wanted to kill me. It was a joke. All of that talk had been a joke back then. Meaningless banter that didn't deserve a second thought.

But there was nothing funny about what he'd said just now. There were no more jokes, no more teasing. There could never be again. *Kill.* He'd made that word come true. He'd pulled the trigger. He'd murdered a friend, a best friend. The guy to my left, the one who had the same eyes as mine, had become a killer.

The drugs, the girls, The Heart. Whatever it was that had changed him, he wasn't my brother anymore.

"Maybe you should have killed me," I said.

"Don't joke about that, Kyle."

"I'm not joking, Anthony."

I looked out the windshield as we passed through green light after green light. How was he not swerving all over the road? Not puking out his window? How did he not have tears running down his face, like mine?

Did he not understand what he did? Was he high? Too high?

Maybe he needed to be reminded.

"Do you know how many people you just damaged? Including me?"

He glanced at me quickly, his lip curled like something smelled terrible in the car. Not even the smallest bit of remorse was in his eyes. "I know what I did, and I don't give a fuck. I told you, he deserved it. It's been a long time coming. He's fucking lucky I didn't pull the trigger months ago."

A monster.

# PRISONED

"No one deserves to be killed. Especially not Paulie."

"Stop running your mouth, Kyle. I don't want to be schooled. I don't want to hear how you don't approve. I'm not in the mood to listen to you at all, so shut the fuck up or—"

"Or you'll kill me?"

He jerked the car to the right, and the tires screeched. We hit grass and then pavement. Anthony slammed on the brakes. I gripped the handle on the door, trying to brace myself for what was about to come. I didn't know if he was aiming for the pole up ahead or if he just wanted to scare me or if he was going to open my door and throw me out. He dodged a fire hydrant and two curbs, coming to a stop at the side of a strip mall.

He panted, but I knew he wasn't out of breath. That was his way of trying to control his anger.

"Look at me."

I waited a few seconds before I released the door. My body was so tense that it ached. My head pounded to the point of nausea, and every time I blinked, I saw the pool of blood. If I wasn't so empty, I would have been projecting bile straight to the floor.

"Fucking *look at me*!"

I wrapped my arms around my churning stomach and glared at him. He didn't even look the same. His eyes were hollow. His lips spread too thin. His cheeks sunken in.

"What have you done with my brother?"

"What have I done with him? I'm in the best place of my life right now. I have over twenty girls working for me, and I'm making a shit-ton of money. I'm about to hire twenty more. Do you know how much cash that's going to bring in—in *one night*?"

That was what he considered a success? Employing women who sucked dick and spread their legs for cash?

He wasn't just lost.

He was gone.

"I don't care, Anthony. I don't care about money, and I definitely don't care about yours."

"You're going to care because I'm going to give you plenty of it to keep your mouth shut."

"You can't buy me."

"That's where you're wrong, sister. I can do whatever the fuck I want because I'm the one holding the gun." He slapped the gun on the armrest, keeping his hand on the butt and his finger on the trigger.

It wasn't pointed at me, but it may as well have been.

"What the—ow!" I yelled as his other hand clamped my cheek. "Get off me."

"You're going to shut the fuck up and listen to me. I'm not going to fight with you, and I'm sure as hell not going to repeat myself." He traced the gun down the side of my face.

I shivered—not just from the feel of the metal on my skin, but also from the power he had over me.

"You're going to leave Atlantic City the second you graduate. You're going to get yourself set up down south somewhere, somewhere like Florida. You're going to go to college that I'm going to pay for. You're going to open a business that I'm going to fund. You're going to get a house that I'm going to purchase in cash. And, every month I'm going to drive down to Florida to check on you, and since my money isn't safe in Jersey, you're going to launder it for me. You're my investment, Kyle. That's your reward for keeping your mouth shut." He released my cheek, but the gun stayed close.

"What if I say no?"

"Then, I'll kill you."

There was no hesitation in his voice. He said it as though he were announcing the weather forecast. And he looked at me as though I were trash on an already littered sidewalk. He could just point a gun at me and shoot.

His way or death.

It was all so simple for him.

"How am I supposed to face Garin and Billy? How can I act like I don't know it was you who killed Paulie?"

"Stop being friends with them if you can't handle it."

"They'll know something is wrong—" I cut myself off when I saw his eyes turn rabid.

"Make sure they don't know." He glanced down at the gun. "There's only two people who were able to see inside this stolen car tonight. One of them is dead; the other is you. If anyone finds out about this, if I hear so much as my name whispered, it will be the end of you."

*The end of me...*

# PRISONED

He might as well have pulled the trigger right then.

Garin and Billy were my whole world. They were all I had. They were my best friends, my family. They kept me safe, fed, clothed.

But there was more.

I loved Garin. Things were going to happen between us. They were about to happen. We were taking it slow, but our relationship was moving forward.

And now?

Now, I had to give that up.

Give everything up.

Give them up.

I looked out the window, at the city outside the glass. Once I stepped out there, things were going to be so different.

They were going to be cold.

Dark.

Lonely.

Every day, I would be ravaged with guilt for not speaking the truth. For allowing Paulie's murderer to roam the streets, the crime remaining unsolved. For being a coward.

I was no longer Kyle.

I was the person Anthony wanted me to be.

# TWENTY-SIX

## KYLE

Plastic—that was all I could taste. My tongue was so dry that it felt like it was made of paper. My teeth were fuzzy, like mold was growing over the enamel. I hoped this prison wouldn't give me Breath's teeth, his rotted gums, his rancid breath. I hoped that, whatever damage had been done, I'd be able to recover from it.

Because, maybe one day, I would get out of here. Breath would open the bars, and Garin and I would walk out with... *his hand clasped in mine, living the life I'd always wanted.*

Why did that thought feel so familiar?

Why was I so groggy?

As I swam through the fog in my brain, it slowly started coming back to me, the very last memory I had. I'd told Breath that Anthony was the murderer...and then everything had turned to black.

Everything was still black. My eyes were closed, my lids feeling much too heavy to open. And there was beeping in my ears. Lots of high-pitched beeping...

Where was it coming from? That noise hadn't been in our cell before.

But the differences didn't stop there.

There was softness, too. The wool blanket we'd used as a pillow wasn't this feathery. It had been hard, cement hard. Our bed was the same, but whatever was underneath me now was cozy, plush, delicate even. And it wasn't cold in here, like it typically was in our cell. If anything, I was warm. Too warm. Sticky...hot.

It must have been from the needle that Breath had stuck in my neck. Those drugs he gave me always made me feel loopy. Garin had said it took at least a day for the meds to work their way out of my system.

Had it been a day?

A day since—

*GARIN.*

More memories started to come back to me. Breath had slashed Garin's entire body. Garin had barely been breathing. He needed help. He needed to go to a hospital. Breath promised he would take him but only if I confessed. Giving him that confession also meant...

*"You'll get the punishment you deserve. Confess and save Garin, or I'm going to kill you both. The choice is yours."*

I'd given him the confession.

Was this death?

Something still beeped not too far from my ear.

"What's beeping?" The sound of my own voice surprised me. It was hoarse, a little deep. So scratchy.

*"Relax, Kyle."*

Relax...Kyle?

I'd heard that voice before. It was the one I'd been hearing since I was put in that cell. It sounded like Garin but up until today it had been a little hazy and muffled. It wasn't either of those now. It was clear.

"Kyle..."

"Garin?"

"I'm right here."

I felt him squeeze my hand, but I still didn't see him. My eyelids were too heavy to open just yet. Everything was heavy. My muscles ached; my skin tingled. Every thought felt like it needed to swim through a sea of peanut butter before it surfaced and actually made sense.

"I need to see you, Garin. I need to see how you're healing. Did Breath make good on his promise? Did he take you to the hospital?"

"Just relax, Kyle. They gave you some heavy medication, so if you're going to open your eyes, do it slowly."

Was it heavier than what Breath had given me in the past? My lids certainly hadn't felt this heavy before. My body definitely hadn't felt this tingly.

"I thought that whatever Breath had put in that needle...I thought it was going to kill me," I said.

I lifted my arm to try and cover my eyes, but it was hard to move. Something was around my wrist, and another something was attached to it.

Wires. It felt like wires.

I finally got my arm up and blocked out the light. Slowly, so slowly, I shifted it down to let in a little at a time. I took a breath after each shift.

A little bit of light and then a little bit of air.

The air came in so easily, much easier than I expected. There was suddenly so much more air in here and much less pressure on my chest.

Why?

I blinked several times, my eyes now fully uncovered but still trying to adjust to the sunlight. Even though they stung and watered from the brightness, I could see Garin sitting in a chair right next to me. I could see his hand on mine. I could smell him.

Clean. He was so clean.

"Breath kept his promise," I said as I studied his handsome face.

I couldn't find a single cut. There wasn't even a scab or a bruise. Not even a scar. That was...strange. Some of his wounds had been so deep; raw muscles had been sticking out of them.

"How did you heal so fast?"

"Heal?"

My stare shifted between his eyes as another thought occurred to me. "How long have I been asleep?"

"Eight days."

"What? Eight whole days?"

He put his palm on my chest to stop me from sitting up. "If you move too fast, you'll get dizzy, and your drain might come out."

I couldn't have been asleep for eight days, nor could he have healed in that time. What Breath had done to him would have taken months to recover from, and he would have been left with scars. But, if he had any, I would have seen them because his beard had been shaved. All that thick, coarse hair…gone.

"How did you get a razor? Did Beard bring you one?"

He took a second to respond. "You've been through a lot, Kyle. You've had a head trauma. I'm sure it's making things cloudy right now."

"Head trauma?" I touched my forehead. "Did Breath hit me on the head? What—" I cut myself off when I noticed his clothes.

He wasn't in the black pants and button-down he'd been wearing since Billy's funeral. He was in jeans and a thin sweater.

"Beard brought you clothes? Did he bring me any?" I looked down and saw the blanket that was tucked over me. It wasn't scratchy gray wool. It was white and knit. And I was in a gown, a light-blue one. And I was lying on a bed with buttons on both sides of the railings that made the bed adjustable.

Why was I in a bed? With a knit blanket, wearing a light-blue gown?

Why was it so bright in here?

*Beep. Beep. Beep.*

I looked over my shoulder, and there were machines behind me—a heart monitor and an IV bag.

"Am I in the hospital?"

"Yes, Kyle."

I glanced back at his face and blinked hard, waiting for the cuts and gashes to reappear. But they didn't, and there weren't any scars. Why was he fully healed, and why was I the one in this bed?

"How did I get to the hospital? Did Breath take me when he dropped you off? Did he do something to me?"

"You got here by ambulance."

"An ambulance picked me up? On Margarita Island? Or did he take us to Caracas?"

There was pity in his eyes—pity like whenever Billy had been high and incoherent. Garin and I would just stare at him while he tried to put words together, but nothing he said made sense.

# PRISONED

Was that me—muddled and unintelligible?

"We're in Atlantic City, Kyle."

Atlantic City?

"I don't get it. You're all healed. I'm the one hurt and...I'm so tired."

It was more than just tiredness that hit me; it felt like a heavy blanket of warmth was sinking me into this bed and about to close out all the light.

"I'll explain everything to you when you wake up. Just shut your eyes, and get some rest."

His hand tightened on mine. Somehow, it made me feel safe. It gave me the encouragement I needed to close my lids again.

"But I just woke up..."

There was that darkness that I remembered. Not the kind I felt in the cell. This was different. This wasn't frightening. My body didn't tremble in fear. It didn't make me search for a way out. In the strangest of ways, it was comforting.

"Relax, Kyle."

I did as he said, and each of my muscles loosened.

"Breathe, Kyle."

My breathing slowed.

Those words...they were so familiar. So was his tone.

So was the dream behind my lids.

# TWENTY-SEVEN

## KYLE

"She's awake."

There was that voice again. The one I'd heard in my head when I was prisoned, the one I'd just fallen asleep to. It was Garin. But, this time, it wasn't in my mind. It wasn't right next to me. It sounded like it was coming from several feet away.

My eyes opened slowly, my lids rising much easier than before. Unlike last time, I looked around the room, taking in the window, the two chairs—one of which had been pulled next to my bed—the TV, bathroom, and closet. I really was in a hospital...but in Atlantic City? That part didn't make any sense. Maybe Breath had flown us back to the States, and an ambulance had picked us up from the airport.

"I haven't told her," Garin said.

I glanced toward the open door, the voice sounding like it came from the hallway.

"I know, I know," he continued. "You have nothing to worry about. Trust me." He looked into the doorway, and our eyes connected. "I'll call you later." He shoved the phone into his pocket and came over to the bed. "Feeling any better?"

As he sat, I noticed he was in different clothes again. Darker jeans, a black button-down shirt. His scruff had grown a little, the black hairs casting a shadow across his cheeks.

"A little, I think. I'm still so tired and so confused."

"The doctor said that's normal. It's going to take your body some time to recover."

"When can I go home? Unless..." My voice drifted off as I thought about the prison.

Were Beard and Breath waiting for me outside the hospital? Would they take me the second I healed?

"Home is an option, right?"

Garin laughed, which confused me more. "Yeah, it's an option. Just a few more days, and you'll be able to go. Your doctor wants to make sure you're stable enough to fly. Your lung is healing well, and so is your head. Your drain should be coming out tomorrow. Then, I'll fly you back to Florida to make sure you get home safely."

"That's not necessary."

"It is. Don't fight me on it. Because last time"—he grabbed the armrests, the tips of his fingers turning white—"I didn't keep you safe."

*Last time.*

"I don't know what you're talking about. What happened to my head? And my lung?"

When he shifted in his chair, I picked up a whiff of his cologne. It was spicy, enticing. It would have turned me on if my whole body didn't hurt, if I wasn't so confused about why he was so healed and I was so battered.

I looked at his hands again. There wasn't any dirt on his fingers or nails. No cuts. Not the least bit of redness. How was that possible?

"Do you remember Billy's funeral?"

I recalled being at the funeral home, seeing Garin near Billy's casket. Garin had come by the table where I was getting a drink.

"Yes," I finally answered, "and I remember going to the bar with you."

# PRISONED

He had kissed me outside the restroom. Squeezed my neck. His touch had brought out more of the guilt. But it was the sexiest kiss I'd ever had, enough to make my skin flush in this hospital bed.

"We left the bar to go to your hotel, I think…"

That was where things became fuzzy. I didn't have a full memory of the car ride, just random flashes of it. I saw the interior, the black leather seats. His hand on my thigh. A green light. Dark…something so dark and hard.

"We never made it back to the hotel, Kyle."

That must have been because of Breath. He'd kidnapped us from Garin's car, injected something in our bodies so that we'd black out, shoved us into a plane and flew us to Margarita Island.

"I know. We were kidnapped and—"

"We got into a car accident."

"We…*what?*"

He pulled his chair closer, sending me his scent again. I didn't know what he was saying, I didn't know what he meant, but I knew there was nothing familiar about this smell. It wasn't the one I'd memorized in the cell. It was too clean.

Everything in here was too clean.

"Listen to me." His hand landed on my leg, and I winced. "A truck ran a red light and hit our car. It was on the passenger side, right in the middle of the hood. You hit the airbag and ricocheted off, slamming against the door. Your head hit the window. The glass shattered, and a piece of it punctured your lung. The blow to your head caused some damage, and you've been in a medically induced coma for the last eight days. The doctors just took out your breathing tube this morning and lowered your medication, so you'd wake up."

It didn't feel like he was talking about me. It felt like he was telling me a story about someone I didn't know. How could all of these things have happened, and I had no recollection of any of them?

Was he lying to me?

I felt the medication in my body, I saw it pumping through the tube that led to my wrist. With each drip, drip, drip of the IV, I thought about everything he had said—head trauma, a breathing tube, days' worth of medication…a coma.

A breathing tube would explain the plastic taste that had been in my mouth.

But what about everything else?

"I don't...understand," I said.

"I probably had a few too many drinks at the bar. I shouldn't have been driving us. My reflexes might have been off, and I didn't slam on the brakes in time. That truck hit us and—fuck, there was nothing I could do to stop it."

I needed him to tell me I wasn't crazy. I needed him to tell me that everything I saw, I felt, I experienced was real.

"Garin, I know we were kidnapped by two guys named Breath and Beard and..." I didn't have to finish. The answer was all over his face.

"I haven't left your side since you were admitted to the hospital, Kyle. I rode in the ambulance, and I slept in this chair."

But he was in the cell with me. We'd both been held captive. We'd both been tortured. I had admitted to Breath and Garin that Anthony had killed Paulie.

And it had all been...a dream?

A dream my mind had created while I was in a coma. None of it was real—not the emotions I'd experienced in there, the words we'd exchanged...the sex. The only thing that was real was the kiss we had shared before we'd gotten in the car and the way he was looking at me now.

"I'm not sure what to say."

"Why don't you tell me about those guys you dreamed about? Beard and Breath—were those their names?" He sounded amused.

It made me feel ridiculous.

The man I stared at was nothing more than a friend from my past who I hadn't seen in twelve years. He was basically a stranger now. The cell hadn't brought us closer. It hadn't reintroduced us; it hadn't made our feelings grow. He hadn't heard me say *I love you*. Telling him my dream wouldn't change anything. It would only make me feel crazier. But there was one thing that seemed consistent during my dream and in this hospital room. I felt it in his grip and in the way his eyes wouldn't let me go.

"You protected me," I said. "You did everything you could to keep me safe."

I didn't deserve his protection in prison. I certainly didn't deserve it out here.

## PRISONED

The secret was still buried inside me. It prisoned me in my dreams, and it fueled me with guilt now that I was awake.

Had Garin known the truth, I wondered if I'd still be alive.

"I didn't protect you, Kyle. That's why you're in here."

# TWENTY-EIGHT

## KYLE

I was chewing on a dinner roll. It wasn't hard or moldy like the rolls I'd eaten in the dream. This one was soft and buttery; it almost melted on my tongue. Then, Anthony walked in. The second my eyes connected with my brother's, I put the roll back on the tray. It was the first thing I'd eaten in almost nine days, and I suddenly had no appetite.

Since Garin had told me about the accident and I'd had a chance to process it all, I knew I would be seeing Anthony soon. I was just surprised it had taken this long, considering I'd been awake for over a day. What didn't surprise me was hearing that my mom wouldn't be making the trip up north. According to Garin, she was staying in Florida to help out at my shop.

My gaze followed Anthony over to the windows.

He stopped and leaned his back against the ledge. "You all right?" he asked.

"I'm okay."

The dream had brought back so many memories from that night in The Heart. I could feel myself huddled on the pavement outside our apartment. I could see the blood flowing out of Paulie's body. I felt myself inside Anthony's car, more scared than I'd ever been. I could hear Anthony give his final orders, dictating the way my life would be.

Twelve years later, the man in front of the windows hadn't changed at all.

But I had.

And the dream I'd had while I was in the coma had changed me again.

"When are you getting out?"

I blinked, wishing I didn't have to answer his question, knowing he'd track me down, no matter what. "A few more days."

I didn't look in Garin's direction even though I felt his eyes on me. I wanted to get through Anthony's visit without getting emotional. And, if I glanced at Garin while the killer was in the room, I didn't think I'd be able to do that.

"I'll drive you to Florida when you get out," Anthony said.

"She's flying to Florida with me," Garin said.

Garin's response came out so fast that I didn't even have a chance to open my mouth. I just stared at Anthony, waiting for him to react.

It didn't take him long.

He looked over his shoulder at Garin, sitting in the back of the room near the closet. "Did you say something, motherfucker?"

When Anthony glared back at me, I shivered. I knew how deadly that stare could be, how easily he had aimed that gun at Paulie and pulled the trigger.

"I think you heard me just fine," Garin said.

"Why don't you get out, so I can talk to my sister alone?"

"That's up to your sister. Not you."

With much pause, I shifted my gaze toward the closet and locked eyes with Garin. He didn't appear fazed at all by Anthony's comment; he didn't look intimidated either. There was no reason for him to. In Garin's line of work, I was sure he dealt with bigger, scarier, more confrontational assholes than my brother.

"Kyle, tell me what *you* want," Garin said before I had a chance to respond.

"It's okay," I said. "Just give us a few minutes."

He nodded. "I'll be right outside."

"Why don't you take a walk?" Anthony said. "I'll come find you when we're done."

Garin stood but didn't take a step. "Let's get something straight right now. I don't take orders from you. I'm only walking out of here because your sister said she's okay with it." He looked in my direction. "I'll be right outside the door. Yell if you need me."

Anthony stalked over to the foot of the bed as the door shut. "I don't fucking like that punk. He thinks he's entitled because he works for the bosses and runs their shitty casino out in Vegas. But you know what? I could take him down in a second. I'm not afraid of that motherfucker or any of the bosses he works for."

Anything I said would only make him angrier. When it came to my brother, I'd learned it was best to keep my mouth shut.

"Why the fuck is he still here anyway? Why hasn't he gone back to Vegas?"

Garin hadn't told me his reasons for staying, and I hadn't asked. But I liked having him around, and I didn't want him to leave. Even though I slept most of the time he was in the room, I felt safe, knowing he was there.

I shrugged. "I don't know. Maybe he feels guilty about the car accident."

"He *should* feel guilty. The asshole almost killed you." He looked toward the door with disgust. "I don't like him hanging around here. I want him gone."

I tried to keep my heart rate down, knowing the monitor would show just how Anthony's demands affected me. I couldn't have that. And I couldn't have him knowing I still had feelings for Garin whether they grew during the dream, during the kiss we'd had at the bar, or in the short time we'd been hanging out in my room.

"It's been twelve years, Anthony. You don't have to worry about me saying anything."

I knew that was the real reason he didn't want Garin around me.

"Lose him. I'm not going to say it again."

Now, I was the one with disgust in my eyes.

I hated my brother.

I hated that he still had this power over me.

I hated that I still feared him.

"He's going to fly me home," I said. "Then, I'll make sure he goes straight back to Vegas."

"He'd better."

As he moved a little closer to me, I finally smelled him. There was nothing clean about his scent. He reeked of cigarettes and booze and women's cheap perfume.

"Take this as your warning."

He was as vile as Breath.

"You don't have to warn me."

"I don't?"

A pang of guilt stabbed the back of my throat. It made it too hard to control my emotions, too hard to keep my heart rate down. Fortunately, Anthony was too angry to notice the monitor.

I kept my voice low, so he wouldn't yell at me about my tone. "No, you don't. I know what I'm allowed to say and what I have to lie about."

"I think you're wrong about that. You went to a bar with him, knowing it would piss me off. Then, you left the bar with him. Where was he taking you, huh? To your fucking bed?" He didn't wait for me to answer. "Do you know this is the first time I've been able to see you since you've been in the hospital? So, yeah, Kyle, I think you need a fucking warning."

"What are you talking about? I've been in the hospital for over eight days now. It's not my fault that you didn't come here to visit me."

He moved to my side and leaned down, so his face was close. Too close...Breath close.

I had to remind myself that the prison wasn't real.

"I came to the hospital every fucking day," Anthony said. "Garin's security wouldn't let me see you until today."

Garin's security?

Maybe I shouldn't have been surprised, given who Garin worked for and that he was back in Atlantic City where the bosses lived and protected one another. But I was. It made me wonder if the accident had really been an accident.

"I'm sure he was just trying to keep me safe," I said.

"From who, Kyle? From me?"

I wanted to give him an honest answer. To tell him again what kind of monster he was. That even his sister needed protection from him.

# PRISONED

But a confession like that would ensure I'd never be discharged from the hospital.

I shrugged again. "Why didn't you just call the police? I'm sure they would have helped you slide through security."

"The police?" He pointed at his pockets. "Do you know how much shit I carry with me?"

*Shit* could have been so many things—dirty money, drugs, weapons. Probably all three.

"I didn't like being told I couldn't see you. I didn't like Garin controlling your medical care. And I didn't like that he gave me a fucking hard time about leaving the room." He pointed at me. "Once he drops you off, he's gone. Forever." Then, he didn't say another word.

He didn't have to.

The anger seething from every aspect of him said enough.

# TWENTY-NINE

## KYLE

As we stepped up to the front door of my house, I reached inside my purse and found my keys. I was about to slide it into the lock when Garin stole it out of my hand.

"My fingers aren't broken," I said. "You could at least let me open the door."

"I've got it."

For the last few days that I'd been at the hospital, he hadn't let me do anything. No one had. Garin made sure I was doted on and given everything I needed. It felt like the nurse was on-call just for me. Garin also hadn't left my side for more than an hour or so; he was only gone long enough to drive to his hotel, take a shower, change his clothes, and drive back.

I didn't know why he had stayed, why he insisted on flying me to Florida, or why he made sure I had everything I needed. In my mind, it was because he cared about me and wanted to spend more time with me—and because, at some point, he'd want to return to the moment we had shared outside the restroom at the bar. That was what *I* wanted anyway. Affection from him. Closeness. To roll over in the middle of the night and see the shadow of his sleeping body next to my bed. For him to drop the hardness that I'd felt since the funeral, wrap his arms around me, and bury his lips against my neck.

I hadn't gotten that. I hadn't gotten anything even close to that.

He pulled my suitcase inside as the alarm went off. I reached for the pad, but his hand reached it before mine. He pressed three-seven-seven-one, as though I'd told him my code.

But I hadn't.

"How did you know?" I asked.

That was my house number when I'd lived in The Heart. It was the password I'd used for everything back then. I still did.

His eyes narrowed, but his smile was missing. "I forget nothing."

My memory wasn't bad, but twelve years was a long time to remember something like that.

He moved to the side, and I stepped into the entryway.

"I flew in my crew and had them clean your place."

People had been inside my house? While I'd been in the hospital?

If Anthony found out, he would lose his mind…more than he already had.

"But how'd you get a key?"

Anthony was the only person who had a spare key. He didn't allow me to keep one lying around.

He trusted no one.

Somehow, Anthony would find out what Garin had done. And, somehow, it would be all my fault.

I would be punished for this.

Garin nodded at my purse hanging from my shoulder. "I made a copy of yours."

I ignored the bleak feeling in my stomach and stepped further inside, noticing how clean everything was. The floors gleamed; the stainless steel was shiny. I didn't have a housekeeper because Anthony wouldn't allow it. I'd never been able to get the place to sparkle like this before. It had never smelled so sweet either.

"Did they make cupcakes?"

"Doughnuts with powdered sugar."

My eyes followed his finger toward the kitchen to the center of the island where three metal racks stood, covered with homemade doughnuts.

A knot lodged in the back of my throat. "You thought of everything."

"I wanted you to feel comfortable. You've gone through a lot."

I was sure that was true, but his eyes were missing the softness he used to reserve for me. I didn't know why I thought it would still be there after all this time. I had to clasp my hands behind my back to stop myself from trying to shake it out of him.

"I do feel comfortable," I said. "I have since the moment I stepped onto your plane." I set my purse on the console table and tucked my hands into my pockets.

Maybe he needed to hear more from me. Maybe he needed to know where my head was, and that would loosen things between us a little.

"Garin, if you're doing this out of guilt, then you should know that I'm not angry about the accident. I don't consider it your fault, and I don't blame you for any of it."

I'd known how much he drank that night, but I'd made the decision to get in his car. I knew the consequences. I wasn't incoherent. What happened after was on me, not him.

He continued to stare at me, his feelings completely masked. "Is your room down the hall?"

I still hadn't broken through.

"Yes," I answered.

He gripped the handle of my suitcase and rolled it toward my bedroom as I went to the kitchen. There was a shelf full of water bottles inside the fridge that hadn't been there before. The other shelves overflowed with fresh food; fruit and vegetables filled both drawers. I was sure my laundry had been done, too, and the sheets washed on both beds, the curtains cleaned and ironed, the lanai couch cushions fluffed and pressed.

The cleanliness, the full fridge, the doughnuts...it still didn't feel like me in here.

I grabbed a bottle of water and struggled with the cap. My strength hadn't returned. My body was still trying to heal. The impact of the crash hadn't just affected my head and lung; my flesh was bruised, my face and chest were covered in cuts, and so were my hands and feet. Garin said I'd taken off my heels when I got into his car. Apparently, I had been a bloody mess when the paramedics pulled me out.

Breath's babies hadn't tortured my feet like I imagined.

The dream hadn't happened.

I'd been in an accident. *This* was my reality.

"I put your suitcase on the end of your bed," he said, stopping on the other side of the island.

The knot was back in my throat as he confirmed our time was coming to an end. He had only promised to fly me to Florida. He hadn't mentioned anything about staying a minute longer. And why should he? I wasn't his girlfriend or his responsibility. I wasn't even his friend anymore. He had a job and a life on the other side of the country.

"Thank you." My fingers grasped the edge of the granite, weakly though. "You did far more than you needed to. I appreciate it—no…" Where were my words? What did I really want to say to him? "I'm grateful, Garin. Grateful that you stayed and oversaw all my care and made sure it was the best I could possibly get. I'm positive the reason I'm standing here right now, so shortly after the accident, is because of you."

I didn't deserve his help. His care. His attention.

But I wanted it. God, I wanted it.

"Do you have everything you need?" he asked flatly.

I nodded. "My meds are in my purse. The fridge is stocked. I'm sure I have enough email to keep me busy for days. I'll be fine."

His eyes roamed my kitchen and slowly returned to me. "It doesn't feel like you in here."

He was right. This house wasn't me; it was Anthony. It didn't matter how many times I remodeled or redecorated; I couldn't find its heart. That was because it had no heart. And no warmth. There wasn't any warmth in my business either.

And there wasn't any warmth coming from the man standing across from me. Somehow, before he left, I needed to feel some from him.

"I'm sure you're anxious to get back to Vegas," I said. "You've missed so much work."

"Anxious? No."

## PRISONED

He had unspoken words. I swore I felt them. I swore that underneath those words was the guy I remembered.

"I—" His phone beeped, cutting him off. He took it out of his pocket and stared at the screen. "Looks like I'm going to be in Florida for the night."

"You're staying?"

He continued to read the screen. "My pilot maxed out his hours when he flew in from Vegas to pick us up in Jersey and bring us down to Tampa. He tried to find a replacement crew but couldn't." He hit a button and held the phone up to his ear. "I'm going to call my assistant and have her book me a hotel—"

"Stay here." The words were out of my mouth before he had even finished speaking. "I have a guest room. Or you could take my room, and I'll sleep in the spare room."

He said nothing.

"Please, it's the least I can do. I want you to stay, Garin."

"I'll call you back," he said and hung up.

I knew the consequences of going against Anthony's warning. I was already in so much trouble with him and would be in even more after he found out Garin's crew had been inside the house. I didn't know what he would do to me, and the thought scared the hell out of me.

But I couldn't let Garin go to a hotel. I couldn't let him be in this city and not be with me.

"You're sure about this?"

I looked at the racks of powered doughnuts. "Go get your suitcase from the car, and send the driver home."

# THIRTY

## KYLE

After a long, steamy shower, I dressed myself in a pair of yoga pants and a thin cotton tank. I squeezed some of the water out of my hair and let the long locks fall down the middle of my shirt, soaking through to my back. There was no reason to blow-dry it. No reason to put on makeup either. Garin had been looking at my bare face for days.

When I left my bedroom, I saw him sitting outside on the lanai. There was a pizza box on the kitchen counter and five bottles of a six-pack of beer next to it. The missing one was in Garin's hand, his cell in the other as he held it up to his ear. I filled the plates with two slices each, tucked the beer under my arm, and joined him outside.

Before my shower, Garin had offered to take me out for dinner or to pick up food from any restaurant I wanted. Our time together was limited; I wanted to spend it in a setting where we could talk and be alone. So, I'd ordered a pizza and told him I'd be out of the shower by the time it was delivered.

It looked like I had stayed in there a little longer than I planned.

Our eyes connected as I slipped through the sliding glass door.

He said, "I'll call you back." Then, he dropped the phone in his pocket.

I handed him a plate, stuck the now four-pack on the table, and joined him on the couch.

As kids, a bit of silence between us had never felt strange. It didn't mean that we had run out of things to say. It had just felt comfortable.

It didn't feel comfortable at all now.

We sat quietly and ate our pizza as questions started to fly through my head.

Why hadn't he responded when I told him I didn't blame him for the accident? Why hadn't he even acknowledged what I said? Why hadn't he softened at all?

"I won't be mad," I blurted out. "I promise I won't take back anything that I said, but I have to know…"

He turned to face me. The Gulf of Mexico was at least twenty yards in front of us, but his eyes had taken on its color. They were deep blue, almost navy. I could feel their gaze penetrating my clothes.

"Did you know the person who hit us?" I asked.

One, two, three seconds passed. His face remained stoic. He said nothing.

Finally, he took a breath and looked back at the ocean. "No, Kyle, I didn't."

While I was in the hospital, I'd learned that it was a hit-and-run. Garin had given his statement to the police, and the investigation was open. The driver still hadn't been found. But that didn't mean it was a random accident.

"I just wondered if maybe you had seen his face, and it was someone you had a problem with or maybe someone the bosses had an issue with and—"

"It had nothing to do with them."

"Then, why did you have security at the hospital?"

He took a bite of his pizza and washed it down with beer. "There's security wherever I am. It's part of my life now."

I looked out to the empty living room and kitchen. Though I couldn't see out to the front of my house from here, there weren't any headlights shining through the windows. "The driver's still out there?"

# PRISONED

He nodded. "Listen, you were unconscious for eight days. I made sure that the only people who saw you were the ones who could make you better. Once you were awake, who you let in was your decision to make. But while I was in control, it was *mine*."

That was why Anthony hadn't been allowed in before I had woken up. I didn't trust my brother enough for him to see me while I was unconscious. That made me appreciate the security even more.

But it didn't explain why Garin was lacking the warmth I remembered.

I finished the rest of my pizza and then grabbed another beer. I wrapped the cap in my tank top to twist it. It took several tries before I found the strength to get it off. "I always wanted to bring Billy down here." I sipped and stared at the water, surprised by the honesty that was surfacing in me. "Get him out of Atlantic City. Show him the Gulf. Let him feel the sunshine. Get him away from all those people."

"What stopped you?"

"Fear." Guilt was the real reason. "Fear that once he got here, he'd possibly only get worse." More than that, I knew Anthony would have killed me if I'd brought Paulie's brother down here.

"Florida wouldn't have gotten him sober," Garin said.

I looked at him. It had been a few days since he shaved, and his scruff was growing in thick, just like it had in the dream.

"You don't think?"

"Only one thing could have helped that kid."

I blinked hard and swallowed, trying to keep the emotion from showing on my face. That one thing...I knew what it was. I had a role in it. I could have given it to Billy, and he would still be alive. But I was too much of a coward to tell him the truth, to tell anyone the truth.

Garin took the beer out of my hand and placed it back on the table. "Let's go for a walk," he said, holding out his fingers, waiting for me to grasp them.

# THIRTY-ONE

## GARIN
## THIRTEEN DAYS AGO

*Unknown* flashed across my screen, and I answered the call just before it went to voice mail. "You'd better have news," I said, unable to hide the irritation in my voice.

Azzo didn't usually take this long to get back to me. He worked hard and fast and was the best PI in the business, which was why he'd been on the bosses' payroll for the last few years. If information existed, Azzo found it. But the waiting almost fucking killed me.

"I got almost everything you asked for," he said. "I'm sorry it took me an extra day, but what I'm about to tell you will make it worth the wait."

"Give me a second," I said.

I muted the phone and looked over at Mario. There was a naked slut standing behind him, rubbing his shoulders. Another one knelt at his feet, sucking his toes. The whore on the ground was for me. But, when she had shown up, stripping off her clothes to join Mario and me in the sauna, I decided I didn't want her. I didn't have the patience for her soft fingers all over me.

I wanted to break fingers. I wanted to make some skin fucking bleed.

"I'm taking this in your office," I told Mario.

"Do what you need to do," he said.

I left the indoor pool and hustled up the stairs to the first floor, rushing down the hallway until I reached the last door. Then, I locked myself in Mario's office and sat on the ledge in front of the windows. "Speak."

"Mario's guy was right; the hooker he'd seen near the alley when he went to collect the evidence from Billy's body had been around when Billy died. She didn't see the murder, but she had a real soft spot for Billy. She'd fucked him a few times in the last couple of weeks...told me she did it for free, too. She said she was headed to meet up with him, and when she got there, he was already dead."

"Jesus fucking Christ." I remembered the conversation I'd had with Billy about some whore. She was the one who had said Paulie owed her money. "This isn't the same one who supposedly worked for Paulie, is it?"

"One and the same. Call it a strange hunch, but I decided to test a sample of the heroin she had on her and compare it to the residue Mario's guy found in Billy's needle. I hit the fucking jackpot, Garin. The junk was identical; it must have come from the same batch."

"So, they bought it from the same dealer; that tells me nothing."

"Nah," he said, "it tells us *everything* because the hooker doesn't buy it. It's supplied to her from her pimp; that's part of her payment. Here's what we know—the hooker had the same size needle on her that was found in Billy's chest, and she had the exact same heroin."

"Don't fucking tell me it was the hooker."

"I can't prove anything just yet, but she would have taken Billy's cash and his heroin...and both were found on him. I think it was her pimp."

"What's his name?"

"Are you ready for this? It's Anthony Lang."

*That motherfucker.*

# PRISONED

If I weren't at Mario's house, my fist would have shattered the window behind me. I would have punched that goddamn glass until I bled out.

Anthony Lang.

Paulie's best friend.

Kyle's brother.

So, if Azzo's information was right, Paulie had partnered up with Anthony. Something must have gone wrong, and Anthony had killed him. Twelve years later, Anthony found out that Billy was looking into Paulie's murder. Maybe Billy talked to the wrong person; maybe rumors started to spread. I'd warned Billy that either of those could happen. But, somehow, Anthony found out Billy was snooping, and he fucking murdered my best friend.

All I needed was confirmation that it was Anthony, and I would murder him.

"Tell me what you have on Anthony Lang," I said.

"He drives to Tampa, Florida, once a month, always around the first. When he arrives, he goes straight to his sister's house and carries inside a medium-sized black duffel bag. He stays about twenty minutes and leaves with the bag. Then, he goes to his mother's house and stays there until he drives back to New Jersey. Usually, it's a one-night visit. On occasion, it's two nights."

"I need more."

"His sister, Kyle, doesn't have a mortgage on her house. She rents the building her shop is in, and the rent is paid a whole year up front. She has zero debt—no car loan, no student loans, no personal lines of credit. She carries no balance on her credit card. Same with her mother."

I didn't like the sound of that.

I hoped to hell she didn't know.

"The mother's house was purchased less than a week after Paulie's death," he continued. "That was where Kyle lived while she attended college."

Two houses. Both paid for in cash. The first house bought less than a week after Paulie died.

That wasn't a coincidence.

But did Kyle know?

"Tell me about Kyle's business."

"It's moderately successful. She takes a salary of a little less than a hundred grand and reinvests the remainder of the profits back into the business. But, with that salary, she's not buying her Lexus in cash, and she's definitely not buying her house outright."

She was cleaning Anthony's money, filtering it through the business and using it to buy the houses and cars and then burying whatever was left in that duffel bag each month.

That wasn't the Kyle I knew. She only hustled as a kid because she felt guilty for taking so much from Billy and me, and she wanted to contribute. She wasn't the type to get involved with something this large, especially because it crossed into her art.

Art was everything to Kyle.

"Is there a guy in her life? Or is this all from Anthony?"

"She dates, but it doesn't look like anything is ever too serious. The steady man in her life is her brother. Unless they're really good friends, the number of texts she receives from him is on the high side, but she only responds to a small percentage. If I had to guess, she's taking orders."

That was my guess, too.

And it started the night Paulie was murdered. I'd gone over the timeline so many fucking times in my head. Kyle must have been outside, somewhere in the vicinity of her front door, when the gun had gone off. I found it pretty strange that she hadn't come out when I was screaming in the middle of the road, and that she was nowhere to be found later that night when the cops and ambulance left. And that I didn't see her again until the next day.

"There's one more piece of news," he said.

I gritted my teeth. "Let me hear it."

"I hacked into the University of South Florida's system; that's where Kyle went to school. Looks like she applied in person, was interviewed by Admissions, and got early acceptance."

After Paulie died, Kyle had missed two days of school toward the end of that week. I'd banged on her front door, begging her to come out so that I could talk to her. Banged and fucking banged. She wouldn't answer. No one did. The banging went on for weeks, even though Kyle returned to school after those two days.

"Let me guess..." I shut my eyes and shook my head. "She applied less than a week after Paulie's murder?"

# PRISONED

"You got it, man. Airline records show Kyle and Anthony spent two days in Florida. She got into school, he bought the house, and they flew back to Jersey."

I had just talked to Kyle about college, and she hadn't known where she wanted to go at that point. She used to tell me everything, and never once had she mentioned Florida.

That was because she hadn't chosen Florida; it had been chosen for her. Just like the house had been chosen and bought for her. Anthony had probably even slipped the Admissions lady a few bucks to get Kyle in early. Then, she came back to Jersey, I cornered her in the alley, and she never talked to Billy or me again. She graduated and moved to Florida.

All these years later, Anthony was still running her goddamn life.

Kyle knew.

Maybe she even saw it.

And I was going to get her to confess.

"I don't have any evidence that puts Anthony in that alley when Billy died or in The Heart at the time of Paulie's murder," Azzo said. "Not yet anyway."

"I'll get the evidence."

"If you're looking to get it from Kyle, I can save you a trip to Florida. She'll be at Billy's funeral."

"You're shitting me."

"Why else would she be flying into Atlantic City tomorrow and traveling back the following day? I'll email you her flight and hotel information."

She was coming straight to me. I'd finally get to look her in the face again.

I'd get to put my hands on her. I'd get to hear either the truth or a lie.

If it was a lie, she was going to be punished.

And she would suffer.

Oh, would she fucking suffer, all right.

"Good work, Azzo. Guessing the hooker wants compensation? And whoever else you had to convince?"

"It's all been covered by the bosses' petty cash, but I'll send you an itemized list in case you want to reimburse them."

"I'd appreciate that."

The bosses paid for a lot, which was one of the perks of running their casino. But this had nothing to do with them. This was on me. And I'd make sure Mario knew that I would pay back every dollar that had been spent.

"I'll be in touch," Azzo said.

And we both hung up.

I paced Mario's office as I put all the pieces together.

Kyle would be coming into town tomorrow and likely spending most of her time with Anthony. I had to come up with a plan that would get her away from him, so I could get an answer out of her.

But I didn't have much time.

When I walked back into the indoor pool room, both girls were on their knees, taking turns giving Mario head. He gripped one by the hair and rubbed the other's tit. His eyes drifted up to mine as the door slammed behind me.

"I need your help," I barked.

He pulled his cock out of the whore's mouth and covered himself with the towel. "Get out," he said to them. When they didn't move fast enough, he snapped, "Fucking hurry!"

They rushed out and closed the door, and he stood from the chair and walked over to me.

He had the biggest goddamn grin on his face—the same one he wore whenever he got to pull out his gun. "Who do I get to kill tonight?"

# THIRTY-TWO

## KYLE

As I walked along the edge of the water, the beer tingled and heated my body; my tolerance had been wiped out from my stay in the hospital. In the short time we'd been gone, I'd taken Garin past the eight homes that surrounded the small alcove that I lived on, down to our private beach where there was the most perfect view of the Sunshine Skyway Bridge. At night, the massive structure was lit up a bright yellow, filling the dark sky with an almost eerie glow. Between that and the moon reflecting off the water, it gave us just enough light to see where we were walking.

When we reached the end of the beach, I stopped and slid off my flip-flops. And then I took in the whole view, including Garin's profile, as I dunked my feet in the water.

During my dream about the cell, I hadn't thought I'd ever see this bridge again, that I'd ever feel the smooth liquid ocean or the rough sand beneath my feet. Even though the prison hadn't been real, it felt like I was being given a second chance at life.

And I needed to appreciate it.

"Can we stay here for a minute?" I asked.

I waited for him to nod before I squatted down on the sand, slipping my legs out in front of me, digging my fingers into a large mound. Garin stood a few feet away, his profile sharp as he looked out toward the water.

The things I'd learned about him in the cell were just random bits of information. They weren't real; they definitely weren't the truth. It was hard to wrap my head around that. Even though I felt like I knew so much, I really knew nothing at all. But I wanted to. I wanted to know everything—what his life was like now, what I had missed in the twelve years that had passed. What was making him so cold beyond the way I had ended our relationship. Nothing I tried had warmed him. But I didn't deserve his warmth. I wanted it anyway. I wanted so much more than that.

"What are you thinking about?" he asked.

"You." I slowly looked up from the sand, not realizing he'd been watching me.

The moonlight glinted off the outline of his thick, coarse scruff and his narrowed eyelids. It illuminated his parted lips. I wondered if it showed my guilt, too.

There was so much of it that I'd been hiding. I needed a break from it. I just wanted to feel something other than the constant pain of what I'd seen, of what I'd done.

My mind brought me back to the dream, to the moment when his mouth had been on my body. Those lips, those fingers—they had made me forget. The way he looked at me, the way he kissed me—that had been my relief. I needed that closeness again. I needed to remind him of that moment outside the restroom at the bar.

I needed to make him want me as much as I wanted him.

"Come here." I held my hand out. "Will you sit?"

He stood, looking down at me while the silence passed between us. He was making me wait, which made me question what he was going to do. That only made the guilt grow.

Why was I doing this to myself?

Why was I craving more when I knew I couldn't have it, especially when I couldn't stop lying to him?

# PRISONED

I'd come out of the coma, thinking I'd told Garin the truth. In reality, the truth had never been spoken.

I wished it had.

But that would have meant everything that happened in the cell was real. That the truth had been tortured out of me, and somehow my life had been spared.

How could I wish to have gone through all of that?

What was wrong with me?

Garin finally sat down next to me, his shoes pushing across the sand as he stretched out his legs. Now that he was closer, the moonlight showed me more of his face, but I didn't need additional light to see how beautiful this man was. His face was an image that wouldn't ever leave my mind. It hadn't in all these years. But now that he had grown into a man, there was a roughness that came with him, an intensity that burned in his eyes, and the most tantalizing curve in his lips.

I couldn't hide what it all made me feel.

I turned toward him and crossed my legs. He leaned back a few inches, moonlight flashing across his hands and a breeze passing through the air. It sent me a whiff of his cologne, a scent I'd been devouring the last couple of days. For the briefest of moments, I closed my eyes, imagining those hands on my body, his scent covering me, his mouth moving across my skin.

His lips.

His tongue.

I took a breath, my lungs not filling as easily as they had in the hospital, and I opened my eyes. "While I was in that coma, my mind took me somewhere. It was a place. A dark place..."

He didn't move. He just stared and listened. His silence was haunting.

"It was a place no one would ever want to visit and no one should ever have to see. But I was there for a reason, and I deserved to be there."

My mind was taking me back to the night I had been in Garin's room, the night Paulie had died, and I was trying to tell him how badly I wanted him. At that time in our lives, I'd always been so honest with him, but telling him how I felt, telling him I wanted more was one of the hardest things I'd ever done. This was even harder.

"You were in that dream, too, Garin. I told you in the hospital that you had protected me, and that's true, but there's more. You were there to show me what I could have had, had my life gone differently." My eyes drifted toward the water; it was easier to look at. "This is going to sound crazy. I shouldn't even think this, let alone say it…"

"You want to go back to the dream."

I squeezed my eyes shut. His words only added to the dirtiness of that thought.

"Yes."

"Tell me why."

I dug my nails into my palms. Admitting this wasn't enough of a punishment. I needed more…I needed pain. "Because I could touch you whenever I wanted. I could tell you how I felt. I could feel you, and I didn't have to let you go. It was just you and me and endless darkness." Finally, I looked up again, and our eyes locked. "I was given a choice, and this time, I chose you."

"This time?"

"Yes. This time." My voice was just above a whisper. "I wanted to before. I wanted it with everything I had. But I couldn't. I had to leave."

It felt like I was back in that alley again, cornered by Garin, telling him nothing but lies to protect my brother. But my brother would point a gun at me and pull the trigger as easily as he had pulled it on Paulie.

"Why?"

"I had to."

"Why, Kyle?"

Here was my chance to tell him the truth. So, why couldn't I do it? It had taken a dream full of torture—torture I believed to be so real at the time—and the threat on Garin's life to make me cave last time. What would it take this time?

Anthony holding a gun to my head?

Or worse…Anthony murdering Garin?

Because, once tomorrow morning came, all of that would be possible.

And, if Anthony didn't kill me, I would go back to being his investment, a way to filter all his cash to make it clean. My payment was an education, a house, and a business. I wasn't grateful. I was miserable.

And I was loyal to a man who didn't give a shit about me. A man who had sucked out all my happiness to cover all his evil.

"Because I *had* to," I said.

"And what do you want now?"

Speaking the word that was in my heart would make this so much harder. But how could I hide it? How could I live with more regret?

"You."

The sound that came from him was a mix between a grunt and a laugh. And then came movement. His knees bent, and his hands moved behind him...even farther away from me.

Was I crazy to want this man? To crave what we had once almost had? To yearn for his coldness because it was better to feel that than nothing at all?

I couldn't control my hands anymore. I reached forward and wrapped them around his calf. Even though his jeans were thick, the heat from his skin poured through the fabric.

His stare intensified.

I slid my hands up to his knee. "I have so many regrets, Garin. I can't live with another."

Everything was so dimly lit, like the cell, and a little chilly from the winter night. But touching him here felt different. The cold was different. The sensation under my fingers was different.

But the pounding in my chest was identical.

"Is this what you want, Kyle?" His hands were suddenly on my throat. His grip was tight. His skin felt like it was scorching mine. "You want to feel me?"

He knelt in front of me, pushing me onto my back. Once I was flat, he hovered over me.

I had a hard time breathing. "Yes," I finally answered.

"That's all you want?"

My mind took me back to the hallway outside the restroom, to the cement floor inside the cell when Garin was peeling off my clothes. The dream and my reality were overlapping, and I couldn't stop it inside my brain. But here, on this beach, it was just us. Nobody walking by on their way to the bathroom, no Breath, no Beard. Just darkness with the feeling of the sand beneath me and the sound of the waves in front of me. His exhales filled me with his scent, his body almost covering me.

"I want more," I said.

He came a little closer and sucked my bottom lip into his mouth, his teeth grinding into it. He'd done that in the cell. It had felt so good then; it felt even better now. "Can your body take more of a beating? Because I'll hurt you, Kyle."

"Hurt me."

His other hand gripped the top of my tank, both hands now tightening in different spots, my breathing only getting worse. "I don't know how to be gentle."

"Then, don't be," I panted.

"I've wanted to fuck you for so long, to feel your cunt dripping over my cock. I almost want to punish you for making me wait all these years."

He was as gritty as he had been inside the prison, as dirty, as feral. And I was as turned on as I'd ever been. I didn't want to wait until we got back to my house where there was a cozy bed waiting for us. I wanted him here, on this beach, right now.

"The wait has been my punishment. Give me what I want, Garin."

I heard the fabric rip as he shredded my tank top right down the center. Then, he unhooked the front clasp of my bra, stripping it off me.

*"This body...how did you keep it away from me for so long?"*

As I heard his voice from inside the cell, I moaned, "Garin..."

His hands left my body roughly to take off his shirt, yanking it over his head. When they returned, one of them squeezed my nipple while the other held my face still. From the way he was positioned, my arms were pinned down to my sides. I couldn't drag him closer. I couldn't use my fingers to emphasize what I wanted. I couldn't touch him.

"Kiss me," I demanded.

The moonlight streaked across his face, showing me that his eyes were locked with mine. I felt the need, the desire. And I felt his hesitation, as though he were battling something deep inside the same way I was.

"Kiss me—"

His lips crashed against mine before I even finished speaking, and I moaned again. I had his tongue in my mouth, his scent in my nose, his body on top of me. It caused the deepest, strongest, fiercest throbbing in my clit.

# PRISONED

As he adjusted me beneath him, his movements were so rough that I winced. I was sore. My skin hurt. My muscles had ached since the hospital. If he heard me, he didn't stop. He didn't lighten up at all.

I didn't want him to.

I never wanted him to.

*"I've wanted to fuck you for more than half of my life. Do you know what that kind of want does to you after a while?"*

I knew. And I felt it, too.

He shimmied my pants down and unhooked his belt, pulling his jeans just low enough that his cock sprung free. I wasn't able to see it; I only felt it slap against my pussy. Then, in one swift, furious movement, he was fully inside me.

"Oh my God!" I screamed.

I wasn't at all prepared for his size, how he filled me completely, how it caused quick flashes of pain. I wasn't prepared for this level of closeness and how much I would cherish it. I definitely wasn't prepared for how much power he had and how much he used when he stroked me.

I didn't tell him to stop.

Garin fucked me like there was an anger inside him. Like his anger made him drive his hips into me, dig his teeth into my flesh, press his fingers into my body. Like he wanted his anger to spill into me.

I would take it. All of it. I deserved it.

And I would enjoy it.

My pussy had finally stretched just enough so that I no longer felt any pain. His hand was off my throat, so I could breathe. I wrapped my legs around his waist. His long, hard, dominant thrusts took over me. He didn't pull out to the tip; he just went halfway and shoved back in. And it didn't happen slowly or gently. There was nothing gentle about this.

"Is this what you wanted?" He didn't wait for me to answer. He just lifted me off the sand and flipped me around, putting me on all fours. Then, he gripped my hips, angling me to his head, as he forced himself back inside.

I tasted sand on my lips as I licked them. "Yes."

This new position seemed to open me up even more, allowing him in deeper. The pain returned, but it was the good kind—the kind that added to the pleasure. And it caused me to shout even louder.

"Am I going to break you?"

My ribs ached from where the drain had been. My muscles threatened to no longer hold me, but I didn't want him to stop. I wanted him to know I could handle whatever he wanted to give me.

He didn't wait for my answer. He just pushed me onto my stomach, taking all the weight away from my limbs, and drove into me with so much power I couldn't stop screaming.

"Am I going to fucking break you, Kyle?" he growled in my ear.

There was nothing to hold on to. The sand slipped through my fingers. The rocks and shells were too small. All I had was the chilly air, the darkness surrounding us, and the incessant pounding of his massive cock.

"No," I panted.

"Then, I'm not fucking you hard enough."

He positioned me just the way he wanted and rocked into me harder than I ever thought I could take. I didn't need to put my fingers on my clit, rubbing it in circles to make the build start. The friction between us was enough, the added closeness, the way he took command of my body, the feeling of him on me.

He gnawed on my neck, chewing the skin around the side of my throat, and across my shoulder. "So fucking tight," he groaned. "And so wet."

The power increased in his thrusting, in his biting.

I couldn't move. I was paralyzed with pleasure, with pain, and both were spreading throughout my entire body.

"Garin, I'm so close…"

I found myself in the air again as he flipped me onto my back. My lungs had a chance to fill, my muscles a moment to relax, but it didn't last long. Seconds later, his power and size were driving right back into me.

"I want you to look at me when you come," he demanded. His thumb landed on my clit, circling my swollen bud.

I moaned so loud that it shook my chest. "Oh my God."

Each time he rocked his hips forward, his abs constricted. They were as tight as they had been in the cell, and the hair on his body was just the way I had dreamed it. He stayed fully inside me, his hips now swiveling, reaching that spot so deep, so sensitive. I knew it wouldn't take much more movement before I was coming.

"Garin..."

"You want more?"

He took my moan as a response, and suddenly, his hand was at my other hole, a hole he had entered in the dream. It was just another similarity that felt as carnal as before.

"Jesus fucking Christ, Kyle. Your ass is *so* tight."

"That feels"—his entire finger was in me, plunging in the same speed as his cock—"so good."

His movements changed again. They became sharp, hard. So deep. And then there was his sounds, his throaty groans. His growling.

I couldn't get enough of it. My body couldn't either.

"Garin," I moaned, "I'm going to come."

His hand left my clit for a second as he pulled me on top of him, but his finger stayed in my ass, his cock in my pussy. I landed upright, straddling his waist, holding his shoulders so that I wouldn't fall.

"Ride the cum out of me."

I bounced up and down on his dick. The fullness was just what I needed. The stimulation on every sensitive part was what brought me to the edge.

"Garin!" I shouted as the burst blasted through me. Just as my navel began to shudder, I felt his long, thick streams of cum enter me.

He rubbed my clit until the screams stopped. Then, he locked his hand around the base of my neck until I had pumped everything out of him. When we both stilled, his face dropped to my breast, his cheek pressing right over my nipple. It was the softest he'd been since my clothes had come off. The very first bit of tenderness I'd felt from him.

He grazed his whiskers over my skin, scraping each of the cuts that the glass window had left. Then, he kissed the same spots. Once his lips had covered them all, he lifted me off him and pulled up his pants and then his shirt.

"Here," he said, handing me my clothes. "Get dressed, and I'll carry you home."

"You don't have to."

"You're bleeding, Kyle."

The light hit him just enough that I saw the blood on his face. It was on his scruff, and there was a swipe of it over his lips. I looked down and saw it was all over my breast, and there were streaks of it on my chest. I didn't know where it had come from—if he'd bitten me or if one of my scabs had opened up.

It didn't matter.

I was such a mess either way.

"Come on, Kyle."

I slipped my arms through the bra straps, wiggled my pants on, threw the shredded tank over my shoulder, and clasped my fingers around his hand. I was only on my feet for a second before he lifted me into his arms.

I didn't say a word. I didn't make a sound. I just tucked my face into his neck and took a deep breath while he walked us home.

# THIRTY-THREE

## KYLE

*"The only thing we have inside this cell is words, Kyle. Don't hold them back from me."*

That line kept repeating in my head. I couldn't get it to stop. I heard it while I was in the shower. I heard it again when I climbed into bed. I even heard it when Garin slipped under the covers, his skin still wet from his shower.

We hadn't spoken much since the beach. He hadn't touched me again. He hadn't asked if I wanted him to sleep in my bed. He just walked out of the bathroom, naked, and got in. He lay on his back and folded his arms under his head.

I didn't want him to leave in the morning. I wanted to tell him that, but I couldn't. I wanted to be with him, but I couldn't tell him that either.

There was no future, no *us*.

Why couldn't I just accept that?

These were the same thoughts that had haunted me in the cell. They hurt even worse out here because I was lying in a bed that could possibly be ours. One that I could share with him forever.

But there were bars between us.

Bars I had created.

I just had to tell him what I wanted.

And I had to tell him what he needed to hear.

"Billy didn't OD," he said.

And then, suddenly, it felt like his hands were back on my throat. But, this time, there was no give; he was squeezing to strangle every bit of air out of me.

I couldn't breathe.

"What do you mean?" The air shuddered out of my lungs. My heart pounded like it was going to break through my skin.

"He was murdered."

No…not again. Garin had to be wrong about Billy's death. Billy was a junkie; he had overdosed on heroin. That was what Anthony had told me. That was what people had said at the funeral.

"I thought they found a needle in him?"

"The needle was in his heart, Kyle. We both know that isn't where an addict shoots up."

I'd seen Billy use plenty of needles in the past. I knew how he prepped; I knew where he injected. His heart definitely wasn't one of those places.

My stomach started to churn.

"So, if Billy didn't do it then…" I had a feeling I already knew the answer to that question. I may have been silent, but inside my head, I was screaming.

"Billy was looking into Paulie's death," he said. "I think he found something out, and I think whoever killed Paulie killed Billy because of that."

Why would my brother do this? I wanted to ask Anthony, but I feared the truth.

The truth would mean I would have to hold in another secret.

I couldn't take another.

I couldn't handle more guilt than I already carried.

# PRISONED

Anthony knew that. He knew I had barely kept it together at Paulie's funeral, and Billy's would have been even worse had I known he had killed again.

"The bosses are looking into it," Garin said. "They'll find the murderer, whoever the fuck he is, and they'll gut him for this."

The bosses would find Anthony. They would kill him. And then they would bury him, so he wouldn't ever be found.

He would finally get what he deserved.

But what about me?

It had only been a few seconds between admitting the truth to Breath and having that needle stuck in my neck, but during that short amount of time, the weight of my guilt had been gone, my conscience cleared.

If I told Garin about Anthony, I would be in that position once more.

I would be facing death, and Garin would more than likely be pulling the trigger.

I sat up and tucked my knees into my chest, hiding my face between them. As I tried to find some air and calm the pounding in my heart, I rocked back and forth.

"Kyle?"

I didn't answer him. I didn't look up.

"Kyle, tell me what's wrong."

"I..." My voice sounded like a whisper. "I can't...breathe."

His hand slipped inside the cave I had made, and it clasped around my chin, slowly lifting, as I made my way out of the darkness. "Did Billy trigger this?"

When I opened my mouth, he pulled me on top of him. I was straddling his lap, his hands gripping high on my throat, but he wasn't squeezing. He was just holding me there, so I couldn't move. I felt his stare through my whole body.

"Tell me."

"Nothing. I—"

"Then, tell me what was on your mind that night in the bar before you disappeared into the restroom."

I tried to remember when we had been sitting at the table together. The details were cloudy, but they began to surface through the fog.

*"Even when I slept, I always wanted to be close to you. And then I left your apartment, and I just couldn't stay anymore. It hurt too much. I struggled so much with it, and I was only..."*

*I was only a witness*, I had wanted to say. But I didn't have the courage. And because he had wanted an answer and I couldn't give him one, I had rushed off to the restroom.

"I don't remember."

"I don't believe you." When I tried to look down, he stopped me. "There was something you wanted to tell me that night, and there's something you want to say to me right now. Stop holding back."

*"The only thing we have inside this cell is words, Kyle. Don't hold them back from me."*

My eyes scanned his. The air hadn't returned, and I was starting to get light-headed. My limbs were all tingling. I didn't know if I would have a voice, so I whispered, "I can't."

"I won't hurt you."

He wouldn't hurt me...until he found out I had been lying to him, until he found out what I had been lying about. But how much longer could I let this eat at me?

And how many more people would die because of Anthony?

# THIRTY-FOUR

## GARIN
## TWELVE DAYS AGO

I sucked Kyle's lip into my mouth, so she would stop biting it. "I want to torture this fucking lip," I said. "Let's get the hell out of here."

"And go where?"

I kissed around her cheek. "To a place where I can give your body everything it needs." I set her back on her feet, still keeping her against the wall in the hallway, and moved my hands to her throat. I squeezed just enough to show her how serious I was but not enough to scare her. I'd tried that earlier. For only a second, fear had passed through her eyes. Then, she had seemed to fucking love it, moaning even when I'd tightened my grip.

She liked it rough.

That was the way she was going to get it, too. Nice and fucking rough. After all those years of waiting, I was going to tear up her pussy when I finally got a piece of it. But I wouldn't be tasting it tonight.

Tonight, I had something else planned.

She grabbed my hand and brought me outside, to where the car was parked. Fuck, she was making this so easy on me. She'd been in it earlier when I drove us to the bar. But, while we were inside, one of the bosses' mechanics had stopped by. He made sure the car was ready for what was going to happen to it.

"My feet hurt," she whined as she got into the passenger seat.

I started the car and shifted into reverse. "Take your shoes off."

She put her bare feet on the dash and turned up the radio, rubbing the back of my neck with her nails. She was dancing in her seat and singing, her hand going lower into the collar of my shirt.

I wished I didn't like the feel of her.

I liked it too fucking much.

I took her fingers off me and pointed at the seat belt. "Put it on."

She wouldn't be wearing it for long. But, for now, it needed to keep her safe before it was ripped from her body.

She laughed like I was messing with her and buckled it over her chest. "Where are you staying *again*? I can't remember if you told me."

It was all working just the way I wanted it to.

"You'll remember the place when you see it."

But she'd never see it.

"Do we *have* to wait until we get there?" She leaned across the seat and kissed the side of my face, her mouth dropping to my neck and back to the corner of my mouth.

I smelled the sweet scent of the alcohol, but underneath it was the scent I really remembered. How could a single smell bring back so many goddamn memories?

*Fuck, Kyle...*

I wanted to pull over, lift her out of the car, slam her on the pavement, and ask her why the hell she had done this. I wanted to tell her how serious this was and to really put the fear in her.

But it was too late for that.

"You want my cock right now?" I moved away from her mouth, so I could see her face.

"*Yes*," she moaned. "Right now."

Her eyelids told me she was almost where I wanted her.

She rested her head on my chest and rubbed her hand over my abs. "God, Garin, you're so much bigger now. So *hard* and muscular." The slurring was getting old, but it wasn't her fault. She wasn't in control anymore. "I'm *so* sleepy."

She was asleep a few seconds later.

As I reached the red light, I pushed her back into her own seat. She slumped against the window, her head leaning into the glass. She clung to the door like it was a fucking pillow.

I took out my phone and hit the number that had been texted to me.

"You good?" a guy said after the first ring.

"Yeah," I answered. "I'm good."

"How long?"

"I'll be there in ten minutes. Get the car ready."

Before I shoved the phone back in my pocket, I pulled up Azzo's text. He had sent a picture about an hour ago that showed the inside of the safe that he'd found in Kyle's closet. He'd told me about it when we talked earlier, but now, I was able to get a look at the masterpiece Anthony had built. The safe was the entire height of the wall and at least five feet wide. It was custom-made and foolproof unless Azzo was the one trying to unlock it. The entire thing was filled with cash. Azzo estimated there was over a million in there.

Under the picture, he typed that he'd left things just the way he found them. He shut the safe, wiped down Kyle's house, and turned her alarm back on.

I was the one who'd given him the code.

The girl may have left The Heart, but there were things about her that hadn't changed at all.

I put my phone away and glanced at her again. She looked so fucking beautiful when she slept. Shit, had things not ended the way they did, had I not been tipped off, she could have been my wife.

But things hadn't gone that way.

And, now, as I looked back at the road, I saw the headlights up ahead. Three quick flashes, telling me it was him.

I ground my fingers over the cheap leather of the steering wheel and leaned over the seat, pressing my lips to Kyle's ear.

"Take a deep breath, baby. This is your last smell of freedom."

# THIRTY-FIVE

## KYLE

"I won't hurt you," Garin repeated, as though I hadn't heard him the first time.

I was straddling his lap, his breath hitting my lips, his stare trying to pull the truth out of me. It was impossible not to hear him. I just didn't believe what he'd said. And I knew that, once he found out the truth, he was most definitely going to hurt me.

But I couldn't let my fear keep me from doing what was right.

Not anymore.

Billy was the second person Anthony had murdered. I was the only one who knew it was him. I had to put a stop to it.

I climbed off Garin's lap and let my feet drop to the floor. The moonlight showed his eyes, his lips. I reached the sliding door that led out to the balcony, leaning my shoulder into the glass. This spot had the best view of the water, and if it was going to be my last time seeing it, I wanted to be as close as possible.

There was no breath to be found. No air.

Just words.

And those words needed to describe when Anthony had put up the first bar of my prison.

"I saw Paulie when I walked out of your apartment that night..."

I was suddenly no longer in my room. I was in The Heart. It was night; there was total blackness, and I saw Paulie from the glow of his cell phone. He went to his car, and I heard his footsteps...his breathing.

Every detail was coming back to me.

I just let them pour out.

When I reached the part where Anthony demanded I get in his car, I wrapped my arms around my stomach and slid to the floor. I was in the corner between the mattress and the windows, and Garin was looking down at me from the bed, just like I had sat and waited in his room all those years ago. But as I looked up, it was Anthony peering out from the car, and I was clinging to the side of the tire. My eyes were shifting between Paulie's blood and Anthony's blacked-out window.

But there was no blood and no window. It was just Garin, the moonlight, and the intensity of his eyes. He didn't make a sound.

I hadn't said Anthony's name. I'd referred to him as *he*.

"I want to rewind my life, Garin." I tucked myself into a small ball. "I want to go back to that moment and not get in his car. I want to run to your apartment and take whatever those consequences were—whether he tried to shoot me or run after me. I just want to do it all over and not hide anything from you this time. And I want to tell you all of it." I tried to take a breath even though I couldn't, even though it felt like the room was closing in on me and I wouldn't be able to push my way out.

"I want to tell my younger self that twelve years' worth of guilt wasn't worth it because I was protecting a person who didn't deserve to be protected." I wrapped my arms tighter around my legs, and I rocked, my nails pressing so hard into my elbows that I could feel them piercing my skin. "It was Anthony. He killed Paulie, and I'm positive he killed Billy, too."

"That motherfucker."

That told me everything I needed to know.

Garin was murderous.

But I wasn't done. He needed to know the rest.

# PRISONED

I picked up the story from the moment I got into Anthony's car and took Garin through the entire ride until Anthony dropped me off much later that night. I told him about the threats. The rules. The orders. I told him about our trip to Florida later that week when I had gotten into college and when Anthony had bought his first house.

"He wanted me out of Atlantic City," I said. "I was his only witness, so he dumped me in a place where I knew no one and where no one knew us. If he could have gotten me to drop out of high school, he would have. But graduating was my only stipulation. Everything else he wanted from me, I would do."

I ended by telling Garin about the financials and how I cleaned Anthony's money and all the assets he had paid for over the years, including my business, both houses, and the cars. And about the safe that was in my closet, only a few feet from us.

"I don't know how much is in there," I said, grinding my toes into the carpet. "I don't have the code, and I've never seen inside. He doesn't allow me to, and honestly, I don't want to."

He hadn't said a word since I'd mentioned Anthony's name. He hadn't moved. The silence should have worried me, and it did, but there was so much relief, too. The anxiety and dread and guilt I had been holding in for twelve years had spilled out of me. Garin now knew it all—the reason I had treated him so badly in that alley, why things had ended between us before they ever really began, why I had left Atlantic City.

"I'm not trying to justify any of this," I added, squeezing my knees into my chest, tucking my chin between them. "I should have told you; there's no excuse for that. All I can say is, he's my brother. I'll never be able to fully explain the kind of loyalty I felt to him. You know I wasn't close to my mom, and he was the only other family I had, despite how he treated me. All the threats and the intimidation."

Still, he said nothing.

"I know what happened to Billy was because of me. My silence is the reason he's dead. That's something I have to live with for the rest of my life—however short my life is going to be now. But there are no more secrets. I've told you everything."

Several seconds passed before he said, "You didn't kill Paulie; Anthony did. And he killed Billy, too." His tone was deep, but he didn't snap at me. If anything, he sounded sympathetic.

"But, Garin—"

"Don't put that on yourself."

He stood from the bed and walked over to the corner. My eyes followed him the entire way. They didn't warn me; they didn't make me fear the closeness between us. When he reached me, he put his hand out for me to grab.

"Come here," he said.

I clasped my fingers around his and followed him to the bed where I sat next to him. My mind quickly brought me back to that night in his room when he had done almost the same thing. But, here, Garin didn't say another word.

The desire to touch him was unbearable, so I placed my fingers on his shoulder, and I waited for him to push them off. When he didn't, I slowly moved up to his face and ran my fingers over his cheek. If this was going to be the last time, I wanted to memorize the feel of his skin—the soft areas and the ones that were rough.

"Garin," I whispered, my palms now cupping his cheeks, "I've loved you my entire life. Leaving you was torture. I wanted to be with you. I wanted to give myself to you. I wanted to move to Vegas with you and never let you go. Getting in Anthony's car to drive to Florida…"

I remembered the tears I had cried the whole way. I remembered the verbal abuse and the threats Anthony had spewed at me.

"It was just awful." The pain was coming through in my voice. "I never stopped thinking about you. I looked you up on social media. I followed your life as much as I could from a distance. And then seeing you again at Billy's funeral, those feelings resurfaced. They never went away. *Never.* But there was so much guilt. I knew when we were kissing at the bar that I could never be what you wanted while I held in this secret and lied to you. I didn't deserve you. But that didn't stop me from wanting more from you."

I suddenly felt how clammy my hands were. "I know there are consequences to what I did. I've known that all along. If I worked for the bosses, they would kill me for lying to them. So, I have a good idea what you're going to do to me."

My heartbeat sped up as I waited for him to respond. The sweat on my hands turned to ice. The tightening in my chest made it even harder to breathe.

"I'm not going to kill you."

# PRISONED

The vibration of his words passed through me, but it didn't bring any relief. There were other consequences besides death…things that would hurt just as much because I'd be alive to feel them.

"But?"

"I fucking hate that you didn't tell me."

His hands went to my waist, and he held me tighter than he ever had. His touch would leave a bruise. I didn't care.

"I hate that you lied and kept it a secret. I don't ever give second chances, Kyle."

My body began to shake as I prepared myself for how this was going to end.

"But I understand why you did it. I can't agree with it, but I get it. And, now, I'd be the liar if I said I didn't feel something for you."

"You…*do?*"

More coldness passed through his eyes. More anger. But then something changed. Something that caught me off guard.

"I do," he said.

I never expected this. I never expected him to understand any of it. I certainly never expected for him to have feelings for me after I came clean.

"Garin, I don't even know what to say—"

Suddenly, I found myself in the air.

# THIRTY-SIX

## GARIN
## PRESENT DAY

I lifted Kyle and pulled her onto my lap, holding her face still while she settled.

*This fucking girl.*

She had finally told *me* the truth, and all it had taken was a little bit of pushing. I didn't have to hurt her. I didn't even have to beg.

But her confession came after years of lies—lies right after Paulie's murder, lies when I'd cornered her in the alley, lies when I'd asked her in the bar, lies up until this very moment.

It had taken everything that had gone down since Billy's funeral—a hospital stay, a plane ride, dinner, a walk, and a fuck on the beach—but the truth had finally come.

I'd never planned on giving her a second chance. Hell, I'd never intended for her to live this long. But the way she had looked at me, how she silently pleaded for me to touch her, how she just wanted me to wrap her up and protect her—it got to me. It burrowed right under that cold, bitter, angriness that I had felt toward her for so long.

So, I'd made myself a deal. If she had the balls to lie to my face again, I'd kill her. But if she told me the truth, I'd spare her life.

I hadn't planned on forgiving her.

I sure as fuck hadn't planned on falling in love with her.

But both had happened.

Shit, the second I saw her all cut up and bloody, the feelings I'd had came straight back.

The situation and what we had gone through wasn't traditional. The deal Mario had helped me broker wasn't either. Kyle should have been dead right now.

She was the first to ever survive.

The first to see the other side of a plan like the one Mario and I had set up.

Saving her was against what everyone wanted. Mario gave me a fucking earful about it. I didn't care what anyone thought, I didn't care about the risks, and I didn't care how much it was going to cost me. I owed big for this one, and I paid up.

The minute I saw all of Kyle's guilt, I knew it was worth it. And when I gave her my cock down at that beach and felt her unravel in pleasure, I definitely knew I'd made the right decision.

All those wasted years because of Anthony, that sick motherfucker. The drugs had gotten to him. The money had gotten to him. And the greed had gotten to him. I'd seen it happen to plenty of guys in the past. No one had fallen as hard as Anthony Lang. And no one had taken out my friends like he had.

I could have made the same deal for him that I had originally made for Kyle, but that wouldn't have been as satisfying. Every time I visited Atlantic City and walked past the boardwalk, I wanted to know his bones had been ground into powder and sprinkled over the sand.

And that was going to happen soon enough.

I continued to hold Kyle's face and stared into her eyes. I could tell she didn't know. If she had, she wouldn't have been looking at me the same way. But that was okay; we all had secrets. It had taken Kyle twelve years to voice hers.

Maybe it would take me just as long to tell her mine.

"If you would have told me back then, I would have protected you," I said. "Nothing would have happened to you. I would have made sure of that."

I saw the guilt hit her, and she tried to look away. I wouldn't let her. There was no more looking away. It was just us now. So, I tipped her chin up and pointed her lips toward mine.

"I'm sorry," she whispered. "I'll be saying that for the rest of my life."

"I don't want you to. It's over. Behind us. We don't have to talk about it again."

"But what about us? You said you have feelings. What exactly does that mean?"

Her voice was so small I could feel her nerves. That was just the opposite from the way she had acted on the beach, almost reaching through my jeans to grab my cock.

"I have something I need to take care of first."

"Of course. I should have figured that," she said. "You live in Vegas, and I'm here and—"

"No, that's not what I meant, Kyle." I leaned my head down, so I could taste her mouth. "I was talking about your brother."

"Oh...right."

"Anthony is fucking dead."

She opened her mouth and shut it real quick.

"You had to know that when you came out with the truth. You don't get to kill people I care about and get away with it."

"I know."

"Did he ever hurt you?"

"No."

I held her face tighter. "Did he ever hurt you, Kyle?"

"No. I would tell you. There isn't anything I wouldn't tell you at this point."

I could feel that she was telling me the truth. Her pulse was steady; she held eye contact. I didn't think I'd have a problem with her lying to me again.

"When are you leaving?" she asked.

After dropping us off in Florida, my pilot had immediately flown back to Vegas. He wasn't out of hours. I just needed a reason to spend more time with her and get the truth out of her. The hospital wasn't the right place for that. She was there to heal.

Florida was the right place, and it had worked.

"Do you want me here for a few more days?" I asked.

"I want that so badly."

So did I. I wanted to spend those days with my face between her legs. What had happened on the beach was too quick; it didn't give me a chance to taste her. But, now, I would have the time.

And why the fuck should I wait another second?

"Do you know what I want?" I asked.

"What?"

I lifted her off my lap and set her on the bed, wedging myself between her thighs. Her shorts were in my way, so I ripped them off her legs and moved my mouth to her cunt.

"Garin," she moaned, grabbing my hair and pulling it.

"Do you want me to stop?"

"Oh God, no."

I swiped my tongue over her clit. She was so turned on that it was already a little swollen. And the taste of it was so goddamn good. I gave her more, flicking the tip of my tongue from side to side. She grabbed the blanket with both hands and lifted it off the bed while her legs spread, and her hips bucked.

This was the sexiest I'd ever seen her.

I stuck a finger into her pussy and felt it clench around my knuckle. "Do you want more, baby?"

"Yes," she groaned.

I gave her a second finger and one in her ass. I liked being back in there again. That tight hole was just begging for my cock. Begging to be spread and fucked so hard.

She'd get it.

She'd get every inch of it…because I knew she could handle it.

In my head, I laughed at the thought.

But in front of me, I watched her arch her back and rock her pussy against my mouth.

I could feel how close she was, and I wanted to give her the orgasm she deserved. There was no reason to punish her and not let her get off, especially when she had been such a good girl today.

So, I licked her harder. I finger-fucked her faster.

# PRISONED

And I felt her come against my mouth.

When she finally stopped moving, I slowly swiped my tongue across her again. I wanted to make sure I got everything that seeped out of her before I swallowed it down.

"Wow." She looked at me from between her legs. "When I was in the coma, I had dreamed of you doing that. But…just…wow."

Of course she had.

I didn't ask her which one was better.

I knew.

# THIRTY-SEVEN

## KYLE

"Hey, Kyle?" One of my employees opened my office door and poked her head through the crack. "The Snyders are thinking they want to go black and white for the wedding colors—"

"Silver font," I said, not bothering to look toward the door to see who was asking or even letting her finish because I already knew the question. It was always the same question. Over and over. "Put their names in script, and keep the rest of the invitation in serif. Make sure they order inner and outer envelopes, and if they want the addresses written out in calligraphy, there's an upcharge for that."

"Thank you," she said. Before she closed my door, she added, "It's good to have you back."

I waved and continued to stare at my inbox.

Work was the last place I wanted to be. Being at the shop meant Garin was gone, and I was having a hard time accepting that. We'd spent over a week together, and from the moment I confessed to the minute I dropped him off at the airport this morning, we had acted like a couple. He had held my hand as we walked around town. He'd cupped my face when he kissed me. He had asked my opinion when he was emailed questions about the hotel and casino, and he listened to the feedback I gave him. And he made love to me. Constantly.

Now, I didn't know when I'd see him again.

I ached at the thought.

I needed him.

I needed more time with him.

And the last thing I needed was work. I cringed at the sight of the emails that were waiting to be answered, at the problems that needed my solving. My mom had run things while I was gone. She told me she'd heard from Garin just after the accident, and he'd kept her updated on my progress, but she needed to be at the shop to make sure the money was filtered correctly. I wasn't surprised when she had acted more concerned about Anthony's next trip to Florida than on my recovery. She didn't care.

Anthony didn't care.

And I didn't care about this place anymore.

The clock on my computer showed it was just after four. I'd been in the office since nine that morning, and I hadn't done a thing. I hadn't returned a single email, I hadn't ordered any of the products that were needed for inventory, and I hadn't met with any of the clients who had come in. All I had done was answer questions when my employees had them and stared at my computer.

I grabbed my bag, locked my office, and walked out the back door, so I wouldn't see anyone out front. I drove straight home. When I pulled into my driveway, my phone rang. Garin's name and number showed on the screen. I hadn't spoken to him since he'd left, but I knew he was in Atlantic City. He'd told me his destination just before he had gotten out of my car and stepped onto the plane.

And, because he was in Jersey, I knew something was about to go down.

I shifted into park and continued to hold the steering wheel. "Hi."

"Hey, you."

I hated that he was so far away. I hated that he wasn't whispering those two words in my ear. And I hated that the tone of his voice told me something was wrong.

# PRISONED

"I didn't think it was right to text you this. I thought it would be better to tell you over the phone."

He took a breath, and I knew. I felt it in my whole body as it started to shake. My throat tightened. My heart pounded.

"It's done," he said.

My eyes closed, and I rested my forehead on my hand, pushing it into the steering wheel. "Anthony's...*gone?*"

"Yes."

I knew this was coming. I knew that was the reason Garin had gone to Atlantic City. When he had told me that Anthony was going to *fucking die*, I knew he wasn't kidding.

So, why was I shocked to hear it?

And why did it hurt?

I stared at my lap, clenching and unclenching my fingers against my forehead. My joints burned. My chest ached. I didn't know why; I couldn't explain it. I wanted it to stop, but it just wouldn't.

"Was it quick?"

"I'm not going to lie to you."

"I don't want you to."

"No, it wasn't quick...and it wasn't painless."

I winced from his honesty and tried not to let my mind wander. Prior to the dream, I hadn't known much about torture. Even though it wasn't real, I felt like it gave me an education on some of the possibilities. Now, I knew what it felt like to have a knife pointed at my throat, to be told I was going to die, to feel a level of pain I had never experienced before. The true meaning of fear, of constant worry, of hurt—I understood all of it now. But I was sure that whatever had been inflicted on Anthony was far worse than what Breath had done to me.

And I had a feeling it had started before Garin had arrived. I hadn't heard from Anthony in two days. That was unlike my brother. He usually made some type of contact every day. I was sure that meant the bosses had captured Anthony, and Garin had finished him.

I wouldn't ask. I didn't want to know.

And I didn't want to know what they had done to him.

Or where they were going to bury him.

Now that I had Garin back in my life and I truly knew what I had lost, what had been taken from me, I blamed Anthony for all of it. I wouldn't miss my brother. And I didn't want to ever visit his grave.

But the thought of more death, more torture, still hurt.

"I'm glad you told me," I said, "and I didn't find out some other way."

I heard talking in the background. Then, there was movement, the rushing of cars, horns honking.

"They need me, Kyle. I'm going to call you back in a little while."

"Okay."

He said good-bye, and we both hung up.

I didn't put the phone down. I lifted my forehead off my hand and stared at the dark screen.

Anthony was gone.

Dead.

I wasn't sure what to say, what to think, how to even process it all. But I knew there was something I had to do, something I wasn't looking forward to.

I swiped my finger across the screen and hit *Mom* in my contacts.

"Hi," I said when she answered. "We need to talk. Can I come over?"

"I just sat down to watch my shows. Johnny's here. I don't feel like having company."

I didn't know who Johnny was. We didn't talk about her friends or the men she dated, and I never met any of them. But his company was clearly more important than mine.

"It's urgent, *Mom*." I added the last word for emphasis because, when I spoke to her, I usually called her by her first name.

"Turn it down, will ya? And pause it, so I don't miss nothing," she said to Johnny.

I heard the TV quiet in the background.

"What do you wanna tell me, Kyle? Make it quick."

"It's really something I need to tell you in person."

"Just spit it out already."

If she didn't want me to come over, I couldn't force her. But I knew what this was going to do to her. She struggled with sobriety. She had relapsed more than once. Losing her son—her enabler, her source of income—was going to destroy her.

# PRISONED

"Anthony's dead." Several seconds of silence passed. "Mom, did you hear what I said? Anthony's dead. He's gone. He's—"

"I heard you. I just don't believe you."

"I wouldn't lie to you, especially not about something like this."

"Then, why haven't I heard this from anyone else? Why didn't one of the guys call me? Or one of his girls? Why hasn't anyone from The Heart picked up the phone and told me my baby's dead?"

"Maybe they don't know yet." It was the only thing I could think of without getting into details, ones I would never share with her. "I'm telling you the truth. I just heard. He's gone, Mom."

"No. No. *No!*" she screamed, the emotion finally coming through in her voice.

Had I not ratted him out, Anthony would have still been alive. But I couldn't take this guilt on, too. I couldn't let this eat at me. Anthony had murdered two of my friends. Had I not told Garin, he probably would have found out anyway. And, if I hadn't put a stop to it, my brother could have killed more innocent people.

"My baby can't be dead," she wailed. "My baby. My *baby*."

I slowly looked up, staring past the steering wheel at the house that was surrounded by palms and thick bushes. The beige stucco front. The two steps I had climbed countless times.

The house that had never once felt like it was mine.

I didn't know where I would go. I didn't know what was going to happen.

But I knew I couldn't live here anymore.

# THIRTY-EIGHT

## GARIN
## TWO HOURS AGO

"You piece of shit," I spewed, spitting the words in Anthony's face.

The boys had done a hell of a job torturing the ever-loving fuck out of him. Every toe but the big ones had been severed and tossed on the ground. He'd been forced to eat his own earlobes. Then, all his teeth were pulled out. The guys didn't even have to tape his lips shut; Anthony had nothing to bite them with.

"Fuck you," he gummed back at me.

"Fuck me?" I laughed. "Yeah, fuck me that I didn't figure this out earlier, and I had to wait so long to kill you."

As I rolled up my sleeves, the blood on my knuckles caught my attention. I fucking hated that a piece of him was on me. My hands had been inside his sister this morning. If I hadn't had his blood all over me, I bet my fingers would have still smelled like her.

The only good part about all this was that it had brought Kyle back to me.

"Why did you do it?" I asked.

His eyelids were swollen, but he still looked at me. There was no life in his eyes. Just a dead stare, as if I'd already killed him. "Fuck you, Garin."

I pulled so hard on a chunk of his hair that I felt his scalp tear. "Give me an answer. You're going to die in this room anyway, so there's no reason to keep it a secret."

He didn't scream like most of the men who had been brought in here over the years. He didn't try to fight his way out of the ropes that bound his limbs to the chair. He didn't cry. He didn't even shit himself, which I'd seen happen before. He stayed still and looked at me with those dead eyes.

"I worked so fucking hard," he finally said.

"So?"

"So, Paulie was going to give it all away, like you pieces of shit deserved some of it."

"You mean, Paulie was going to tell the bosses?"

"Yeah, motherfucker." When he spit, a clot of blood dripped down his lip. It ran across the front of his shirt and landed on his lap. "He was a pussy. Couldn't handle doing business without you guys wiping his ass for him." He spoke slow, and without teeth, it was hard to understand him. "When I found out he was gonna tell you guys, I killed him. I wasn't sharing nothing with you. I did the work, took the risk. You weren't gonna get a fucking cent of it."

"And look where that got you." I clenched my fists together and stepped back, so I could get a good look at him. "What about Billy?"

"What about that fucking junkie? He was asking all around town about Paulie's murder. I got tired of hearing whispers about it. Then, I found out he was fucking one of my top girls. It had to stop, so I got rid of him."

I gritted my teeth. "He was my best friend."

"Yeah?" More blood dripped from his lip. "Some fucking friend you are. You left him in Jersey where you knew he was going to die."

I wasn't going to let this piece of scum make me feel bad for my decisions, and I sure as hell wasn't going to justify my actions to him or anyone else. I'd done everything I could to help Billy. I didn't care if Anthony knew that or not.

# PRISONED

I walked toward his chair again, stopping inches from his legs. "I was with your sister this morning."

"This morning? That's impossible. I told her to stay the fuck away from you."

It was only minutes before his death, and this asshole still wanted to control Kyle.

"It's not impossible." I pulled out my cell phone and clicked on my photos, bringing up a picture of Kyle and me.

I'd taken it when we got back from dinner last night. We were in the living room. She was sitting on my lap, my face kissing her neck. In the photo, I'd included plenty of the background, knowing I was going to show it to Anthony.

"Look familiar?" I watched the anger spread across his face. "I've been there, at *your* house, since I flew her home from the hospital."

"She'd better not have given you nothing."

I leaned in, getting really close to him. He smelled like death already.

"She gave me everything I wanted. I know all about the houses and cars and her business. And I saw your safe." I laughed, wishing I had strangled this asshole when we were kids. Things would have worked out so differently. "You took her from me once. I promise you, that won't happen again."

He rocked in the chair, trying to head-butt me. "That's my fucking money."

Money made him buck. It made him moan. It made him show real emotion for the first time since I'd stepped in this room.

He was one greedy motherfucker who didn't give a shit about anything else.

"The money will be of no use to you when you're dead."

Looking back at my phone, I found the button to record a voice message and pressed it. I couldn't take a video; I didn't want Kyle to see what we had done to him. I didn't want her to have to see his face ever again. I held the phone out toward him, so it could catch everything that was about to be said.

"You ruined so many fucking lives, Anthony. But there's one person who had to put up with your abuse the longest. You destroyed everything she wanted, and you owe her an apology."

"Who? My whore of a sister?"

I nodded toward one of the guys standing on the far wall. He took the signal and walked over to Anthony, whipping the back of Anthony's head with the butt of his gun. Anthony grunted, a clot of blood shooting out of his mouth.

"Let's try this again," I said. "Apologize. Now."

"I'm sorry."

"Mean it, asshole."

He slowly looked up. "I'm fucking sorry, all right? I wasn't a good brother to you, and I know that. But you finally got Garin. I hope he's everything you wanted, you cunt."

This motherfucker.

After everything he did to Kyle, and this was the best he had. I should have expected that from a guy who killed his own best friend.

I turned the recording off and slid the phone in my pocket. Then, I reached behind my back as one of the guys handed me a blade. It was nine inches, just long and sharp enough to do what I needed. I let Anthony watch as I folded my fingers around the base. I wanted him to know what was going to happen. I wanted him to see how much it was going to hurt.

"Do you have anything else you want to say?" I asked.

A string of drool hung from his lip, and he licked it away. He had no teeth to show me, but it didn't stop him from trying to smile. "I should have killed you when I still had the chance, you worthless—"

Before he could say another word, I jerked my arm forward and stabbed the blade into the middle of his throat. A rush of blood squirted out from the wound. It filled his mouth and gurgled on his tongue as he tried to choke in air. His chest pumped, and his shoulders twitched until his head slumped forward. Then, all his movements stopped.

One of the guys went over and checked his pulse. "He's dead, Garin."

He reached for the blade, and I handed it to him. He would clean my prints off the weapon, and then he'd destroy it.

"Grind that fucker up and bring him to the beach," I ordered to all the guys in the room. "I want to lie on his goddamn bones the next time I'm there."

As I walked out, Mario joined me, and we went outside to his car.

"You did good, kid." He patted me on the back. "I thought you were going to tell him how much you've been fucking his sister. You know, more salt on the wound."

"I won't talk about her like that, even to a dead man."

"Oh, fuck," he said, stopping several feet from his car. "This is more serious than I thought. Does that mean you're not going to tell me anything about your trip to Florida?"

I laughed. "That's exactly what it means."

He pulled a cigar out of his pocket and lit it. "Are you going to tell her?"

"That I saved her life? Nah. She doesn't need to know that."

"You know that's not what I'm talking about."

I put my arm around his shoulders and shook his meaty muscles. "Let's go get something to eat. I know you get hungry after you watch someone die."

He took a puff and blew the smoke behind me. "That's my boy."

# THIRTY-NINE

## KYLE

I dropped my phone on my lap, unable to listen to my mother's sobs anymore, and continued to stare at the front of my house.

Anthony's house.

He wouldn't be calling me later to bark about the amount of cash I needed to move. He wouldn't text me, asking for the daily numbers. He wouldn't be coming to visit at the first of the month. He would never give me another order again.

He was dead.

Gone.

It was all over with.

I found myself getting out of the car and unlocking the front door, standing in the foyer as my eyes wandered over the inside. Nothing felt like it was mine. None of it felt right. It was as though I'd seen it all before in a magazine, but I hadn't touched any of it. I hadn't owned it. I hadn't felt comfortable around it.

It all reminded me of my brother.

I walked over to the kitchen window and stared out onto the water. The view was beautiful. Serene. Relaxing. So many nights, I had gazed at this scenery and wondered what was next. I had tried to plan for my future, to see past everything Anthony had taken away from me, and to find happiness in the things he had given me.

But I couldn't.

Anthony had chosen Florida. He had chosen both houses. He had picked the building where the shop was, he had influenced what I was going to sell and what services I would offer, he had chosen the employees who worked there.

It wasn't mine. It wasn't even close to mine.

None of it.

And I didn't love it.

This was my prison.

*He* was my prison.

But he was gone. There was no one keeping me here anymore. No one was making me stay in Florida. No one was making sure I went to work in the morning.

The bars had been lifted.

So, what the hell was I going to do with my freedom?

I opened a bottle of wine from the fridge and brought it into the bathroom, setting it on the edge of the tub with my phone. I ran the warm water, stripped off all my clothes, and left them in a pile on the floor. Once I added in some bath salts and lit a few candles, I climbed in.

I was still sore. My muscles hadn't fully healed. The cuts and scrapes and bruises were just starting to lighten from my body. My appetite hadn't completely returned, and my stomach still had a hard time processing everything I ate. The doctor had assured me that this was all normal. I needed time and things would all gradually return to the way they had been before the accident.

Time was something I had now.

Just as I closed my eyes and tried to shut my brain off, my phone rang from the side of the tub.

"Hey, Garin," I said as I answered.

"Are you okay?"

"I think so."

I looked at the bottle of wine that was now half gone. They were sips that I didn't remember taking, and I couldn't recall when the candle closest to me had blown out. In the shred of light that was left, I saw the outline of my body in the water. My skin looked so dark, almost dirty.

Dirty like I had been in the dream.

"It has nothing to do with losing Anthony," I said. I felt like shit for saying that, but it was the truth. After what Anthony had done to me, it was hard to mourn him. Hard to feel anything for him at all. "I just don't know what to do now. I can't be here anymore—that, I do know."

"Come here."

"To Jersey?"

"No, to Vegas. I'm flying there in the morning. I can come down to Florida and get you, and we can fly there together."

I sat up quickly, the water splashing over the side of the tub. "You want me...in Vegas?"

"It's where I live, where I work. So, yeah, it's where I want you. Come live with me, Kyle."

He wanted me. He wanted me to live with him. He wanted me there, so I could touch him every day, so I could kiss him whenever I wanted, so I could tell him to his face that I loved him.

I took a deep breath. "Come get me."

"That was easy."

"It's a little late for me to play hard to get since you've already had me." I stepped out of the tub and wrapped myself in a towel. "Besides, I'm done playing, Garin. I want you more than anything. And I want us."

"You're going to have it all, everything you've ever wanted. I'll make sure of it. Close your eyes, and get some sleep, baby. I'll be there when you wake up."

# FORTY

## GARIN
## PRESENT DAY

"Mmm," I groaned, rubbing my nose against the side of Kyle's throat.

I'd missed this neck, the scent of her skin. I couldn't live without either of them now. And I'd missed how she always had a part of her touching a part of me.

She stirred as I climbed into bed, and when she tried to roll over, I pushed my chest into her back, so she couldn't.

"I hope that's you, and I'm not dreaming this," she said.

It made me smile whenever she brought up the dream. She never told me many details about it, but I wished she would.

I kissed her shoulder all the way up to her ear. She was so warm, her skin so fucking soft. I loved that she slept naked, so I could touch her without having to rip any unnecessary clothes away.

"Oh!" She ground her ass over my cock that had been hard since I walked through her front door. "Now, I know I'm definitely not dreaming."

I smiled again.

*This girl.*

"Should I get up and shower, so we can go to your plane, or do you want me right where I am?"

I growled into the back of her neck. So willing. So submissive. We'd spent so much time in this bed during my last visit here.

But before I slid inside that pussy again, I had somewhere I wanted to bring her.

"I was thinking we could stay here one more night and go to Vegas in the morning."

She rolled over as I lightened my grip. There was worry in her eyes, and her hand immediately went to my face. I kissed the side of it.

"Are you having second thoughts about me coming with you?"

"Oh, no, baby. You're coming to Vegas with me, but there's one thing my town doesn't have, and that's an ocean."

"I don't get it."

"I want to take you to the beach, Kyle. Like when we were kids." I watched her face as she realized what I was saying, and then I kissed her when she leaned forward.

"My favorite place…you know that." She bit her bottom lip as she grinned. She knew that drove me fucking crazy. The only teeth allowed to bite that lip were mine. "But none of my suits have holes in them. It won't be the same."

"I bought you a new one. See? Some things never change."

"You didn't."

I nodded. "It's in your bathroom. Go put it on for me."

Knowing I was going to push Vegas off for one more day, I'd had Mario's assistant go buy some suits for Kyle and me. I knew it would bring back a good memory for her. The only ones I wanted her to remember were the good ones.

She gave me another kiss. This time, it lasted a little longer. "You're too much," she said. And then she disappeared into the bathroom.

I got out of bed and went into the kitchen, grabbing a bottle of water out of the fridge. Since I'd asked her to move in with me just last night, that hadn't given her much time to pack. But there wasn't a single box anywhere in here. I hadn't even seen a suitcase in her room.

"What do you think?"

I turned toward the entrance of the hallway where she was standing in just the bikini. "I prefer you naked." I walked over to her, hoping I could ease the scowl off her face. "That's only because your body is too fucking gorgeous to be covered."

"Garin…"

"You look incredible. Every guy on that beach is going to be jealous of what I have." I wrapped my hand around her throat, smelling the toothpaste on her lips. "Are you ready to go?"

"Yes."

"I noticed you forgot to pack. Does that mean you're having second thoughts?"

She pulled away from my mouth and licked her lips. "I don't want to take anything with me."

"Nothing?"

"Just a small bag for some of my clothes, cosmetics, and jewelry. But I'm leaving the rest. I need a fresh start, and I need to leave my old life here, behind me, where it belongs."

"Are you going to rent out the house?"

"I want to sell it." She took the bottle of water out of my hand and drank quite a few sips. "The deed is in my name, and there's no mortgage. I don't have any debt to pay off, so I came up with an idea."

"I'll introduce you to my financial advisor. He's great. He'll—"

"I don't want the money."

I took the bottle out of her hand and pulled her into my arms. "What are you going to do with it? If you give it to your ma, you know what's going to happen."

"I want to donate all of it to the community center. They did so much for me, for all of us. I want to make sure they can continue taking care of the kids who live in The Heart. I want them to have more than we did, Garin."

Before we were old enough to hustle, the community center was where we had gone when our stomachs were empty and aching. They'd given us a roof, beds, and clean sheets when our power had been shut off. They'd dressed us in warm clothes. A donation as large as Kyle's would only benefit the kids and give them extras they didn't even know they were missing.

Kyle was nothing like her brother. Hell, she was nothing like me either.

She was better than both of us.

"Whatever the amount is," I said, "I'll match you."

Her arms tightened around me. "I want to sell my business, too."

"Let my team help you. They'll fly here, they'll get everything ready to sell, and they'll draw up all the paperwork for you to sign. They'll make it so much easier for you."

She looked around the kitchen, as though she were saying good-bye to it all. "I would love that."

"Good." I slapped her ass, but before I pulled my hand away, I grabbed the bottom of her cheek. "Go get some towels and sunscreen, so we can go."

On our way to the beach, Kyle asked the driver to stop at the grocery store. She went in alone and returned a few minutes later with two bags, packing them into the cooler that she had insisted we bring.

"Do you get driven everywhere?" she asked as she got into the backseat.

"I have two drivers, one for each shift. It's rare for me to drive, but it's happened."

"If you need a driver twenty-four hours a day, then when do you sleep?"

I ran my hand over her thigh. The dress she had put on was white and sheer; it was almost as soft as her skin. "I don't plan on ever sleeping when you're in my bed."

She giggled. It was a sound I fucking loved. It showed me how happy she was, and it was so different than the laugh I'd heard at the bar the night of Billy's funeral. No one would ever know the torture and verbal abuse she had gone through based on that laugh.

She was so strong—stronger than she even realized.

When we got to the beach, I dropped the cooler, the towels, and the sunscreen onto the sand, and I brought Kyle straight into the ocean. Once the water became deep enough, I swam out a few feet and waited for her to catch up. I was still able to stand, so I wrapped her legs around my waist and held her close to my body.

"This water is a little warmer than the Atlantic," she said.

"That wouldn't have mattered when we were kids."

"Are you kidding? Ice water wouldn't have stopped us." She rubbed her feet over my ass. "Would you have held me like this? To keep me warm?"

I groaned. "Shit, Kyle, I wanted to. I always wanted to."

"I know." She circled her arms around my neck and kissed me. "I've been thinking about jobs and what I'm going to do when I get out there."

"You don't have to work. I'll take care of you."

She tightened her grip. "I do have to work, and I want to work, but thank you for saying that." She dipped her head back to get all of her hair wet. "I'm thinking I want to start using canvases again, get back into creating real art. Anthony wouldn't let me sell any of my designs at the shop, so I stopped painting. I think he feared I would make a name for myself, and the shop would come under investigation. But, now, I have the time to do it, and I don't have anyone telling me I can't."

"I'll build you a studio in our condo."

"You don't have to. I can paint in the kitchen or something."

"There are five extra bedrooms, Kyle. I think it's okay if we convert one of them into a studio."

"Five?"

I nodded.

"And a plane? And two drivers? Wow, things have really changed."

"For the both of us." I lifted a hand, so I could grip her face. "You'll get used to it, I promise. It'll be overwhelming at first. But just at first."

"Will I be mingling with the bosses' wives?"

"None of them live in Vegas. But, when I fly back to Jersey every few months, you'll be coming with me, and you'll be mingling with them then." As I moved us a little deeper into the water, she clung to me even tighter. "I have something I want you to listen to, but only when you're ready."

A line appeared between her brows. "What is it?"

"I recorded a voice message from Anthony." I didn't like her expression, so I cut her off before she could say anything. "Look, I can't fix what he did, I can't make it better, and I sure as hell can't rewind what happened. But he owed you an apology, and I made sure you got one."

It took several seconds before she responded, "I'm not ready to hear it."

"That's okay. It's there when you are."

Her legs dropped from my waist, and she grabbed my hand. "I have something I want to show you."

She led me out of the water and unfolded the towels, spreading them out next to each other. We both sat, and she reached into the cooler. "I got us lunch, but I'm really not in the mood for sandwiches. I'd much rather have this." She handed me a plastic sleeve of powdered doughnuts. They were the same kind I'd bought when we were kids. "The ones you had made were good, but they were too fancy. These are my favorite."

"Get over here."

She laughed so hard as I grabbed her by the waist and pulled her onto my lap.

"How many packs of these did you get?" I asked.

"More than enough."

"Enough for me to cover your pussy in powdered sugar and lick off every speck?"

"Oh, yes, there's plenty for that." She took out one of the doughnuts and popped it into my mouth, laughing again as I coughed out some of the sugar. "I thought about soul mates a lot when I was having that dream. The whole concept really and how I believe they're revealed only once during our life." She looked at me over her shoulder. "You're my soul mate, Garin."

I kissed the side of her neck, loving how the sun and the salt made her smell. "Do you want to tell me more about that dream?"

"No, not today. Today is all about the beach."

I pressed my lips against her ear. "Tonight is all about the powdered sugar."

"And tomorrow is all about Vegas," she said. "But don't worry; I'll tell you sometime soon."

As she looked out toward the water, she closed her eyes and took a deep breath. She was leaving it behind—every threat Anthony had ever made, every rule, every bit of control. As long as I could help it, Florida was where it would all stay.

"I'm ready to get out of here." She turned around to face me again. "And I'm ready to start my life with you."

# FORTY-ONE

## KYLE

We pulled up to the front of Garin's hotel, a massive high-rise situated in the middle of the strip. The front was all glass. Deep blue lights shone onto the cars, illuminating the entrance. The brick pavers that lined the front were spotless. Everyone was so nicely dressed, everything so well-manicured.

Our doors were immediately opened by the valet attendants. "Welcome back, Mr. Woods," one of them said.

Garin shook each of their hands. "This is my girlfriend, Kyle Lang," Garin said to the men.

"Miss Lang," each of them said as they shook my hand.

Garin pulled me closer to him and placed his hand on my lower back, escorting me to the front door. "Don't get used to the *Miss*. It's not going to last for long."

I looked at him, my brows drawn together, my lips pursed. "What's that supposed to mean?"

He smiled at me. "Mmm, I want to bite that lip right now."

"Garin..."

His stare intensified. "You know exactly what that means." He glanced at the doorman. "Javier, it's nice to see you."

"And you, Mr. Woods," Javier replied back.

"This is Kyle," Garin said. "She'll be living with me now, so you'll be seeing much more of her."

"We'll make sure she feels right at home, sir."

I waved at Javier and thanked him, and I smiled as we stepped inside. I couldn't hide how good all of this felt, having Garin so close, his hand on my body, having him introduce me to his staff, to finally be in his home.

A home that would now be mine.

And, although I'd only seen the entrance of the hotel, it felt more comfortable than my house ever had.

"Do you know all the names of everyone who works here?" I asked. "There must be hundreds of employees."

"Some departments have a high turnover, so I don't get a chance to learn them before they leave or get fired, but I know most of them."

That impressed me.

So did the lobby. It was stunning, extremely contemporary, full of brightly colored glass chandeliers, exotic arrangements of flowers, and soft, shiny marble. I didn't smell smoke even though I knew there was plenty of that in the casino in front of us. Crowds of people walked past us, congregated by the slot machines, or stood in front of the restaurant. But the space was so vast that it could handle all the people, which was good. I didn't feel shut in at all.

"I'm going to show you the whole property a little later and take you to my office, so you can see where I work. But, first, I'm going to take you upstairs."

He'd fucked me three times on the plane on the way here. The look in his eyes told me he wasn't quite done with me. I loved that about him.

"Why do I get the feeling that I'm not going to be able to walk tomorrow?"

I'd learned that Garin really liked to take his time. His movements weren't slow at all. They weren't rushed. They weren't half-assed. They were strong, rough, forceful, making sure I was constantly filled with

# PRISONED

a mix of sensations. But I never got his cock before I got his lips, his tongue, before he savored and licked every part of my body.

He leaned into my ear while he turned us down an empty hallway where we were finally alone. "You're right about that, *Miss* Lang. You won't be walking. Not after what I plan to do to your ass."

He slapped it so hard that I yelped.

But I liked the pain.

He knew I liked it.

At the end of the hallway, there was a single elevator. Garin pressed the button and held me while we waited. It took a few seconds before the door opened, and a middle-aged woman walked off, carrying a bag of cleaning supplies.

"Your condo is all clean and ready for you, Mr. Woods," she said with a heavy accent.

"*Gracias, Isabella. Hiciste la cama con sábanas y cobijas nuevas?*"

"*Sí, señor,*" she said, smiling at me as she walked past us.

I stared at Garin as we stepped inside the elevator, shocked at what I'd just heard. "You speak Spanish?"

He'd spoken it in the dream; he'd understood everything that Beard had said and translated it for me. But I didn't know that, outside the dream, in real life, he was fluent. The two years of Spanish we had taken in high school hadn't given us enough skills for a reply that lengthy. I couldn't help but wonder where he'd learned it.

Garin placed his hand on the tablet that was embedded in the elevator wall. It read his fingerprints. A second later, he pulled his hand off and tapped the screen. It showed he had access to all the floors, but he selected *PH*.

"Garin? Will you answer me?"

He turned away from the tablet as the door shut, and the elevator began to rise. His eyes narrowed as he focused on my face. "Yes, Kyle, I speak Spanish now."

He moved behind me, pressing his chest against my back, his hands circling around the top of my throat. That seemed to be his favorite spot to hold. He tilted my neck, so he'd have better access, and he kissed all the way down and across my shoulder. He ground his dick into my ass, eventually letting his hand slide to my pussy, swiping my clit before he brought it back up to my throat.

I moaned. The forcefulness of his movements, the way he was pushing into my ass, was such a turn-on.

"You want more?"

"Yes."

"Fuck," he hissed, "my soul mate wants more."

My eyes popped open, not even realizing they had been closed. I'd called him that on the beach yesterday, but he hadn't said it back to me. "I'm your soul mate?"

He didn't answer me right away. He just held me tightly and kissed all around my neck. When he reached my ear, he pressed his lips really close and whispered, "I believe our soul mate is revealed only once during our life. Maybe it's a glimpse of a stranger. Maybe it's our best friend. The timing may not always be right. But, when they're shown to us, we know it's them. Then, life happens. We grow. We age. We develop scars. And we remember that glimpse. Some are lucky enough to spend the rest of their lives with that person. Some, like me, only have memories."

I couldn't breathe. My body was shaking, my knees on the verge of giving out. It wasn't because his hands were on my throat or that he was holding me too tightly.

It was because those were *my* words he had spoken.

Words I had said while we were in that prison.

A prison that was supposed to be a dream.

And a dream that I'd had while I was in a coma.

"Now, you have more than just memories," he said. "You have me. You have us. And, now, we have forever."

His hands left my body, so I turned around to face him.

His eyes told me everything I needed to know.

And, when I opened my mouth to speak, nothing came out.

But something came out of his.

*"Breathe, Kyle."*

# ACKNOWLEDGMENTS

Jesse James and Heather Ludviksson, this book started with the two of you. I'll never forget all those late hours on my lanai, breaking down each layer. I love you both so much. Thank you for being such amazing friends.

Steven Luna, thank you for giving this story all the love and care it needed. As I've said to you so many times before, you treat my words as though they were your own. Thank you, thank you, my friend.

Shari Ryan, you're the most patient, loving, caring friend, and the creations you put together are simply breathtaking. Thank you for giving this book the most gorgeous face, and thank you for everything you do for me. Love you, lady.

Jovana Shirley, it's such an honor to work with you. You add the most beautiful glow and the most stunning designs to every book. I'm so appreciative of everything you do and everything you teach me.

Linda Russell, thank you for bringing me on and for working so hard on this project. Since the beginning, you've known exactly what it needs, and you've rocked it out, lady. You amaze me, and I just adore you. XO

Julie Healey-Vaden, I am so grateful to have you, your constant support and your brilliant brain in my life. You are one of the most amazing women, and your passion has made me a better person and a stronger writer. *Prisoned* wouldn't have been the same without you. I, most especially, wouldn't be the same without you. Love you and your bossy ass.

Donna Cooksley Sanderson, you have been the most incredible sidekick and partner in crime throughout this whole journey. Thank you for always letting me lean on you and for being there whenever I need you. I have so much love for you. xx

Sunny Borek, it has been such a privilege and an honor to work with you on this book. I will never be able to thank you for all the time and dedication you put into my words. Beard loves you, and so do I. <3

Kimmi Conner Street, you are the most beautiful friend. Thank you for everything—and I mean *everything*. Your hugs, your encouragement, your time, your wonderful insight, and especially your friendship. Love you so much.

Jennifer Porpora, you've supported me since the beginning, and I can't tell you how much it means to me. Thanks for being a part of this, for giving me the best advice, and for making *Prisoned* so much better because of it. I love your face, and I love you.

Rose, my sweet friend, thank you for all your patience and for translating all of my crazy words. You brought such an awesome twist to this novel, and I appreciate it so much.

Gia Riley, thank you for all the pep talks and for all the virtual tissues you sent my way. I especially thank you for all the laughs. You knew just when I needed them, and each one was appreciated. You, my friend, are amazing. Chomp, chomp.

Special love goes to my COPA ladies, Clarissa Federico LaFirst, Dee Montoya, Melissa Mann, Stacey Jacovina, Heather Hawley, Katie Kinnetz, Katy Truscott, Allie Burke, Liz Milner, Katie Amanatidis, Missy Domson, and Diane Dacey. I'm so grateful to have you all in my life.

Mom and Dad, thanks for your unwavering belief in me and your constant encouragement. It means more than you'll ever know.

# PRISONED

My Midnighters, you are such a supportive, loving, motivating group. Thanks for being such an inspiration, for holding my hand when I need it, and for always begging for more words. I love you all.

To all the bloggers who read, review, share, post, tweet, Instagram—Thank you, thank you, thank you, will never be enough. You do so much for our writing community, and we're so appreciative.

To my readers, I cherish each and every one of you. I'm so grateful for all the love you show my books, for taking the time to reach out to me, for your passion and enthusiasm. I love, love, love you all.

# DID YOU ENJOY PRISONED?

Reviews mean the world to authors, and they are the most powerful way to help other readers learn about my work. If you enjoyed *Prisoned*, I would absolutely love it if you left an honest review. Even if it's short, as little as a few sentences, it can still help so much.

# MARNI'S MIDNIGHTERS

Getting to know my readers is one of my favorite parts about being an author. In Marni's Midnighters, my private Facebook group, we chat about steamy books, sexy taboo toys, and sensual book boyfriends. Team members also qualify for exclusive giveaways and are the first to receive sneak peeks of the projects I'm currently working on. To join Marni's Midnighters, go to www.facebook.com/groups/1597153177180837/.

# ABOUT THE AUTHOR

Best-selling author Marni Mann knew she was going to be a writer since middle school. While other girls her age were daydreaming about teenage pop stars, Marni was fantasizing about penning her first novel. She crafts sexy, titillating stories that weave together her love of darkness, mystery, passion, and human emotions. A New Englander at heart, she now lives in Sarasota, Florida, with her husband and their two dogs, who have been characters in her books. When she's not nose deep in her laptop, working on her next novel, she's scouring for chocolate, sipping wine, traveling, or devouring fabulous books.

Want to get in touch? Visit Marni at…

www.facebook.com/MarniMannAuthor

http://twitter.com/marnimann

www.instagram.com/marnimann

http://marnismann.com

MarniMannBooks@gmail.com

# NEWSLETTER

Would you like to qualify for exclusive giveaways, be notified of new releases, and read free excerpts of my latest work? Then, sign up for my newsletter. I promise not to spam you. Go to http://marnismann.com/newsletter to sign up.

# ALSO BY MARNI MANN

A Sexy Standalone (Erotica)

*Wild Aces*

Trapper Montgomery had been passed from one abusive home to another. They were all the same—the taste of blood on his tongue, the sound of broken bones in his ears. But when he finally escaped the system that tore him apart, he dedicated his life to avenging those who had laid their hands on him, who spit at him, who told him he was nothing. He was ready to fight…until he met Brea Bradley.

The Unblocked Collection (Erotica)

*Episodes 1–5*

Derek Block seeks revenge. Frankie Jordan seeks professional dominance. He wants her; she wants him. Lines that can't cross begin to blur. Things start heating up as real estate gets real…

The Shadows Series (Erotica)

*Seductive Shadows*

Charlie is a passionate, sensually inspired art student, desperately seeking an escape from the abusive past that haunts her and a tragic accident that emptied her heart. Scarred and unable to love, her yearning for physical pleasure leads her into a tantalizing, dangerous world of power and seduction.

*Seductive Secrecy*

Can Charlie and Cameron overcome the destruction of their clouded pasts, or will the revelation of more painful, shocking secrets pull them back into the shadows?

The Bar Harbor Series (New Adult)

*Pulled Beneath*

Drew travels north to settle her grandparents' estate, but she finds more questions than answers as the truth starts unraveling. What she didn't expect to find was Saint, whose reputation is as tumultuous as his past. With Saint's scars so deep and Drew's so fresh, can the pair heal from their painful wounds, or will they be pulled beneath the darkness of their pasts?

*Pulled Within*

Rae Ryan has lived in a storm over which she has no control. Plagued by nightmares and a terrible family secret, she carries her scars as much on the inside as she does on the outside. Can she survive the storm and become a part of the light she so desperately desires? Or is she destined to remain pulled within?

The Memoir Series (Dark Fiction)

*Memoirs Aren't Fairytales*

Leaving behind a nightmarish college experience, Nicole and her friend, Eric, escape their home of Bangor, Maine, to start a new life in Boston, Massachusetts. Fragile and scared, Nicole desperately seeks a new beginning to help erase her past. But there is something besides freedom waiting for her in the shadows—a drug that will make every day a nightmare.

*Scars from a Memoir*

Two men love Nicole; one fills a void, and the other gives her hope of a future. Will love find a way to help her sing a lullaby to addiction, or will her scars be her final good-bye?

Made in the USA
Lexington, KY
14 October 2016